Transplants

A Novel

Daniel Tam-Claiborne

A REGALO PRESS BOOK
ISBN: 979-8-88845-721-4
ISBN (eBook): 979-8-88845-722-1

Transplants
© 2025 by Daniel Tam-Claiborne
All Rights Reserved

Cover Design by Elisha Zepeda

Publishing Team:
Founder and Publisher – Gretchen Young
Editor – Caitlyn Limbaugh
Managing Editor – Aleigha Koss
Production Manager – Alana Mills
Production Editor – Rachel Paul
Associate Production Manager – Kate Harris

This book is a work of fiction. People, places, events, and situations are the product of the author's imagination. Any resemblance to actual persons, living or dead, or historical events, is purely coincidental.

This book, as well as any other Regalo Press publications, may be purchased in bulk quantities at a special discounted rate. Contact orders@regalopress.com for more information.

As part of the mission of Regalo Press, a donation is being made to the Seattle Chinatown International District Preservation and Development Authority (SCIDpda), as chosen by the author. Find out more about this organization at: https://scidpda.org

No part of this book may be reproduced, stored in a retrieval system, or transmitted by any means without the written permission of the author and publisher.

Regalo Press
New York • Nashville
regalopress.com

Published in the United States of America
1 2 3 4 5 6 7 8 9 10

For Lynn and Anne

To migrate is to disappear, and then to be reborn.
To migrate is to be reborn, never again to disappear.

—Sami Nair and Juan Goytisolo

1

Animals were her first love. Guinea pigs, prairie mice, salamanders with bright pink spots. Garden snakes she could curl in the palm of her hand like yarn. Even before Lin was old enough to talk, she was fascinated by how they felt. The sticky webbed feet of a salamander like cupping a sweet rice cake between her fingers. A snake's lacquered skin: a cold cucumber before being minced into vinegar salad.

Like nearly everyone born in the year 2000, she grew up an only child. She had cousins: first cousins—the real ones—and the so-called cousin children of her mother's friends and neighbors, a nod to the carefree, reckless procreation of generations past. But Lin shied away from them like she did from all people. She much preferred to hide behind the strong calves of her mother's legs anytime they walked into the tailor's or bought vegetables at the market. In middle school, she was so anxious about talking to the sunbeaten laoban—who sat with his shirt rolled up over his belly, a lit cigarette dangling from his open hand—that she sooner chose to skip a meal than dare ask to buy a jar of blue-foiled yogurt or a red package of sesame seed cookies.

Lin had a remarkable memory for words, phrases, and formulas. She made perfect grades despite hardly speaking a word in class. She walked the halls of her high school avoiding eye contact, counting the cracks in the hexagonal tiles, and waiting to hear "Fang Xue Ge" pipe in over the tinny loudspeaker to signal the end of the day. Her classmates and teachers held no interest for her. The animals she kept at home were much more than playthings: they were all she had.

"No more," her mother Qi Fei said, standing inside the pet store on Wukang Road. "Don't you own enough of these damn things already?"

It was July, the summer before Lin would start her first year of university, and broiling. A single desk fan bolted to the wall oscillated cigarette smoke and the smell of stale urine from one end of the room to the other.

"Hao kelian," Lin mouthed. Along the shelves were rows of cages, stacked crookedly on top of one another like scaffolding for a construction tower: a three-high mound of pug-nosed mutts next to an empty fish tank, a pair of broad-shelled tortoises skating in puddle-deep water. She'd rescued dozens already, over the years, from suffering a similar fate. If she couldn't free herself from the indifference of humans, Lin reasoned, then sparing these animals was its own minor consolation.

"You promised," Lin whispered, not wanting to rouse the shopkeeper. She crossed her arms in front of her chest. "Do you think I made valedictorian just to kiss Fan laoshi's ass?"

Since Lin first entered primary school, it had been her mother's idea to give Lin pets as rewards for good grades. When she was six and still refused to talk to anyone, the doctors worried she was biantai, born with a personality disorder, or worse. For hours when her mother was at work at the accounting office, Lin crouched by the side of the thin stream, watching the fish. She'd made noises at them: sing-song flourishes, the sounds of shamans. It wasn't long before their neighbor noticed she'd even befriended the choleric shar-pei he kept chained to the front gate that snarled its teeth whenever anyone but her approached.

Lin knew about her mother's experiment, of course. She had no false conceptions about Qi Fei's enthusiasm for purchasing living creatures, despite her refusal to so much as venture into Lin's bedroom. Her mother thought that giving Lin a pet of her own might help to socialize her better, a temporary bridge between the animal and human worlds. If her daughter could start relating to rabbits, the logic went, it surely wouldn't be long before she could look her first-grade teacher in the eye or not run screaming from the postman every time he knocked on their front door.

"This one," Lin said, her voice rising from the back of the store. She'd settled on a row with calicos and tabby cats, Persians and bobtails, long-haired Turkish Angoras and short-haired Bengals. Her hand rested against one cage, where a black cat with a white smudge on the bridge of his nose stooped to drink from a dish of water.

"Absolutely not," her mother said, shaking her head. "You know how I feel about cats."

Lin knew that in her mother's world, like in much of the rest of China, pets were practical. They served a purpose. Dogs were not things you took inside the house: they made sure someone didn't go breaking into your property or walking off with part of your crop yield. A person only ever took a cat home if they were trying to scare away the mice burrowing holes in their sheetrock.

But mice or not, Qi Fei had no use for cats. Cooperation and sacrifice, she'd maintained, were the cornerstones of modern China's success. Men and women striving together to form a better tomorrow. And more than any other animal, cats represented to her its moral antithesis: lazy, pompous, interested only in themselves. She made clear that if Lin was given the chance to care for one, it would only be a matter of time before she exhibited those qualities herself.

But Lin was undeterred. "You said anything, Ma," she repeated, her voice the low drone of a storm cloud.

"Just look at it," Qi Fei said. The black cat pushed his wet nose through the front of the grate, lapping his tongue against Lin's finger. "Yan ren er mu."

Lin rolled her eyes. Hadn't she been the one deceiving her mother? Above all, Qi Fei hated to be wrong, so Lin took great pains to prove that her experiment was paying off. She knew what it took to sustain her mother's generosity, even if it meant having to talk directly to the waitress when they went out for dinner or call the electrical company whenever there was a power fuse that needed resetting.

"What if—" Lin started, but her voice trailed off. What else did she have to barter? She'd already graduated first in her class. She'd passed the gaokao with aplomb. And in a month, she would start university. She didn't know how else to appease her mother if not with high marks on a page.

"Maybe it's not too late for me to fanhui, too," Lin said. The cat's tail was raised like an unanswered question, his coat glistening.

"Not possible."

"I can unenroll from university," Lin said. "Sell lotto tickets at the fuli caipiao instead."

"Enough," her mother replied. Even Lin knew it was an empty threat. Like every young person in the country, Lin had been taught to follow the masses. She would graduate from a good school, get a good job, marry a good husband. There was nothing either of them could do to change it.

"I'll make a friend," Lin said suddenly. "In university. A real human friend." Before her mother had a chance to respond, she added, "And I promise this one will be my last."

Lin took the black cat home. The white smudge on his nose looked like a bolt of lightning, so Lin named him Boom, after the English sound for thunder.

More than any other subject, Lin was fascinated by English. Surrounded by her animals at home, Lin watched re-runs of *The Big Bang Theory*, practicing the cadence of the words, the rising sound of a joke, the pacing of each phrase. Lin had already committed hundreds of words and phrases to memory. But the word "thunder" was new. The strong sound of it clapping against the clouds. The force of a gale wind that might sweep her and her animals up away from Yuci and drop them somewhere new, a world apart. A place with no other people.

But, despite her hopes, where Lin landed couldn't have been more different. Her gaokao score was good enough that she could have placed into Hunan University, renowned for its veterinary sciences program, in the south of the country. Lin had never been so far away. Even during Golden Week trips with her mother, they'd always opted for local travel if they traveled at all: the Yungang Grottos in the north of the province or the barren grasslands of Inner Mongolia.

Lin and her mother lived modestly by Yuci standards: a two-bedroom walk-up with a balcony and shared courtyard in an area zoned for development. The apartment had been given to Qi Fei by the county government, along with a lump sum, as part of a settlement after Lin's father died in a mining accident when Lin was three.

The thought of a fresh start that far from home was exhilarating. Lin had watched enough foreign shows that she would have gladly considered leaving the country, too. But as tempting as it was to go, Lin feared that her pets wouldn't survive the journey. Nor would they be any safer in Yuci under her mother's charge. So, she made a concession not to venture far, choosing instead to matriculate at the local agricultural university in Qixian, the next town over. The student body there numbered twenty thousand, more than twice the size of the entire town where she lived.

Lin decided she would come home every weekend, frequently enough that she could leave extra food and water on Monday morning and be back on Friday night in time to manage any potential calamity. As it was, she still brought as many of her pets with her to Qixian as she could: a cage of gerbils, two garden snakes, and Boom.

"Don't forget about that new friend of yours," her mother said, when it was time to go.

Qi Fei helped her with the move, each of them lugging a pet carrier and a checker-print suitcase on the back of a motor rickshaw, making the half-hour journey from Yuci to the university's campus on move-in day in August. University will be nothing like high school, Lin thought. The American movies Lin watched treated it like a gateway to another universe, new ideas and possibilities she couldn't yet fathom. How hard would making a friend be?

At the front gate, her mother cupped Lin's hands in her own. She closed her eyes, whispering something under her breath.

"What is it?" Lin asked, bracing for another argument.

Qi Fei pulled a red envelope out of her pocket and thrust it into Lin's hands.

"Pet food," she said, and then, almost mournfully: "Let's hope your classmates like them as much as you."

The three other girls Lin shared a room with didn't care much for her pets. Or rather, they did—were excited to stroke a stiff finger to mat down Boom's fur or watch the snakes slither across their tank—until it became clear that Lin had more interest in her pets than she did in their friendship. Ming, a farm girl, was raised on a sheep ranch in Inner Mongolia. Cai Cai, a fellow Shanxi native, was tall and fiercely competitive. Mei-ying, sophisticated and demure, had traveled the farthest, almost eight hundred kilometers from the coastal city of Dalian. They asked her questions about her hobbies, what movies she liked to watch, where she disappeared to every weekend.

It felt like an affront not to respond. But Lin stayed quiet.

"Have you heard the mute?" Mei-ying would repeat, like a bad joke, to any of the other first-years on their hall who would listen.

Their dorm room was narrow as a train car, two sets of bunk beds stacked against the wall like matchsticks. The four of them took turns using the vanity and wash basin by the door. The shared bathroom with spigots for boiling and cold water was located at the end of the hall. A communal table along with four olive-green stools slumped in the center of the room for study or meals or playing cards.

But Lin kept almost exclusively to her own bunk. She'd always done things on her own, exercising a fierce independence that bewildered her teachers and classmates. While her mother had always attributed Lin's difference to something she was born with, Lin knew it was more circumstantial than anything else. Her aversion to people was the disappointment of not meeting their expectations. From a young age, she feared what others thought of her: she wore her hair short, had a house full of pets, preferred speaking English over Guoyu. She hated singing patriotic songs on the schoolyard or brandishing the red scarf of the Young Pioneers knotted tight around her neck. During the Monday morning flag-raising ceremony, she feigned dizziness to avoid attendance.

But as Lin got older, she saw that her unwillingness to conform to convention touched on something more entrenched. Anything she said or did made her feel like she was being judged. In a society that valued the whole, she'd been trapped by the limitations of what she, as an individual, could do. And at the university, she was physically trapped, too. Unlike in high school, Lin couldn't retreat home to her animals at the end of the day. She fashioned a makeshift curtain out of gauzy blue fabric and fastened it to the wooden beam above her bunk. At night, after curfew and lights out, Lin pulled out her phone, shrouding herself in the stark white glare of her own private oasis. She had no idea how she would keep her promise to her mother to make even a single friend.

Lin had known all along that pets weren't allowed in the dorm, but her roommates, for the first two weeks, seemed to tolerate them enough.

Then September came—sandstorm season—and Lin sealed the single window with plastic and duct tape to prevent dust from seeping in under the frame, just like she'd always done at home. But pretty soon the dorm room began to smell like the pet shop on Wukang Road. Lin tried everything she could: she got up early—tiptoeing around the room in the quiet dark—to change the cages, lay down a fresh bed of straw, replace the water. At night, she kept the cages beneath her bed, and before she left for class, she ferried them on top, careful to make sure they got enough light.

"Can you believe the mute?" she overheard Mei-ying say. "Doesn't she know it's against school policy to keep animals in the dorm?"

"There's a reason people leave them outside," Ming piped up.

"Someone should do something about it," Cai Cai added, with a sneer.

Their threats only served to draw Lin further into herself. She lived in fear that she would come home after class one day to find her pets confiscated, one of her roommates ratting her out to the dorm supervisor, or worse, the dean. The only thing stopping them, Lin knew, was her remarkable proficiency with English.

On the first day of English class, the foreign teacher, Travis, went around the room making each of the students introduce themselves. He was wearing a button-down shirt tucked under a navy-blue sweater, his shoulder-length hair twisted in a bun. Each of the students answered with their names and hometowns, but when Lin didn't respond immediately, Travis paused.

"What's wrong, cat got your tongue?"

"What does it mean?" she asked in English, her face blank. She'd never heard the expression. In high school, it always felt tedious speaking to Wu laoshi in what was a second language for them both. But Lin had never met a foreigner before, much less talked to one. The other students had gawked when he walked in, too: a real waiguoren in the flesh. *Where was he from? Could he speak Chinese? Did he know how to use chopsticks?* A hush came over the room when he'd begun to speak.

"It means to be shy, you know, not talkative," Travis said. "Is that you?" Some of the other students in class who could understand him snickered. Shy was an understatement. The word he was looking for was jianmin, pariah.

But Lin sat up straight in her chair.

"No," she said, "the cat doesn't have my tongue." She looked around the room, as if surveying a fiefdom. "I have his."

By the third week of class, Travis had already cycled through the more basic lessons on food and clothing and was onto animals: farms, zoos, aquariums. At university, English was required for all students. But Lin's roommates—who were also biology majors—couldn't care less about the language. They were more than happy to skip class just as long as they passed. So, in exchange for Lin doing their homework, they promised to keep quiet about her pets.

On the blackboard, Travis drew pictures of animals in white chalk with the English words written next to them. It would have been a good study aid, Lin thought, had he not drawn the animals so badly that it was impossible to tell whether something was a walrus or an elephant because they both had a tusk in the same place.

"This is the word for giraffe," Travis said, before stepping back and scanning the letters, Lin suspected, to make sure he'd spelled it correctly.

"What's that one?" Lin asked, pointing a finger at a lumpy shape with crosshair markings and a bushy tail.

Lin had never been much of a notetaker in class. She could stare at a cross section of a pancreas or a list of world capitals organized alphabetically and have no trouble committing the information to heart. But she found herself scribbling furiously in her notebook in Travis's classes. Not vocabulary or sentence fragments, but the things she noticed about him. His mannerisms, his gestures, the way he looped his l's on the chalkboard. His nervous habit, after assigning an activity for the class to do in pairs, of pacing from the podium to the window and staring up at the oak tree with its sun-dappled leaves. His hands drawn to either side of his hip, chin tilted skyward, his mouth slightly agape.

The class now seemed to be glowering collectively at Lin—at her newfound loquaciousness—but her attention was rapt. Lin sat in the same seat every day, at the very front of the class. She could express herself in English precisely because it didn't feel as though she was expressing herself at all. It was like adopting a wholly different persona, in a pretend world, like learning an animal language.

"Oh," Travis said, "that's a pony." From his throat erupted a noise Lin associated with the old cowboy Westerns she'd streamed back home. But the rest of the class exploded in laughter.

"What is it?" Travis asked, confounded. "It couldn't be any worse than my drawing." Calling a baby horse a pony—and not, frankly, a small horse—didn't make any sense to Lin, so why should their sounds be any different? Horses neighed in English, bees went buzz, and dogs—most idiotic of all—woofed. The only sound that came at all close to mirroring the Chinese equivalent, Lin decided, was a cat's meow.

Had Travis ever been to a zoo? Owned a pet? Walked far enough away from campus that he could see the stray dogs curled up in restaurant entranceways cruelly shooed away with a straw broom? Nearly a month of notes during class and still Lin felt she wasn't any closer to understanding her teacher. This bizarre person who Lin saw her own likeness in—recognized, in other words, as being *human*—in some ways more resembled the animals she cared for, each with their own distinct personality, striking features, curious habits. It nagged at her incessantly, this sense that he was both like her and yet completely different, a new creature to be understood.

"Look, if you want to see some *real* animals," Lin said, taking him aside after class, "I've got them." She smiled the same smile she made when she first bought Boom from the pet store. "I can show you."

On the afternoon they first got lunch together, the sandstorms had already dusted the campus in a thin silt. The restaurants that lined South Yard had thick cloth tartans draped over the front doors, a defense against the dust and the cold. Walking alongside Travis—close, but not close enough to draw suspicion—Lin first had to peek between the slats in the curtains to check whether anyone else from her class was sitting inside. She didn't want to draw any unwanted attention from eating alone with the foreign teacher.

Lin eventually settled on a small stall at the edge of South Yard, far from the normal student traffic, and after the lunchtime rush. There was a glut of plastic wrappers partially blocking the sewer drain out front. Stray cats were passing in and between her legs with hunks of scavenged huotui dangling from their mouths. She let her eyes linger on their scrawny bodies, their frayed tails. Would Boom have been out here, too, had she not intervened? She felt a swell of pride. As helpless as she was, she still had the power to alter another creature's fate.

When they sat down, the waitress—who looked no older than Lin—approached the table with a notebook in her hands.

"Dian shenme ne?"

Travis's eyes widened and searched the room. "Can you ask for a menu?" Travis asked Lin, opening and closing his hands like a billfold.

But there were no menus. The names of the dishes were scrawled on a sheet of butcher paper affixed to the wall, clear as day. Not only could he not speak Mandarin, but he evidently couldn't read it either. One mystery solved. Lin sucked in her breath, the way she did when she was made to order at restaurants with her mother.

"Two bowls of noodles," she said. And then added: "a hardboiled egg in his." She pointed down at the spot in front of Travis where her eyes were fixed.

"Thanks," Travis said, when the waitress had walked off. "I'm sunk without pictures."

The foreign men Lin saw in TV shows and western movies all looked older to Lin—taller, fatter, with broad shoulders and beards that covered their lips and chins. But Travis was slight and wiry; freckles blossomed on the sides of his face like wild lilac. She was surprised when he told her he was only twenty-two, just three years older than her.

Her eyes edged up from the table to meet his. "Did you just graduate?" Lin asked. Travis nodded.

"Not much you can do with a communications degree." He ran a finger over the edge of the plastic tablecloth. "You've probably never even heard of Tennessee."

Lin shook her head. "Why come all the way here?"

"I don't know, try something different," he said. "I'm still figuring out what I want to do with my life. To be honest," Travis paused, wiping away the sticky film that collected on his hand, "this whole teaching thing, I'm kind of winging it."

Lin discovered that Travis was clueless about most other things, too. It was his first time in China, a country he'd only ever learned about from history textbooks and cable news before he arrived. He was talkative—funny, even—in class, but otherwise was speechless. He had to point and nod to accomplish the most basic tasks. He didn't know the first thing he would do when he left school, and China was never a place he imagined living. But Travis was also, for Lin, like no one she could ever have imagined befriending.

To her surprise, Lin offered to spend more time with Travis outside of class. She didn't feel nervous when she talked with him. Maybe it was because of the way her animals also blinked their wide eyes at unfamiliar things or straightened up, crooning, when they'd done something well. There was no judgment in the way Travis looked at her, and in him she saw the possibility of a new reality, another way to exist in the world.

"What's that?" Travis asked. The xiaomaibu in South Yard was lined with composition notebooks, headphones, plastic toy helicopters dangling from the rafters. Travis pointed at an electrical outlet attached to a vial of clear liquid.

"It's to prevent mosquitoes," Lin said. "They hate the smell." Travis pushed his nose up to the vent and breathed deeply.

"It's not for humans," Lin laughed, tugging at his sleeve.

"I hoped it would smell like apple cinnamon or something," Travis said. "Like a Glade PlugIn." Lin nodded but didn't respond. It was one of the first things she'd written down in her notebook about him: *explains things in ways I don't understand.*

Travis lived in teacher housing on the far side of campus, in red-brick flats that he explained looked like old one-room schoolhouses where he was from in America. But when Lin came over, the place he lived more closely resembled the ancient manors in Yuci's laocheng than anything else: a stand-alone house with shared living room and two bedrooms, one on each side. Luxurious by campus standards. A far cry from the glorified barracks she was forced to cohabit.

"They have a scent like that for mice too," Lin said, "maybe we should buy it." She'd already gathered up the essentials: mop, toilet paper, hard plastic containers to keep his food intact.

"What do you know about mice?" he asked, teasing, by the checkout line.

"I buy them to feed my snakes," Lin replied. "But if I knew they were living in your walls, I'd catch them there instead." Travis's eyes grew wide.

"But I thought you liked animals?"

"I do."

"You're an enigma," Travis said, shaking his head. "Has anyone ever told you that?"

Lin had always been practical. She did her best to care for each individual creature while it was alive, but she wasn't afraid of death. She never named her gerbils, certain that they would die too soon. Guinea pigs were composted, tossed like overdone potatoes into the backyard to fertilize her mother's crops. Even the translucent fin of a goldfish seemed to exemplify her own mortality, that one day she too would find herself belly-up at the surface of the water.

"And your rabbits," Travis asked. "What do you do with them when they die?"

"Eat them," she said, as naturally as opening an umbrella in the rain. "They taste especially good in stews."

Lin brought lunch from South Yard to eat with Travis at his house. He lived alone, and Lin relished any opportunity to avoid being in her dorm room. She wasn't getting along with her roommates any better now than when she moved in six weeks ago. One afternoon, she'd forgotten to lock the cage, and one of her gerbils popped out, peeling across the floor when Lin wasn't there. He skittered around the room for close to an hour—darting Ming's advances—until Cai Cai called, screaming, telling Lin she was going straight to the dean, English homework be damned.

Eventually, Lin broke down and asked Travis if she could bring the cages over to his place.

"You won't have to worry about them at all," Lin said. "They're very independent. And I'll do all the work." She'd run out of options. If Travis said no, she feared she'd have to drop out, pack up her crates, and return home. But Travis was unfazed.

"I don't mind at all," he said. "You know how good I am with animals." He grinned, and Lin, finding him both stupid and irresistible, smiled back.

She'd never thought that someone else might share this connection. If Travis could value her pets, maybe he could understand her, too.

"Just don't kill them while I'm sleeping," she said, "or let them out of the house."

"I swear I won't mess with them," he said. He pushed his pair of chopsticks down into the mound of rice and raised three fingers in the air. "Scout's honor."

"Scout who?" Lin asked. She was still swallowing a piece of eggplant when Travis reached for her hand and brought it to his heart.

"It means to promise," he said. His skin was warm against hers, his heart thudding in his chest. Lin wondered if time had slowed, or if she'd momentarily stopped breathing herself.

"You're doing me a favor," Travis continued, "it'll give me something to do after class."

Lin knew that Travis was bored. When he was hired, the waishiban assured him there would be other foreign teachers on campus, but so far, it was just him. After class, Lin often found him sprawled on the couch in shorts and a T-shirt, phone cradled in his long fingers. She insisted on getting him out. They'd walk around campus, Lin pointing out the characters for noodles, soup, skewered meat, if only for a chance to play teacher, watching Travis marvel at their hidden meanings. With freckles and pale skin, Travis stood out like a raised nail. Like a professor twice his age, he wore square glasses that sat crookedly on his nose. Still, his cuteness was undeniable. He had wavy hair and, when he spoke, his Adam's apple twitched nervously in his throat.

The other freshmen eyed Lin conspiratorially, wishing they'd drawn whatever lot had netted the foreign teacher's attention. Her roommates began to get bold, saying things loud enough that Lin could hear them when she walked the halls.

"That's Lin, too good for the Chinese boys," Mei-ying would say, and then, putting a hand over her mouth as if to muffle the sound, "She's got chongyang meiwai." The words sounded to Lin both coarse and ridiculous. As if she was literally burning up, becoming consumed, by whiteness.

By then Lin had started wearing her hair down instead of in a bun, where it curled to meet her collarbone. In high school, she was used to being envied by her classmates for being a xueba, but never for her ability to attract boys. When she smiled—as she did when she was with Travis—dimples appeared like small flourishes on either side of her face. But it wasn't Travis's whiteness, exactly, that was inviting. He could have been any color under the sun, blue or polychromic or magenta. All she knew was that he, like she, might well have been an alien species.

But even Lin wasn't naive enough to misconstrue the subtext behind her classmates' words: With whiteness came money. Travis laoshi had a good passport and could go places. And Lin, they all seemed to be sure, was looking for a way out.

Word spread fast. Out at the big track, where Lin sometimes walked laps after dinner, she caught other students—people she'd never even seen before—stopping to give her a dirty look before turning away. She found a note—*Chinese men can't even find women to fuck*—scrawled on a blank page in her notebook. Her contraband animals no longer kept her up at night; she had much bigger things to worry about. And yet, she'd done nothing to rouse suspicion. The only touch she'd ever exchanged with Travis were the hugs he insisted on every time they parted, tiny bursts of heat and breath that Lin could still feel on her face long after she left.

September passed, giving way to colder weather. Leaves collected in dull bunches along the brick walkways. The plastic film on the window in Lin's dorm began to bulge and contract, like a patient attached to a ventilator. At night, Lin stared up at the mess of wooden slats above her bed. Her private oasis began to feel more like a coffin, an early grave.

By the end of October, Lin couldn't hold in her curiosity any longer. By then there were two more foreign teachers at the school: tall, brutish men with names she couldn't remember. It didn't matter. As far as Lin was concerned, Travis was the first of his kind. She'd started to have dreams about him, things she'd never done with anyone. Travis running his hands below her waist, his breath hot in her ear.

That morning, Travis surprised the class by bringing in pumpkins to carve—a green mesh satchel slung across his back—and Lin noted the heft of the bag as it cascaded off his shoulders, the tightness in his grip as he plopped a pumpkin down on each table.

"An American tradition," he said proudly, looking on.

In his backpack, he ferried over a handful of kitchen knives from his house and a bowl to collect the phlegmy seeds. The pumpkins were dusty and dark green, half-flattened like flying saucers. Alien transporters.

Lin made up her mind then that she was going to go over to Travis's house that night. She was concerned about what people might think. She didn't know the rules, or if there were even rules at all. She feared that if it happened—*really* happened—that this time it wouldn't just be yaoyan, the small, unfounded rumors that circulate in the track or by the campus square, it would be full-blown feiwan: a scandal. So big, even the dean would have to get involved. Even still, she resigned herself to a simple fact: *If everyone believes it already, then it may as well be true.*

Lin bought cheap food in South Yard: dumplings, two kuai sausages roasted over a charcoal spit, a plastic-bagged bowl of cold noodles. But the food was a ruse, a decoy as much for herself as for anyone who happened to cross her on the road. When she came close to the cluster of red-brick foreign houses, she stopped short. Outside, on the hexagonal tiles that led to the front door, she saw Boom. She had to squint to see clearly in the dim light, but the cat was unmistakable: the same white spot on his nose, golden eyes, tail lifted in a perpetual state of wonder.

He didn't look hurt or injured, and when Lin rushed over, almost scaring him, she realized it had been a week or more since she'd last seen him. Had he been out of the house the whole time? She had to stop to remember if she had refilled his food and water bowls. Boom jumped up from the path onto the windowsill of Travis's house. The square windows, with the orange shades drawn over them, and there he was, walking back and forth in front, like a runway model. Boom: confident and carefree. Boom: a crash of thunder. Boom: that most electrifying English word.

Lin crouched down, letting Boom brush past her fingers. She never forgot things like feedings, but suddenly she felt her life splintering. There was so much inside, ready to burst, that it was impossible to bring her mind back to that old life before she met Travis. She had already come too far. It was as unimaginable as believing that Boom might ever concede freedom now that he'd tasted it, the safety of the indoors already a distant memory.

"Look who I found," Lin said, when Travis opened the latch on the screen door. "I thought you promised not to let him out."

"I didn't know how to tell you," Travis said. "He got out when I was teaching one day and—"

"I'm not angry," Lin said.

"He always comes back."

"I know," she said. She set the bags of food down on a stool by the door. She forced out the next words, not giving herself the chance to change her mind. "I've been thinking about you."

With one hand, she led Travis to the spare bedroom on the opposite side of the house, the empty room where Travis never slept. She was insistent. There was a square bed in the center of the room facing a set of windows with the blinds drawn. She sat down on the bed and felt the hard heft of the mattress against her thigh. She put Travis's hand on her knee and walked it slowly up the fabric of her jeans, resting it on the metal button beneath her navel. The heat from the radiator felt hot on her face, and she was grateful when she could turn to him and close her eyes.

She tasted a hunger on his lips, a quiet desperation. Travis wrung the shirt over his head and shimmied his pants to the floor. The speed with which he was laid bare startled Lin: an animal stretched out on his hands and knees, ready to ravish his prey. Lin lay down flat on her back. She let him remove her clothes, paw every inch of her skin. She looked up at the ceiling with its square gray panels, not unlike the ones in the room where she'd grown up. A pink speck of insulation showed at each of its corners like the plume of a parakeet. She wondered if there had been birds up there—a whole menagerie—all along, would it have changed how she felt?

"I like you, Lin He," Travis said.

Lin nodded, swallowing a knot in her throat. She had expected he might have done this before, but it didn't feel practiced or rehearsed. She was surprised by the fine hairs that covered his legs and arms, how some parts of him felt smooth while others were jagged and rough. The way he mouthed words that she couldn't make out. His breath quickening as he swayed and surged against her. She liked the sensation of being weightless, of feeling the heavy presence of Travis above her, as though she could sink down into the mattress and forget all about her roommates, her mother back home, even the animals sleeping just beyond the closed door. With their clothes off, they were like two creatures in the wild with only their nature to cling to.

"You should stay," Travis said, a giddy lilt to his voice. They were lying side by side, Lin's head swimming. She felt a sharp pain throbbing between her legs like a bruise. Outside, it was threatening to storm.

Still, Lin was surprised by how light she felt, how comfortable she was in her own skin. She tossed the sheets back, baring herself to the halogen light. No, Lin decided, she couldn't stay. But there would be time. It was more than just speaking in English with Travis. There were no societal conventions, no thousands of years of expectations to underperform. For the first time, Lin realized she could feel accepted—wanted, even—in all her startling difference.

She gathered her clothes from the heap on the floor, slipping on her jeans first and then pulling the jacket over her head. She was careful not to let the screen door slam when she went out. The night was cool, and Lin could almost make out the stars through the gauze of clouds. Boom was somewhere out here, too, his fur shimmering under the night sky. And she was proud of him. In her nineteen years, she'd overlooked something essential: that her pets were still confined by her beliefs. To be truly free, she realized, was to crawl out from under her, to take on a new life all their own.

The path back to her dorm was shrouded in a dense mist. Lin strode across the crooked tiles, past the faded red pagoda—a thatch of weeds growing in its hutch—the crop fields wrapped in plastic film, the spaceship hull of the cafeteria. She exhaled at the chilly air that seemed to twinkle with her breath. There was nowhere she would rather be.

2

The train was packed so tightly that Liz Chen could barely stand. One hand on the fabric cover of the seat she was pressed up against, the other wedged into the metal luggage rack that lined the top of the berth. In the seats in front of her, four women were squeezed around a square table, a bag of watermelon seeds propped against the windowsill. Each wore a matching turtleneck sweater and a pair of Fanta-orange sweatpants with a confidence that could only come with friendship.

It was rare to see a group of women traveling alone. Most of the girls Liz saw at the university were already coupled up, walking arm in arm with their boyfriends from class to the cafeteria. Parting ways at the entrance to the gender-segregated baths. Disappearing in the high brush just beyond the teacher flats. At night, phone flashlight pitched at the ramshackle path, Liz prayed she wouldn't bump into one of her students—their bodies tangled on a stone bench, coat slipping from their shoulders—though she couldn't say she didn't envy their ardor.

The women on the train looked to be about Liz's age: fresh out of college, starting their first jobs. But they were also about the age Liz's mom was when she'd had Liz. How Pearl must have looked in her prime: trim bangs swept to one side, narrow hips, high cheekbones.

It wasn't long after Pearl and Liz's father got married that they emigrated from China. He was doing research for an American academic before taking an opportunity to study in the states. There were hardly any photographs that survived the journey, so Liz had always had to look in the mirror and squint. But it was hard for Liz to picture her mom's life all those years ago, in the rural Fujian village where she'd grown up, before being whisked away to the suburbs of Ohio.

It must have been a shock for her mom to go from being forbidden to date in high school to needing to be married by the time she graduated college. Liz couldn't imagine how anyone could learn the first thing about relationships that way. Or sex. But Pearl had told Liz that there just weren't that many choices for women when she was young. Figures, Liz thought. It was no coincidence, then, that she'd had to settle for the kind of man who would eventually leave her.

No one in China seemed to think about marriage the way Liz did now: hoping to put it off indefinitely, but at least long enough that she could stop feeling utterly disappointed in men. Pearl had always told her to take her time, not to rush into anything. But if her mom had been alive long enough to see Liz through graduation, Liz was sure she'd have told her to start looking for a husband by now, too.

Liz heard a shout rear up from the aisle a few rows behind her and quickly turned her head.

"Then you're left in the dust," Collin's voice hollered, "unless I stuck by you."

Liz stared hard at the ceiling and sighed. She would have liked to believe the intrusion was an anomaly. A product of the zhapi at dinner or the cans of Xue Hua still making the rounds between them. But even just a month into living in Qixian, Liz was inured to such displays—Jim, Collin, and Travis having their own fireside karaoke in the train car—just as she had become used to the standing-room only trains from Taiyuan, the spitting and shouting, the smell of stale smoke gathering in the air vents like tear gas. Worse still was that Jim and Collin had actually convinced some of the other passengers to join in.

"Everybody, now," Jim called out, his mouth framed by a firetruck red goatee. He slowed down and enunciated each syllable, like speaking to a classroom full of children. "You're the sunflower. *One more time!* You're the sunflower."

The sight of the three men—boys, really—in collared shirts, holding a primer on American hip-hop might have been funny, Liz conceded, if she hadn't felt a different set of eyes trained solely on her. Aunties. Wire-frame glasses and gray hair matted down to their scalps. Eyebrows squinted in a V. She could hear the conversation ringing in her head:

"Are you with them?"

"No," she could protest.

"Those boys have no suzhi." No class. Liz would nod. "And you?"

"Look at me. I'm just like you," Liz would say. She would get that far and freeze. *So long as you never have to hear me speak.*

The train screeched to a stop, and Liz's hand juddered from the metal railing. She was getting restless. There was an ache in her calves that got worse the longer she stood. The boys had moved onto another song by now—one she didn't recognize—and Jim and Collin were talking to a man over twice their age, his face smeared with soot.

"American?" the man asked them in English, almost gleeful.

What the fuck else? Liz muttered under her breath.

Crews dressed in rumpled navy uniforms pushed through to the furnace, presumably to deposit more coal. Liz stared out the window, at the crests of brown smokestacks that dotted the arid landscape. Hardly a speck of green in sight. And then, just beyond the billowing plumes, she recognized the thatched roofs of the Foreign Affairs Office, the cluster of dorm buildings the color of Pepto-Bismol, as the campus. Almost there, she whispered to herself. An incantation. A prayer.

"Would you mind?" a voice asked, tapping her on the shoulder. It was Travis, face flushed, phone in hand. "Battery's dead."

"And?" Liz asked. Travis waved the phone in the air, an identical model to her own. "What makes you think I've got a charger?"

Travis rolled his eyes. "Come on," he said. "I'm not that drunk. Give me a little credit."

It was Liz's curse. She was the kind of person who prepared for every calamity: hand disinfectant, insect repellent, sunscreen in January. She flopped her arm over her satchel-sized purse.

"We're almost back," Liz said. "I can see the campus from here."

"Just charge it, would you?" he asked. Liz endured a few more glares from the aunties. She was careful not to make eye contact with Travis, but her cover was as good as blown. The only thing worse than being associated with the foreign men was being mistaken for fawning over one of them instead.

"Don't say I never did anything for you," Liz said, snatching the phone and plunging it to the bottom of her bag.

The streets were dark by the time the train pulled into the station. Only the new fog lights that flanked the university paifang were visible in the distance, a skein of white atop the horizon like the layer of film on fresh soymilk. Jim and Collin had hopped off the train and were exchanging handshakes with a group by the station exit. Liz barreled ahead. She was desperate to separate herself from what she saw as the perfect portrait of American exceptionalism.

"What's the hurry?" Travis shouted, a Hongtashan wedged between his lips. "We already missed curfew."

Liz hadn't checked her phone, but to do so now would be pointless, an act tantamount to willing a miracle into existence. It hadn't been her idea to stay out that late. If Liz had had it her way, they would all have cooked a big meal together for Thanksgiving. Bought fresh chicken and gooseberries and potatoes at the market. Invited over some students. Sat around the living room and talked about what they were grateful for. Liz wanted to believe, from the first day she arrived at the university, that she and the other foreigners could be more than glorified strangers, forced to live together against their will simply on account of their nationality. That they could be each other's confidants in a place far from home. Something, perhaps, resembling family.

But Jim and Collin had vetoed Liz's proposal two to one, and Travis, who could have brought the vote to a tie, sided with the other two.

"Golden Hans *is* kind of perfect," Travis said. He cited the wide aisles, large steins of beer, whole pork loins and beef shanks that were paraded to each table like prize animals at a state fair. "What's more American than that?"

It didn't matter that the boys had dragged Liz to Golden Hans, the only restaurant for miles with even the wispiest semblance of Western food, every weekend since she'd been in Qixian. Liz's presence was out of her own obligation more than anything else—an appeal to her supposed *Chinese sensibility*—preferring the will of the group over the individual, the collective over the self. If any of that bullshit was to be believed.

"I'm exhausted," Liz shouted over her shoulder.

"Tell me something new," Travis said, staggering alongside her. Behind him, Jim and Collin had their arms around each other's shoulders—Collin thin and lanky, Jim stout as an ox—swaying like tall stalks of corn before the thresher.

"I wanted to go home hours ago," Liz said. "The gate's locked now. How do you suppose we're going to get in?" They'd gotten back late before, but Liz had never missed curfew.

"You should have said something earlier," Travis said, cracking open the can of Xue Hua bulging from his jeans pocket. "And don't worry about the gate. Just follow my lead."

It was three kilometers from the train station to campus. Though it would've been faster to hitch a ride from one of the three-wheeled motorbikes or the black cabs with the dazzling faux-taxi marquees idling at the entrance to the train station, Liz didn't want to bother with having to corral the drunken men into a car, to have to explain—yet again—what a bunch of foreigners were doing in a backwater town, to apologize to the driver at the campus gate after a dispute they would almost certainly get into over the price. After a month of living with the other foreign teachers, she was tired of always being the one to clean up after them. She was tired of being the mother she didn't have.

Still not slowing her pace, Liz turned to Travis. "I've kind of given up," she said, and then added: "You know saying anything wouldn't have made a difference anyway."

What Liz wanted to tell him was that ever since she'd arrived in China, she'd felt invisible. It wasn't just the way the other foreign teachers treated her—making plans without her input, dominating conversation—but the way the whole town did, too. She was never asked how long she'd been studying Chinese, never once praised for using the simplest phrases: a *two, please* to the man who peddled lamb skewers outside the swimming pool or a *thank you* to the woman who ran the grain store in South Yard. She wasn't doted on like the foreign men for the endearing pitch of their accents, their frothy heads of blond hair.

Liz had tapered bangs that came to a stiff point, jet-black hair that waterfalled past her shoulders. On the surface, her Americanness wasn't obvious. She would only have to change her outfit—donning a pair of overalls or a denim skirt, a blouse with a frilly lace collar or a T-shirt with a mangled English phrase—to blend in with any one of the girls on campus. It made her feel indistinguishable, like she might well have ceased to exist.

Travis pulled a lighter out of his pocket and ran his finger against the coils until the flint caught. He only smoked when he was drunk. Liz hated the way he did things just to fit in, that he succumbed so easily to the slightest hint of peer pressure.

"Why does it seem like you're always angriest at me?" Travis asked.

"Because you should know better."

Of all the places she could have gone in China, Liz had never imagined she'd end up in Qixian. Growing up, Liz knew she was different. She and her brother, Phil, were the only Asians at her high school in Akron. She got her eyes pulled, got called ugly names. She was told more than once to go back to a country she'd never been to, like the one she was born into somehow wasn't hers to claim.

Everything Liz had learned about China—pitched fields for growing wheat, roads lined with white-ringed cedars, the red-shingled village where her parents lived—was from her mom. But almost immediately after Liz's dad left, Pearl stopped saying anything about China. It was as if the entire country was jettisoned from her memory as quickly as the man she married. Liz would have erased it too if she could. Why else endure the tormenting from her classmates? But she realized that if she never set foot in China, there would always be a part of her she'd never fully understand. Phil was increasingly reluctant about her going, but Pearl's death only bolstered her resolve. Liz felt like she had to hold more tightly to her identity, like she had something to prove.

When she started looking for a way to go to China after graduation, teaching seemed like the most feasible route. She had friends going to teach English in Japan, Paraguay, Spain. Why not China too? But none of the schools Liz applied to in the big cities accepted her. They said they required master's degrees, years of experience. No matter that she'd studied English in college, tutored ESL students in the afternoons after class. She knew other Americans who had skated into Beijing and Shanghai on little more than their passports. In interviews, she noticed she kept getting asked the same question: *Are you a native English speaker?* Yes, she'd said. But looking at her Chinese face, no one could really be sure.

The more she researched, the more Liz learned that rural counties, typically short on foreign teachers, were more willing to bend the rules. She found a university in Shanxi Province, four hundred miles from Beijing, that wanted to hire her. But even then, there was a problem with her visa. She didn't arrive until early November, a month after Jim and Collin, and three months after Travis. It was unclear what accounted for the delay. Liz was the only one with a TEFL certificate, another supposed requirement, and the battery of health tests and X-rays she was made to undergo had all come back clean. The waishiban cited only "bureaucratic obstacles" that, Liz suspected, could be hurdled only with bribes. She wondered if it was a holdover from when her parents emigrated from China in the '90s, under circumstances that were never entirely clear.

Liz was assigned to live with Travis. Travis—unlike Jim and Collin, who had been friends in college and all too happy to room together—lived alone, and China was less uptight about gender than Liz had given it credit. The red-brick duplex functioned like a perfect mirror: Each of the two halves had its own bedroom, bathroom, and kitchen. In the center was a shared living room, with upholstered wooden furniture and dog-eared paperbacks that had been passed down through generations of foreign teachers. But the first thing Liz noticed when she arrived from the airport and Travis greeted her at the door was a cage of gerbils and a cat's litter box near the entrance.

Liz warmed to him immediately. Travis introduced her to Qixian's drum tower, what remained of its city walls. In South Yard, he pointed out the restaurant with the best knife-cut noodles, which boba tea counters used real milk, the cheapest doufu hua for breakfast. She learned how to judge air quality by standing at the big track and squinting at the mountains in the distance. When the mountains were any more defined than a slushy gray inkblot, they went running together off campus, past the crop fields where farmers toiled past sundown, and into the back roads of neighboring villages. Travis knew the town in a way that felt inherited. Like he'd had his own guide.

It was true that Liz was harder on Travis than she was on the other foreign teachers. Travis had been at the school the longest, could at least speak passable Mandarin, and was, after all, sleeping with one of his students.

They were nearly back to campus now, and the glittering neon paifang was sharpening into view. Jim and Collin were a few blocks behind, still making broken conversation with students they'd met on the train.

"Does Lin know where you are?" Liz asked. Travis straightened up, the end of his cigarette flecked with ash.

"What do you mean?"

"Like where you are right now," Liz said. "Or that you went out tonight?"

"No, why should she?" Travis gave a shrug that was meant to appear nonchalant, but she couldn't take him seriously. He looked like a cartoon snowman sucking on a twig pipe.

"What if she needs to feed her pets?" Liz asked. "Also, would you stop with that? The other guys can't see you, and you really aren't impressing me."

The gate to the school consisted of a cement barracks and a bright row of waist-high metal fence posts fastened with security cameras. Just beyond it was a musical fountain, where waves danced in controlled loops to driveling Kenny G ballads for sixteen hours without pause. But now, the fountain was silent and the waves dormant, allowed their nightly rest. As Liz and Travis approached the gate, one of the guards poked his head out from inside the barracks, where another was asleep in a folding chair.

"You again," the guard laughed, crossing his arms. "Curfew was an hour ago."

Travis pulled out the rest of the pack of Hongtashan from his jacket pocket, the gold lip of the wrapper visible. But the guard waved him off.

"No chance," he said. "Not after what you laowai did last time."

Travis stared at the guard, saying nothing, still shaking the pack of cigarettes. Liz sighed, tugging Travis off to one side.

"He says he won't take it," she said. "It must have been something serious you guys did last time?"

Travis's face turned a pique of red and he grimaced, pushing Liz aside. "I go through," he shouted in staccato Mandarin. "Wo! Guo! Qu!"

He was banging on the metal fence post with both hands, trying to force the gate open. The guard shook his sleeping coworker awake and soon they were both standing at attention, night sticks in hand.

"What do you think you're doing?" Liz hissed under her breath. "Do you want to get us banned from leaving campus?"

"Bu hao yi si," Liz said. "I'm sorry for the misunderstanding." Even though she spoke Mandarin with her mom growing up, her vocabulary was limited, and it took considerable effort to read characters. She looked at the guards, whose faces contorted as she spoke, the familiar shame rising in her chest. It was bad enough she couldn't be taken seriously as a native English speaker. But she didn't expect that people would sooner choose to believe she was born biantai—off—than entertain the possibility that someone with her face could have learned Mandarin as a second language.

"And who are you?" the first guard asked. "His translator?"

"I'm an English teacher here too," Liz started. "We live—"

"We've never seen you before," the second guard jeered. "How do we know he didn't pick you up?" He pointed his baton to the lit area toward the train station.

"Pick me up?" Liz asked, but as soon as the words left her mouth, she realized what they meant. Xiaojie. Whore. Her face twisted into a scowl.

"We're going to need to see your papers," the first guard said, "your residency permit."

"It's back at my house," Liz explained.

"Mei banfa," the guard replied. He shoved both hands into his pockets. "Better keep it moving or take it to South Yard." Liz had heard of the red-lit area of identical pay-by-the-hour hotel rooms just beyond the campus boundary. Pink gauzy curtains, no bedside table, plastic liner over the mattress. Students liked them, Liz learned, because the staff were more discreet than their roommates, and it was preferable to freezing outside in the cold.

But Liz didn't want privacy—certainly not with Travis. She wanted to go home.

"Un-fucking-believable," Liz muttered under her breath. She turned and walked away from the gate before the guards could question her any further.

The air outside was acrid and still. Qixian was the heart of vinegar country, where the dark liquid, pungent and thick, was bottled and shipped to every other province and exported abroad. But the factories had to compete with the coal mines, which operated from daybreak until dusk. It was only in the dead of night that the sky opened up, blooming with the blistering scent of tonic and salt. A much more welcome smell, Liz learned to appreciate, than the rotting-broccoli stench of sulfur that peppered the air with black streaks.

"Hey, wait up," Travis said, trailing after her.

"What did you do to piss off the guards like that?"

Travis paused. "We may have climbed over the gate."

"You what?"

"Me and the other guys were coming back late from something, and the guards were asleep. They didn't catch us, but I guess they must have recognized us from the security footage."

"No shit," Liz said, shaking her head, "you don't exactly blend in." Then she added: "It sure would have been nice of you to tell me that before I got accused of being paid to sleep with you."

She stopped short, letting the wind send a gust of vinegar air at her back. Her ex, Andrew, who Liz dated right up until she boarded the plane to Qixian, had the same blue eyes and dirty-blond hair as Travis. She would never admit it, but had Travis not been with Lin, and if she didn't already know what she knew, she might have been interested in him too.

Travis shot her a puzzled look, and Liz wasn't sure if he hadn't understood the exchange with the guards or if he would've only cared about the implication if he'd been the one put on trial.

"Look, about Lin," Travis said, rubbing his hands into fists. Liz's ears perked up. She'd only ever had a conversation with Travis about Lin once, when she first arrived:

"Do you ever feel weird about dating a student?" Liz had asked.

"We're not dating," Travis insisted.

"Sure, but are there repercussions for teachers and students commingling?"

"We're not commingling."

"Ok, but are there rules against *fucking* them?"

Since then, Liz had dropped the subject. It felt strange that they never talked about it again, considering that she told him all about Andrew. How they met in a biology lecture class that they both immediately dropped. How Andrew, when putting on a Southern drawl, tricked her into believing he was a descendant of Davy Crockett. How he was the only one with Liz at the hospital the day her mom died.

"I don't know what you're thinking about Lin," Travis continued. "All I'm saying is that she doesn't need to know my whereabouts. If Lin needs to feed her animals or whatever, she knows where to find the spare key. She doesn't need my permission. She's just in and out, no big deal."

"If this is your attempt at comforting me," Liz said, "you're doing a poor job."

Travis never described his relationship with Lin as anything remotely romantic. He preferred the term *language partner*, invoking the words anytime he knew Lin would be coming over. Liz marveled at the lengths he went to avoid being seen with her in public. Whenever Jim or Collin brought Lin up, he would change the subject. At group hot pot dinners, when they bragged about the girls they'd fucked at Florida State, Travis would laugh, and Liz quietly drowned her vegetables in a bowl of sesame sauce.

Back home, she wouldn't have tolerated it. She had friends who would've backed her up. But there was a certain distance she'd learned to live with in Qixian. She never told Travis that she went to bed crying most nights, knowing he wouldn't understand. Though she would hardly have had any reason to consider it before, Liz longed for the company of another woman. She'd wanted to believe that dating a Chinese girl instilled in Travis a certain sensitivity, a power of perception. But she was terrifically mistaken.

"Honestly, why does everything always have to be about you?" Liz caught herself breathing fast, bursts of vapor igniting in the air.

"We're just helping each other out," Travis said, ignoring Liz's question.

"Let me get this straight. Lin can't keep her pets in the dorm for fear of being kicked out of school. And you're—what exactly? Lonely?" She laughed. "Get over yourself. The world's not exactly fair."

"Look, this isn't what I signed up for either. You're Chinese," he said, wiping his lips with the back of his hand, "shouldn't this be easy for you?"

When Liz arrived on campus, she was given four classes of first-year English majors to teach. She'd taught before, but rarely to an entire room—forest-green chalkboard, wooden podium, thirty-five desks bolted into the floorboards—and never to students who looked like her. She was thrilled. But, almost immediately, she could tell her students didn't share the same enthusiasm. They didn't say anything about it—wouldn't have dared—but Liz knew they must have wondered what they did wrong to be stuck with her, when all the other first-years got to be taught by *real* foreigners.

"And that makes me some kind of expert?" Liz shot back. "It's not like I've been here before either."

"That's not what I meant," Travis said. "You're the one who came to China to find yourself or whatever."

"That's the whole point!" Liz exclaimed. "My parents left before I was born and I'm trying to figure out what all this means to me. I don't know any better than you do. I'm *Chinese American*, not Chinese. There's a difference."

Travis shrugged. "Could've fooled me."

"At least you have people here," Liz said, swallowing a lump in her throat. "I've never felt more alone." Liz had wrongly assumed it would be easy for her to make contacts. Maybe it was the inadequacy she felt with the language. The cultural miscues that might arise. None of the Chinese teachers at the university were close to her age, and most of her students could barely be counted on to attend class regularly, let alone socialize after.

At the end of the day, Liz was a huayi, not a native-born, which began to sound increasingly to her like the Chinese word huaiyi: to doubt. It was the worst of both worlds: too Chinese for America, not Chinese enough here. So instead, she'd tried to make inroads with Jim and Collin. She went out of her way to understand the cultures they were born into, the bizarre rituals they shared. Baptism. Sculling. Rushing. All of it, a waste. And there was no one she'd tried to get to know more than Travis.

Liz inhaled sharply, rubbing her nose with the edge of her finger. She half-expected Travis to see her upset and offer a hug, the way he did sometimes after they parted ways before class. She would have accepted it too. The desire for touch—any touch—outweighed any pride she could still muster.

But when she looked up, Travis's eyes were full of scorn.

"You know what this is really about?" Travis asked. "You're jealous." Liz felt a cold like poison seeping into every artery and vein.

"Hope you enjoy sharing a room with Jim and Collin tonight," she said. "You always side with them anyway." Liz set off toward the opposite end of campus. "And don't you dare follow me," she shouted, without turning around to face him.

Travis may have been at the school the longest, but only Liz knew about the secret entrance, past the heaps of leaves to be incinerated and broken stone shingles that lay just beyond the student dorms. The gate that surrounded the campus was shorter there, sloping down to meet the pavement. Liz hoisted herself up over the lip of the wall—tiptoeing around the curlicues of derelict barbed wire—and onto the red dirt path.

There were no guards and no cameras, and yet Liz couldn't help but feel watched. She dreaded thinking about seeing Travis back at the house but running into Lin would be almost as bad. Lin had a habit of holing up in Travis's room—sometimes, Liz was certain—even when Travis wasn't there. She had to feed the gerbils and the cat, sure, but Liz suspected there was something else. She didn't seem to interact much with other people. All those classmates and yet no friends of her own. Lin would come around in the dead of night, when Liz was already in bed, and leave by the next morning, stealing away in the cold chill of dawn.

Who is this girl? Liz asked herself, brushing her teeth in the morning or crawling under her sheets at night. This girl who had roundly inserted herself into Liz's life and yet seemed to want nothing to do with her. They rarely saw each other, much less had a proper conversation. It was like Lin somehow knew Liz's schedule better than she did, could predict Liz's next move before Liz could even think it. And yet, as easy as it was to judge Lin,

Liz couldn't help feeling sorry for her, too. Having Travis as her only confidant? she thought. Maybe she's just as lonely as me.

The house was quiet when Liz pulled back the screen door and turned the skeleton key in the lock. The front door creaked open with a heft that nearly startled her. Just then, Liz felt the soft crunch of something beneath her and, in the dark, saw a pair of eyes so round and bright she thought it was a rat. She screamed, sending her purse skittering to the floor. Boom sprang up onto the couch and slipped through the crack in the open window.

"Goddamn cat," Liz muttered. "One more thing Travis doesn't have to deal with."

Liz flicked on the light switch and stooped to the floor. She gathered back into her purse what had fallen out—gray shawl, change purse, tissue paper—before spotting the power bank and phone that Travis had asked her to hold on the train.

Liz glanced down at the blank screen and, instinctively, pressed her finger to the glass to make sure it still worked. The time flashed, as did a green text bubble with three messages. There was just a phone number but no name. Liz knew she shouldn't read them, but she couldn't stop herself.

Tonight, I will give you a surprise, the first text read in English. Liz expanded the second two.

This afternoon, I took a nap and dreamt of you. And then, suddenly, a longer message in Chinese:

You're going to dinner again in Taiyuan but didn't invite me. I feel like I must be a burden. Do you understand what I mean?

Liz knew immediately that it was Lin. She didn't know if Lin was actually teaching Travis or if Travis had been learning characters on his own. But either way, the texts in Chinese, the unsaved number. Further proof of Travis's desire to keep things under wraps.

Still, Liz couldn't make heads or tails of them. Perhaps they'd been in a fight and Lin had been the one to resolve it? It was infuriating to only read half the conversation and not the texts from Travis that prompted them.

Like seeing a reflection in a mirror but never knowing the person standing in front of it.

It surprised Liz how good Lin's English was, how seamlessly the two of them were able to communicate. They had each other, and yet Lin might as well have been alone.

Liz reached into her bag. She wouldn't have been able to explain what made her do it, but she copied Lin's number into her own phone and composed a new message.

Hi Lin, Liz wrote, *this is Liz, Travis's roommate*. She paused, and then added an exclamation point before hitting send.

If Liz had been jealous of Travis, it was because of this: He'd managed to befriend a Chinese student and she hadn't. She yearned to be that close, to imagine how her own life might have played out had her parents never left China. To see her experiences reflected through what could have been. To truly belong to a place. What she wouldn't give for that.

She texted again.

I think the two of us should meet.

3

It's getting colder, her mother Qi Fei texted. *Do you have enough to wear?* Lin was in her dorm room, the light from her phone throwing shadows across the white walls of her bunk.

Gou le, she texted back. It was the first week of December, the time of year when the days became hard to tell apart. Faint glow of red in the ashen sky when she rolled out of bed for class. Dark pallor that hung thick as a curtain before she was even hungry for dinner. There were long lines at the taps to fill her thermos with boiling water, crowds at the hot food section of the underground supermarket, frozen streaks in her hair when she left the bathhouse—or Travis's—and headed back to her dorm.

Lin's phone dinged again. *I can bring another coat if you need it. Maybe an extra blanket.* The vents on the radiator rattled like a train car. It was warm enough in the dorm, but in class, Lin had already begun to wear cotton sleeves over the top of her jacket, gloves that she rubbed together under her desk.

I'm fine, Lin texted, knowing better than to bring it up. Her mother had always been overly worried about her. Lin wasn't sure if it had something to do with her father's accident—how one morning he was in their kitchen, spooning babao zhou with youtiao, and by the evening, when she came back from kindergarten, there were two men rapping on the door in his place. They wore the same blue jackets smudged black with coal as her father had, but their heads were cast down, an envelope sealed with the company insignia in their outstretched hands.

It's no trouble, her mother wrote. *I can ride up tomorrow.* It didn't help that Lin was her only child. Even in high school, when Lin had nowhere better to be, her mother made it a point to schedule dinners together. She signed them both up to volunteer on weekends, convinced it would help

Lin build character. She needed to know about every school assignment and when it was due. Lin imagined her mother riding to Qixian on her electric scooter, barking her name from the other side of the gate. No, the last thing Lin needed was another embarrassment.

Lin didn't respond to the message, hoping her silence would be answer enough, but her mother texted again: *Jiao ge pengyou le ma?* Lin froze. She heard Mei-ying shift in the bunk above her. Lin was certain she would sooner crush her in her sleep than feign friendship. Ming and Cai Cai, doubtless, would be all too happy to assist.

Lin's weekend trips to Yuci had become less frequent since she started seeing Travis. Her animals retreated to the back of her thoughts. She'd kept up her end of the bargain not to buy any more pets, but she couldn't stop her mother from hoping she'd actually make a friend. After her father died, Lin knew she was everything to Qi Fei. She still wanted to make her proud, yearned for the warm feeling that rose in her when she could meet her mother's expectations and exceed them. If only to prove that she—both of them—were worthy of more than other people's pity.

But the truth was that Lin hadn't fared any better with her new classmates than she had with those in high school. There was Travis, of course, but there was no way she could tell her mother about him.

"I don't want you watching those shows," Qi Fei had told her, of the episodes of *House of Cards* and *Silicon Valley* that Lin used to stream before bed. "You'll fill your head with wrong ideas." Ever since Lin was little, she'd been warned about foreign influence. Her mother suggested instead that she watch Qing dynasty period pieces—coquettish women dressed in silk qipao—or modern romance dramas with their shrewd and charming men. Growing up, her mother sang songs extolling the motherland and defaming the West. "Foreigners have meddled in our affairs for too long," she decried. But even now, with America heaping levies on imported steel and solar panels, every family that could afford it seemed to be sending their kids on a plane to attend school across the Pacific.

I've been busy, Lin texted back. *Studying.* It wasn't entirely wrong. Qi Fei encouraged Lin to study English, so long as it never detracted from her other classes. Lin always had to temper her interest as simply another subject she excelled in. But she'd already learned more in a few months with Travis than she had from a decade of reading textbooks.

The irony wasn't lost on Lin that Travis was the only friend she had at university and probably the last person her mother would've chosen for her. Qi Fei had been adamant about not consorting with foreigners, but she'd never considered whether a waiguoren could also be Lin's teacher. Things with Travis were good, better than good. If teachers were to be esteemed, then perhaps she'd had nothing to fear all along.

Just be careful, her mother wrote back, as if she, too, knew how easy it was to convince oneself of anything.

The next morning, she got a text from Liz. *Yumaoqiu this afternoon?* it read, next to an emoji of a racket. Lin still hadn't replied to the text Liz sent on Thanksgiving, the night Travis hadn't returned her messages, and she'd woken up to a call that he'd slept over at a love hotel.

"Just me, though," he'd explained, with a chuckle, as if to head off any misunderstanding. It wasn't the first time he'd had so much to drink that he'd forgotten to respond, but Lin tried not to take it personally. She and Travis never talked about it, but Lin felt weird about the texts she sent him that night. Lin approached dating like she did a school assignment: by studying. The websites she read stressed that to ensure a harmonious relationship, you had to avoid conflict. She'd meant the part about feeling like an inconvenience. Why else would Travis keep her a secret? But she'd had to follow it up with schlock she'd copied from the internet, not really sure she believed it. *You must be irresistible yet nonchalant, offering but withholding.* Lin didn't even know what her arrangement with Travis could rightly be called.

Lin appreciated Liz's efforts to reach out but had been reluctant to text her back. Even if Liz was born in America and spoke English, she was still Chinese, subject to the same expectations Lin had spent her whole life eluding. She was wary of Liz, afraid that she thought of her the same way her roommates did. Or worse, that she harbored feelings for Travis. How much could she hear from her side of the house? Lin could practically draw a line midway down the couch and coffee table in the living room; the two sides couldn't have felt further apart.

Still, with her guilt mounting, Lin agreed to meet Liz at the badminton courts by the big track. For her birthday years ago, Lin's mother had gifted her two rackets in plastic-backed cases, the second more out of aspiration than necessity. Lin retrieved them from the luggage under her bed, the vinyl still sticky and untouched.

"Nice to finally meet you," Liz said, smiling, when they shook hands across the sagging net.

Lin smiled back. The truth was that she'd seen Liz many times. At the xiaomaibu, where she and Travis shopped for supplies together when Liz first arrived. Alone at the edge of campus, her head bundled in a scarf. Through the parted blinds in her room, dressed in pajamas and an oversized sweatshirt. Lin had almost begun to feel sorry for her. It was hard to come over to the house as often as she did and not think about the other woman who lived there. Liz always kept the door to her side closed. Lin could never tell her that she'd been inside, once, back when the room was still empty, and she'd slept with Travis for the first time on Liz's bed.

"I see people playing all the time," Liz said. "I've been so curious to try."

"I've never really played either," Lin said, handing her a racket. "We can make ourselves foolish together."

They batted the birdie back and forth, occasionally stooping to reset for a serve, the wind carrying more sound than their voices.

"It's getting cold," Lin said, remembering Travis's lesson on greetings. *When in doubt, talk about the weather.*

"I grew up by a frozen lake," Liz replied, "the cold doesn't scare me." She was wearing joggers and a light fleece. Lin had on three layers, a pair of thermal underwear underneath her blue track pants, wondering why they were out playing badminton in December.

"My pets don't like the cold," Lin said, not sure how to respond. She was still getting used to people. Her animals couldn't talk back, one of the things she liked about them. For hours, she could unspool stories, grandstand, get annoyed. All the while, never worrying about what they really thought of her. It was its own kind of freedom, the ability to be unapologetically herself.

"Aren't pets scared of lots of things?" Liz asked. "Water? Cold? I heard they can die of loneliness."

"No different from people," Lin said. She smacked the birdie past Liz's outstretched racket. And then, suddenly, she asked: "What are you scared of?" They were standing near the net, close enough to hear each other breathe.

"Losing myself," Liz said, "feeling like I might float away." Lin imagined the waxy plastic kites with cartoon faces that she and her mother used to fly in the park back when Lin was a kid.

"How do you mean float away?"

"The longer I'm here, the more I'm afraid I won't recognize myself." Liz paused. "I don't want to be mistaken for that kind of foreigner."

"What kind of foreigner?"

"The ones who come to live in a new country," Liz said, "but still act like they never left."

They had stopped playing. Lin was holding the shuttlecock in her hands like something injured. She wanted to say something else, but Liz's eyes darted away.

"What about you?" Liz asked. "What are you afraid of?"

Lin had a ready answer too. But she couldn't tell Liz the truth: that what she feared most, in that moment, was to lose Travis. The warm buoy of acceptance she'd gone her whole life lacking. To give it up now, after having felt it, was almost too painful to bear.

"High places," Lin said, unconvincingly. For as long as she could remember, every step in her life had felt preordained. But, deep down, she was just as clueless about what she would do after graduation as Travis had been. Before him, she hadn't met anyone who'd ever introduced her to the possibility of following a different path.

"You'd love Ohio," Liz joked. "Not a hill in sight." Lin laughed too. She liked that Liz seemed interested in her life in a way that didn't feel probing. She wondered for the first time if Liz had also chosen to come to Qixian on her own. Whether all the foreign teachers had made these decisions for themselves. If there was an entire country of people who thought like this, Lin decided, she would like to get to know them, too.

A few days later, at Lin's request, Travis invited Lin out to dinner. Lin was giddy, determined to make a good impression. She wore her nicest outfit:

army-green parka with the feather hood, wool sweater, rhinestone jeans with fake jewels over the back pockets.

It was the way she sometimes dressed when she and Travis went to eat off campus. Next to the Jia Jia Li department store, Dico's had recently opened, a KFC shanzhai that specialized in fried chicken. Travis would order two chicken burgers, and together they would eat in the hard-molded plastic booths by the window.

Lin didn't care much for the food at Dico's, but she couldn't deny Travis's insistence, his exuberant joy, like a puppy eager for his morning walk. Perhaps it had been his way of tricking himself, Lin thought, a momentary departure from the soft tofu and stewed eggplant, the chicken thighs plated with tiny bones, that she knew he'd never gotten used to eating.

"They never taste as good as they look in the pictures," he'd said, in between bites of fries. But Lin knew that he craved them nonetheless. He was always trying to rationalize his trips to Dico's—like the ones he took with Jim and Collin to Taiyuan—on some innate cultural allegiance. But the truth felt undeniable: There would always be something about China that would never be enough.

Lin was waiting inside the restaurant in South Yard when she heard Travis approach. He ducked his head through the beaded curtain, Collin and Jim following close behind. Lin didn't know anything about the other two men save for the few stories Travis had told, which made them appear both charming and strange. As they clamored in, the sound of their voices besieged the narrow space.

"What are we doing?" Travis said, swinging his leg over the wooden bench. "Noods? Dumps? Dishes?"

"Not hungry," Jim said.

"Come on, nothing a few watery beers can't fix."

"I'm serious," Jim replied, smoothing his fingers over his beard. "I'm sick of this food."

"You want to go to Dico's?" Travis asked. "We don't really have a lot of options."

"Don't mind him," Collin said, "he's having a China day." He picked at the menu on the table. "We just saw a mother hold a baby taking a shit over a trash can. Not surprising he lost his appetite."

Lin crossed her legs under the table, then uncrossed them. She kept waiting for Travis to introduce her, to so much as glance in her direction.

"Where's Liz?" Lin asked, suddenly wishing she was there. Collin and Jim didn't look up from their phones. Travis shrugged, shouting out a toneless order to the waitstaff. Lin didn't offer to help. She tried to pay attention to their conversation but was having a hard time following. Everything was a reference to a TV show or a movie or a piece of music she'd never heard of. Lin felt, for the first time, that no matter how far she'd come in the language, there was so much more she wanted to learn.

"Lai le," the waiter said, as bowls brimming with cloudy broth arrived. Shanks of pink ribeye tossed with flat noodles. Lin could hear the cooks rolling out and pounding the dough against the metal countertop before boiling the strands in water. She felt the hairs on her arms stand up. Every sound was like a firecracker in her mind. Exhaust fans humming above the stove. Plastic chopsticks vibrating in a sanitizing machine. Toilet paper spinning on a trivet in the center of the table.

"Banquets are next week," Jim said, stirring chili oil into his bowl. He lifted three fingers to the waitstaff, then pointed at the fridge. "Gotta prime the old liver."

"Lube it up," Collin chimed in.

"Banquets?" Travis asked.

"Every class organizes a banquet at the end of the semester to honor their teacher. What, did your students not tell you?"

"Is that right?" Travis said, acknowledging Lin for the first time.

The waiter placed three large bottles of Xue Hua on the table and snapped off the tops. Collin handed one each to Jim and Travis before clinking them together. Lin wished more than anything that she could disappear. It was a terrible mistake to have come.

"Each student has to toast you as a sign of respect," Collin said. "You know, like we're actual teachers or something."

"And it'll be worse than this," Jim said, bringing the bottle to his lips. "Baijiu." He knocked back an imaginary glass, shuddering from the burn.

Lin didn't want to get involved, but she felt compelled. "Then the teacher must toast with every student," Lin said, turning to face Travis. "A sign of gratitude."

"Let me get this straight," Travis said. "So if I have thirty students and I'm taking two shots with each of them—"

"After everyone has toasted with you, there are no rules," Lin said, with a smirk. "In our culture, it's impolite to refuse." She watched Travis's face, a freight train falling off a cliff.

"How am I supposed to stand after?"

"You're not," Lin explained. "The boys will carry you home."

"I'd much rather have one of the girls take me home," Jim said, licking the grease from his lips.

"They say it's so easy here if you're a foreigner," Collin replied.

Lin couldn't tell whether the two men were joking. She started to feel sick. Travis had stopped looking at her, and it was like he was one of her animals again: wordless and inscrutable. Lin wondered if the dinner was less an invitation and more payback for something she did.

"Check out this word Lin taught me," Travis said, pulling out his phone. Just hearing her name from his mouth, she could almost forgive him. But he looked nervous, trying to direct the conversation elsewhere. Lin felt like she was losing the ability to read him, if she'd ever been able to at all.

On the way back from dinner, Lin stopped at the forking path that connected Jim and Collin's house with Travis's. She knew that Mondays were usually when Travis went over to watch bad reality TV. Housewives ripping at each other's hair. Half-naked coeds on a tropical island. "The best remedy for missing home," he'd told her.

"Not feeling it tonight," Jim said. He slapped his belly like he was testing a melon for ripeness. "Gotta sleep this one off."

"God forbid we can't teach in the morning," Collin laughed, touching the back of his hand to his forehead.

They staggered down the lamplit path. When they were safely out of sight, Travis turned to Lin and motioned to his own door. She missed the autonomy she'd had when she first started coming over. Increasingly, Travis was setting the rules, limiting the nights she could stay. Lin didn't want to go, would have even preferred her own dorm room after what had happened, but knowing she had to feed the gerbils and the snakes anyway, she relented.

The lights in his room were off. On the desk near the edge of the bed, Lin took off her clothes. Parka, sweater, glittery jeans. Travis tossed her bra and underwear with his own clothes in a heap on the floor. The wooden planks under the mattress rattled when they laid down. She let him touch her. It was easier when she imagined that his hands were like one of her runty-nosed gerbils piddling around on her lap.

"Turn around," he instructed. Lin still hadn't gotten used to his stubble raking her skin or the way an elbow sometimes forced its way into her side. He pulled open a drawer, wrapped himself up, and Lin felt him push his way inside her. She didn't have to look back to know how his face would go rigid, his body trembling like a tuning fork, fingers seizing her flesh with such force that a typhoon couldn't pry him off.

Travis rolled to his back, sat up against the headboard. The bed was sticking out at a different angle, the mattress going in one direction and the wooden platform in another. Heat was exuding from the radiator in translucent waves. Travis yawned, and Lin looked at how his jaw tightened and clenched, Adam's apple baleful at his throat. She lay on her back, quietly fuming. Above her, mice scurried in the ceiling space, and Lin wondered if they'd become more emboldened ever since Boom started spending more time outside.

She pounced.

"I don't like when you spend time with them," Lin said, "you act different." She waited, holding her breath.

"You're right," Travis said.

"Really? That's great, so you won't—"

"I won't invite you to any more meals with them. Which reminds me, do you have to come over right before dinner?" He'd told Lin where he kept his spare key without ever dictating when she could use it.

"I didn't know you cared when I fed them."

"Well," Travis said, "I guess I do now." And Lin felt something within her rupture and snap.

Lin gathered her clothes. In the shower, she scoured her skin with soap, washed it clean with scalding water. When she was done, she walked out of

Travis's room and closed the door. Though she was normally careful not to draw attention, she must have slammed it hard, because as she unhooked the latch on the front door, she saw Liz's head peek out from her side of the house.

Lin felt caught, a woman trapped in a magician's box just before getting sawed in two. *Everything all right?* the visage seemed to say. Lin didn't respond, not wanting to give away any expression. She pointed down to her wrist as though gesturing at a watch and ran into the cold dark. At the dorm reception, Lin darted past the night ayi who stood guard at the front desk. The large clock nailed to the wall behind her read 10:55, five minutes to curfew. Her hair was damp, a plastic bag of toiletries in her hand. It was enough to pretend she'd come straight from the bathhouse, but her lips were too wet, and her cheeks burned unnaturally.

In mid-December, Lin's class held its end-of-semester banquet. One hundred kuai per student to the class monitor bought enough tables to seat thirty-five at one of the larger restaurants in South Yard. It was timed to celebrate the end of classes, but there were still two weeks of final exams to get through before winter break.

"Is it 'better' or 'best'?" Cai Cai asked, scrutinizing the beaded ends of her mascara. Lin was in her dorm room, her roommates practicing the handful of phrases they wanted to use to toast with Travis. "What about this?" Cai Cai asked, and then, switching to punctuated English: "You are my best-liked teacher?"

It had been a week since the dinner without a text or call from Travis. Lin put on a pair of high-waisted leggings and a faded blouse before donning a coat, determined not to make the slightest effort. Mei-ying and Ming took their last glances at the foggy mirror epoxied to the concrete wall before they all headed out. Lin stayed a few steps behind them on the walk over. Her roommates giggled and preened, arms linked in a line, their conversation swirling over and around Lin but not meant for her ears.

Lin, of course, was accustomed to eating alone. Her roommates hadn't once invited her to a meal, had never even asked to grab a clear bag of jiaozi to share with them in the dorm. But she had a vain hope that she might fare better with them than she had with Jim or Collin. At least there would be less room for misunderstanding. She was still Chinese, after all. Their intentions, even if chiding, would be clear as glass.

"No idea," Ming said, her eyes glued to her phone, "my app isn't working." Lin had stopped doing her roommates' assignments ever since they made her move her pets out of the dorm, but their English hadn't remotely improved.

"Ask the mute," Mei-ying said, gesturing behind her.

"If it's English, she would know," Ming said. "I'm just not sure she can speak Guoyu anymore." It wasn't the first time Lin had been chastised for speaking English or spending time with the foreign teachers.

"You can say 'favorite,'" Lin said, reluctantly, doing nothing to help her case. "Like this: 'Travis, you are my favorite teacher.'" The sound of the words almost made her mouth sour.

"Why 'favorite?'" Mei-ying asked, steadying her heels over the cobblestone path. "If he asks." She was wearing a red dress cinched at the waist with a white belt and a gleaming silver buckle.

"I don't know," Ming asked. "What's 'favorite' about him?"

"Lin should know," Cai Cai piped up. "She's the one fucking him."

At the restaurant, Travis was sitting at the center table, in the seat of honor, a shot glass extended in his right hand. The class monitor had just finished his welcoming remarks, and each of Lin's classmates tapped a glass at the edge of their tables, held it up in Travis's direction, and drank it down in a single gulp. Travis's table was already full by the time Lin walked in with her roommates, so the four of them squeezed in at another table on the far side of the room.

The restaurant was fancy by campus standards. Cloth tablecloths. Glass zhuanpan. Porcelain bowls shrink-wrapped in taut plastic. Lin still had on her coat and a set of arm warmers that came up past her elbows. The thermostat by the door was broken, and the standing heaters looked like prison wardens, bearing down on her from the four corners of the room.

The first dishes clattered onto the table: cold pork juanjuan, spinach and peanuts, egg and tomato soup. Lin popped the plastic of her silverware with her chopsticks, but she wasn't at all hungry. The tablecloth was flecked with dots of chili oil, globs of paste like a painting spread over a great canvas. Lin stared down at her rice bowl rounded like a burial mound.

"We should have come earlier," Ming lamented, filling a dish with vinegar. "Maybe we could've gotten to him first." There was a nervous hush in the room, everyone wondering who would break the spell. Mei-ying plucked the stout bottle from the table.

"Watch me go."

It was no secret that Mei-ying was one of the worst students. She could hardly even respond to Travis's customary "how are you?" at the start of each class. And yet, when she floated across the room and sidled up next to Travis, the slit in her dress seemed to move from the outside of her thigh to the space between her legs. She raised the glass to her puckered lips.

"To my favorite foreign teacher," she said, leaning over as she poured.

Travis clinked glasses and downed the shot. He turned the glass over when he was done to show that not even a single drop was left. The ultimate sign of respect. Bitterness spread in Lin's chest like a blaze. There were shouts of "Ganbei" and chairs shuffling as a crowd began to form around Travis. There would be no stopping him now.

Back at the table, Lin filled up her glass with baijiu too. Her eyes watered from the first sip, but the next two went down easier. She looked over again at Travis's table. He had on his usual teaching clothes—a button-down shirt and pair of loose khakis—but his top button was undone. Over the lip of his shirt, Lin could count the sprigs of hair sprouting from his chest like a weed.

"Slow down," Cai Cai said, her voice dripping with contempt. "I'm sure Travis didn't forget about you."

Lin saw the way the boys in her class looked up to Travis, the way the other girls blushed when they passed him, like glimpsing something forbidden. It wasn't uncommon that, on days when Lin came over to Travis's house, there would be a random student waiting on the doorstep, hoping simply for the chance to talk. Lin had, she admitted, felt some of the sheen rub off on herself.

Now, suddenly, all that confidence had vanished. Lin missed the days when she and Travis used to get lunch together or talk in the halls after class. She hadn't anticipated that anything between them could evaporate so quickly. It wasn't just when he was with the other foreign teachers. Travis couldn't care less about her, and Lin had no idea why.

New dishes slid across the glass disk. Lin lifted a spool of limp fentiao into her bowl. She poked at the noodles with a chopstick and then, thinking better of it, filled her glass up again. Ming and Cai Cai stood to line up with the others and, in their place, Mei-ying returned to the table. She picked up a peanut and placed it delicately between her lips.

"Was it worth it?" she asked.

"Was what worth it?" Lin replied, feeling her head spin. Mei-ying stretched both arms across the table and took Lin's hands in hers.

"Some of us still got everything we wanted," she said, so smug she was almost beaming. "And look how far that got you."

Lin hadn't realized it then, but by sleeping with Travis, she'd crossed a line. She might have been able to fool the ayi at reception, but she could feel the way her roommates glowered at her when she came back from Travis's at night, as though she was tainted, like they seemed to be asking: *Who would ever want a girl like you now?*

Lin snapped her hands back, flinching at the sight of the cartoon sheep arm warmers she wore over her coat. She remembered the way her mother used to dress her for school, always insisting on a puffy coat even if it made her bulge like a marshmallow. Who was she kidding? She was too short. Her glasses hid her face. She had a pimple under her nose the size of an eggplant. Maybe if she tried harder—wore more makeup or bought better outfits—then all of this wouldn't have happened. The worst thing Lin could imagine had come true. It wasn't her own reticence that had made people unwilling to befriend her. It was that she'd been a disappointment all along.

Another roar went up from across the restaurant and Lin saw Travis standing at the head of the table, a girl squeezed under each arm. Of course, he'd have his pick of willing companions. Lin knew better than to wait and see if Travis would ever make his way over. She was foolish to think that Travis needed her acceptance as much as she did his. As she rushed to the door, she caught a glimpse of Ming and Cai Cai teetering back to the table. She began to see herself as her roommates did. First, she'd given up her body to a foreigner. Pretty soon, she'd lose her Chineseness too. What they were really saying was this: *You're not one of us anymore. Maybe you never were.*

Outside of the banquet hall, the wind was blowing hard, leafless trees swaying like figure skaters. Lin zipped her coat all the way up to her neck and donned the hood. She didn't expect anyone to mourn her absence, least of all Travis. But she didn't know where to go. She couldn't go to her dorm, not with the specter of her roommates coming back. And it was too cold to stay out. She was seething, but through the fog of her mind, a plan began to take shape.

Lin turned the key in Travis's lock and pushed open the door. She didn't know if Liz was home or what exactly she would say to her if she was, but she collapsed in a heap on the couch. The light in Liz's room was off and the door shut. It was late enough that she could have long been in pajamas and already asleep.

Lin slumped forward before quickly straightening up. She felt the room spin, her stomach lurch. Just then, she heard the sound of a key, startling enough to make her jump.

"Lin," the voice said, raising a hand to her heart. "You scared the shit out of me." Liz turned on the lights. There was a wobble in her step. She slumped her purse and jacket over a stool by the door and took off her shoes.

"Water?" Liz asked. She was wearing a white blouse and a long skirt. But her eyes were bloodshot, her cheeks flushed. She didn't look in much better shape than Lin.

Liz disappeared and returned from her kitchen with two ceramic mugs, the water steaming. In China, hot water could cure any ailment. But how would Liz have known that?

"You must have had your banquet, too?" Lin asked, her words more lopsided than she'd intended.

"I made some of my students drink for me," Liz said. "Or else I wouldn't be standing."

Hao lihai, Lin thought, holding back the urge to compliment her. She'd neglected to tell Travis that, as the teacher, he could have his students drink on his behalf. But surely someone else could explain that now.

"You're more like us than I thought," Lin said. Liz smiled, and for a moment, there was a radiance on her face that Lin didn't expect. "Do you have banquets like this in America?"

"God no," Liz said. "We'd get put in jail if we made our students get drunk like that." Lin pictured a system of rules. People who lined up in queues, who didn't lace milk with melamine, who cared for their fellow citizens. A place where a person wouldn't be made to feel any less for their difference.

"And Travis?" Liz asked. "I mean, how was your banquet?"

"Fine," Lin said, her tone unconvincing. Liz had told her about the kinds of foreigners who never leave home. She pictured Travis's face drawn over the cartoon characters on the kites she used to fly—the line spooling farther and farther away—until, finally, snapping off in the wind. No, Travis was not the special creature she'd once believed him to be. Whatever uniqueness she'd seen in him had been overblown. Lin wondered if there would ever be anyone who could make her see herself in the world the way she thought he had.

"Just don't tell me you're in love with him," Lin blurted out.

Liz laughed, a full-throated roar that started in her belly and gushed from her mouth. But Lin's face was crumpled, tears spreading in the corners of her eyes.

"I'm sorry," Liz said, composing herself. "I didn't mean to make light of things." She reached her hand to Lin's face and brushed a hair from her cheek. The motion of it was so tender that it almost made Lin retreat. No one—not Travis, not even her mother—had ever touched her that way. Lin didn't know how to process any of it. She wasn't sure whether to feel jealous or jilted or ashamed. But she'd also never had someone to confide in, to reassure her that everything was going to be fine.

"I know what you're feeling," Liz said. She took a deep breath, steadying herself against the armrest. "I didn't want to be the one to tell you. But back home, in America, Travis has another girlfriend."

4

The pool was closing earlier and earlier each day. The sign scrawled in red characters on the door cited low student interest, which was true, but Liz also suspected it was because the lifeguards wanted to get home before dark. At dusk, the last slivers of sunlight poked through the dark streaks of pollution, dense as a layer cake. The radiant pinks and purples were almost beautiful if not for their insidiousness. They held up the sunset like a sagging curtain, lowering it slowly before, inevitably, taking the sky and clouds along with it.

That afternoon, when Liz walked in, there were only a handful of students wading in the shallow end. Knowing how to swim was a marker of status anywhere in China, but especially in Shanxi Province, landlocked and hundreds of miles from the nearest body of water. It almost guaranteed that you came from a wealthy family. Liz had one student who owned a real LV handbag and drove a Mustang, but if her classes were any indication, most students at the university never used the pool as anything more than a place to shower.

The complex, though pleasant enough in November, was now drafty and cold. Cracks high in the glass facade drew fierce wind that blew in rattling gusts. A series of sudden blizzards had swept in from the north, a whiteout reminiscent of Liz's childhood in Akron. It was the heaviest snowfall since Qixian had started keeping records, white mounds lodged in the boughs of trees and amassed on the eaves of pointed roofs. Her students were afraid of the cold—a sure way to get sick, they'd said—so today, like most days, Liz had the locker room to herself, changing into her one-piece before stepping out in thick flip-flops.

Liz dog-paddled out to the right lane. She wasn't a strong swimmer, but by then her ability to do much of anything felt so limited that it hardly mattered. Authorities had been blindsided by the swiftness and intensity of the storms. There was a run on plastic shovels and the only plows in the region had already been dispatched to presumably better resourced cities farther east. The roads off campus were too icy to run on and the big track, where Liz used to do laps, was closed, too, cordoned off by groundskeepers who used it to dump snow they collected with dustpans and rakes meant for clearing leaves.

Liz alternated breaststroke and the crawl—her motions long and fast—with an almost manic energy. She squinted as her face crested the surface, her legs doubling over herself as she kicked off at one end and throttled back toward the other. The shock of the water ran through her body like a current. She relished the sensation of cold striking nerves, a reminder that there was still something left in the world with the ability to make her feel.

Most days, Liz snoozed her alarm, skipped breakfast, waited until the last possible moment to pull a gray sweater over her head and trudge off to class. Liz liked her students, gave them each an English name that she bestowed like a new mother, but she had no idea whether anything she taught was making a difference. There were no textbooks; Liz made up new lesson plans each week. Nobody from the waishiban ever sat in on a class, and Liz wasn't sure they'd care if she stopped coming altogether. She walked the same path from the teaching building to her house methodically, worried she might lose the nerve to do even that if she had to go any other way.

Outside of the pool, Liz spent almost all her time at home. She cooked meals for one on her tiny hot plate and resigned herself to changing into pajamas by 6 p.m. What else was there to do? She wouldn't have chosen to go, but the pool was one of the few places left that could make her forget where she was. She learned to swim faster and longer than she ever had before, savoring the meditative quality to the strokes. The endorphin rush of near exhaustion.

Initially, Travis used to knock on her door to ask if she wanted to go with him. When Liz turned him down, he started calling half-heartedly from the living room.

"Last chance," he said, "Jim and Collin are waiting on the porch."

Liz couldn't have cared less when he stopped completely. By then, she acknowledged Travis's presence only if she had to, barely leaving her room if she knew he was home. She waited to hear the screen clang against the door frame—footsteps becoming faint, the dull vibration of the heating pipes—to know that she was, once again, alone. She was tired of making excuses for why she should spend more time with them. Because they speak English. Because I'm lonely. Because they're all I have.

It seemed like nearly every night they gathered to watch *The Real Housewives of Orange County*, set off firecrackers they bought at the xiaomaibu, and tomahawk glass Tsingtao bottles against the brick fence. More proof that being an American was license to do whatever they damn well pleased. Sometimes Liz wouldn't hear the door in the living room slam until midnight or later. Whatever else they did to pass the time, she didn't care to know. It was just as well that the campus, mired in the aftermath of a snowstorm, felt like an island unto itself. They already lived in a place free of consequence and responsibility: a world entirely of their own devising.

When Liz looked up from her final lap, she realized she was the last one in the pool. The other students had left, and she could hear the lifeguards—men in their mid-fifties, who wore swim trunks underneath thick green Communist-era jackets—chain-smoking and playing cards on the other side. But when she stood up to try and locate the source of their voices, she discovered she couldn't see them at all. She could barely see anything. The heat from the water had collided with the cold air seeping in from the walls—the swirl of condensation billowing like a club's fog machine—until the other half of the pool dropped out of view.

Liz stared into the water, which reached her chest in the deep end. On the shallow side, it barely made it past her knees. Liz assumed this was because the lifeguards were lazy. The low water level meant that they could continue to stretch out on beach chairs, sinking their spent cigarettes into the dregs of their glass tea thermoses, without ever having to do their jobs. The pool was practically designed to prevent drowning.

Not that Liz wanted to drown. If she was going to die anywhere, she knew it wouldn't be in a rust-colored pool in the middle of rural China. But as Liz stared out at the fog, she felt like she was standing on the edge of some alien colony, watching the last, dying gasps of any world she'd previously known. If I disappeared tomorrow, she asked herself, would anyone even know I was gone?

Liz brought her legs up into her arms and expelled the air from her nose slowly, feeling her body sink as she did. The weight of the water, like the little neuroses of everyday, bore down like a too-big coat. Liz had started to wish that her old life, her friends and routine back home, could be swept up that easily into dustpans and transported to Qixian. She didn't miss home so much as the person she was when she was there. Confident. Warm. Outgoing. Even if I could explain all this, she thought, would anyone really understand?

Her brother, Phil, was still living in Ohio—in Cleveland—but he had a real job, at the city planning commission, with a good salary and benefits. Phil had always been the model child—their mom's favorite—and he didn't let Liz forget it. His teachers described him in his flawless report cards as *astute and hardworking* and *possessing a quiet strength*. Phil earned a full ride to Washington University in St. Louis, and yet, he still insisted, even years after graduating, that he was cheated out of the Ivy League.

Liz kept her distance partly because she felt like she could never live up to him, but partly so that she wouldn't have to bear the brunt of his judgment. Phil's discomfort with his own background, Liz believed, stemmed from their mom's reluctance to acknowledge it. He seemed to resent being Asian and resented Asian girls even more for dating white guys, who, despite his best efforts, he would never be. He never approved of Liz's relationship with Andrew and couldn't understand why Liz wanted to go to China at all.

"There's a reason everyone who can get here does. If I were Mom and Dad, I would've left that shithole, too."

But when Pearl was in the hospital with leukemia, Liz was halfway through her senior year of college, and Phil's voice on the other end of the line was the only thing that kept her from dropping out.

Near the end of last week, feeling like she'd reached a breaking point, Liz called him for the first time from China. She nearly cried when he picked up the phone.

"Look, just come home if you can't hack it," Phil had said. "I tried to tell you, didn't I? I've got a guest room with your name on it."

Liz felt a tug on her body, a jolt that sent her head piercing through the surface of the water.

"Ni gan ma?!" she heard over the din of slapping water. One of the lifeguards was in front of her, his hands on both her shoulders. He was shirtless and thin, with ribs grooved as tire treads. His lips were pulled tight in a grimace, but were quivering at the corners, his coat tossed in a heap by the side of the pool.

"I was—" Liz started, breathing heavy, "I was practicing holding my breath."

The lifeguard shook his head, raised his arms to the ruined ceiling, before sloshing off toward the ladder. It seemed a good enough answer. Or maybe the pool was closing, and the lifeguards had somewhere—anywhere—they would rather be.

It was noon on Saturday, and Liz was still lying in bed when she got a text. She ignored her phone. Mustering even the slightest energy seemed hopeless. Around her room were laminated posters with words for fruits and vegetables in Mandarin that she hadn't bothered to take down since she arrived. The remnants of some more adjusted teacher's life she would never know.

Her phone buzzed again. It was Lin. *Bring warm clothes*, she wrote, next to a snowflake emoji. *Or whatever you Midwestern people wear in the winter.*

Liz smiled. She hadn't wanted to see anyone. But the pool had closed for maintenance, and she didn't have a better excuse to say no.

At the big track, Liz hopped the wrought-iron fence. The snow was up to her knees, the runoff from other parts of campus packed on like thousand-layer bread. But the middle of the track was untouched, a blanket of white so blistering it almost made her dizzy. Liz took a few steps toward midfield before dropping onto her back. Lin lay down next to her.

"Any plans for the holiday?" Lin asked. Winter break was six weeks, longer than any school vacation Liz had had in the states.

"I'm not sure yet," Liz said. "All I know is that I want to get out of here."

"Where would you go?"

"I don't care. I'm just ready to leave."

"You don't want to go home?" Lin asked. Liz shook her head.

"My brother would give me endless shit if he knew I was coming back after only two months. Besides," she said, "I'm already here. I might as well go somewhere new."

"I've never really traveled anywhere," Lin said.

"Why not?"

"My pets mostly. I think about it sometimes, but it seems kind of scary to be that alone."

"You'd be fine," Liz said, kicking out her legs. She spread her arms out to either side, too, demonstrating the motion to Lin.

"I don't think my mom would let me," Lin said. "She tends to worry a lot." She turned to face Liz. "Doesn't your mom miss you?"

Liz's heart seized. It took everything in her power not to break down on the spot.

"My mom's dead." It was only then that Liz realized she hadn't told anyone in Qixian. No one had ever asked.

"I'm so sorry," Lin said.

"It's OK. If she was still alive, she'd want me to be here," Liz replied, biting her tongue.

"And your dad?"

One of the few memories Liz had of her father was hunched over the square table in their Akron kitchen, a cigarette perched between his lips. He'd taken the English name Ron, since Rongxing was too hard for his colleagues in the political science department to pronounce. He wore glasses with big circular lenses, but Liz could barely picture his face anymore.

"He left when I was five."

"Where is he now?"

"As far as I know, he could be anywhere," Liz said. For years, she'd begged Pearl to tell her where he ran off to. Eventually, as the years passed with no news, Liz found it easier to imagine him dead.

"I barely knew my father too," Lin said, her cheeks pink with cold. "He died in an accident when I was three." Liz made a mental note. Absent fathers. Maybe they had more in common than she thought.

Lin propped herself up on her elbows. "Why did you come to China?"

"My mom grew up in Fujian but never really talked much about that time," Liz said. "It was like she intentionally avoided it. I always figured she would tell me one day, but now it's too late to ask."

The truth was that Pearl seemed to love America, even when Liz found attitudes of the country so baffling or problematic that Liz was sure she'd take offense. "You should be grateful you were born here," her mom had repeated, regardless of whether they were driving past the Cleveland Clinic or a homeless encampment off I-80. When Liz complained about her classmates' teasing, her mom insisted that nothing about her and Phil made them any different. America was the land of promise she'd never had. And if Liz worked hard, she would grow up to have the same opportunities as any other American.

Liz stood up, gazing at the dotted path of their boots from the fencepost to the middle of the track, the two arcing imprints flattened symmetrically in the snow. She smiled at her accomplishment, this small act of truancy, with a lightness she hadn't felt in weeks.

"What about you?" she asked Lin. "I take it you're going home?"

Lin rubbed her mittened hands together. "My mom will want to see me," Lin said. "To be honest, I'm not that close with a lot of people."

"Well, it's good you at least have someone," Liz said, watching her breath waft toward the sky. "Me, I'm just—" She made a fluttering motion with her hands.

"Free as a bird," Lin said. She turned to look at the silhouettes on the ground behind her. "Or an angel."

Before Liz knew it, she and Lin were hanging out nearly every day. In college, Liz was put off by the handful of spoiled, cliquish Chinese girls she associated with privilege and corruption. Her mom had gone a step further. "The people there are so backwards," she'd told her, making chiding sounds with her tongue. "They don't think the way we do." It seemed ironic to Liz, considering her mom had once been one of those supposedly backwards people herself, to say nothing of any relatives in China she still had left.

But Lin, to her credit, was none of those things. She and Lin texted constantly, linked arms to brace against the cold, talked shit about other people in English. Liz made her a playlist with all her favorite songs, and the next day, Lin came back humming Lucy Dacus and Japanese Breakfast. She was patient, funny, inquisitive—the little sister Liz had never had.

When they met up, Liz avoided the house, not wanting to invite Travis's questioning. So instead, they took walks around campus: past the bathhouse and the hulking cinder-block library, around old campus, with its curious rounded doorways. Everything was masked in a perpetual haze, giving it the guise of a projection film reel. The air was so thick Liz could feel it sticking to the back of her throat like stale taffy. They stood on the edge of a pond that, though recently filled and landscaped, still had streaks of trash writhing under its frozen surface.

One afternoon, they talked for so long that by the time they returned to Liz's porch it was dark. Liz motioned for Lin to stay, and together they began to gather snow from her walkway in huge, gloved handfuls, packing it down into rounded mounds. A larger sphere for the base, a smaller one for the middle, and a final orb for the head. Travis was out at dinner with Jim and Collin and wouldn't be home for at least another hour. Lin had evidently been thinking the same thing, because she piped up at once.

"Travis told me he's going home for the holiday," Lin said. "Do you think he's going to visit his girlfriend?"

Liz froze, feeling her face go warm. She'd completely forgotten what she told Lin after the student banquet, but especially the part she'd made up about Travis's girlfriend.

"I didn't know he was going back to the states," Liz said, unable to meet Lin's eyes.

Before she met Lin, Liz found it hard to give her a straight face, too. She didn't know what Lin saw in Travis, but it seemed obvious that he was taking advantage of her. Even worse, she worried it was how her own classmates in college had also seen her.

Growing up, Liz had never been attracted to Asian men. There were nearly none in her town, so by the time she got to college, she was immune to their advances, finding them about as salacious as her own brother. Americans—those most prototypical Midwestern stock—were the only men she'd ever desired. When Liz started dating Andrew her junior year, she was elated. He was tall, popular, could play "The General" on guitar. She'd never questioned their relationship. But the more she thought about it now, the more she remembered how he showed her off to friends, the way his hand gripped her waist a little too tightly when they entered crowded rooms.

"This is my little Asian princess," he would announce at parties, like a rarity to be beheld. Liz, for her part, played the role flawlessly. Sometimes she tucked a strand of tinsel in her hair. For Halloween, she dressed up as Mulan sporting a tiara, as a joke.

Liz began to wonder about the cost of that attraction. As if, in order to be worthy of Andrew's attention, she'd had to represent a certain kind of woman: demure, unspoiled, submissive. She feared that she'd cheapened herself and, in doing so, had come to believe that men who looked like she did weren't worth as much, either.

It would have been easy to apologize to Lin, to say she'd misremembered the whole episode with Travis, and take it back. But she suspected that Lin might suffer from the same affliction.

"What did he tell you about her?" Lin asked.

"Only that they'd been dating since college," Liz said, warily.

"Are they on a break?"

"It's complicated," Liz said. "It's probably best not to ask." She trained her eyes on the snowman that came up just past her waist. "I think it's still missing something." She ran into her house and grabbed a carrot and two anise stars from her pantry. On the way out, she pulled a glittery pink cowboy hat—another abandoned relic—off the top of the coat rack.

"What should we name it?" Lin asked.

Liz eyed the creature sideways. She rummaged through the pack of Hongtashan on the lip of the bookshelf near the door, then dabbed an indentation in the side of the snowman's cheek before wedging the cigarette inside. When she stepped back, the man was giving her a lopsided smile, like he'd just emerged, drunk and horny, from a nightclub.

"Travis," she said, with a chuckle, and looked over at Lin, who covered her face with both hands. But whether it was from crying or laughing, Liz wasn't entirely sure.

"Look, if it were me," Liz said, lowering her voice, "I'd break up with him." Lin was way too good for him anyway. Liz felt bad for lying, but it seemed impossible that Lin wouldn't get hurt. She couldn't understand why anyone would choose to get involved with a foreigner. At the end of the day, they would only ever leave you for home.

"What about my pets?" Lin asked finally.

"Your pets?" Liz replied, as if that was the most traumatic part. "Leave them to me."

Lin waved bye from the porch as Liz slipped behind the screen door into the house. Her clothes were damp from the snow, and she promptly peeled them off under the glow of the overhead fluorescent. She turned the water on in her green-tinted bathroom and let the temperature climb on the water heater's gauge. The water left a tingle at her back where it fell, soaking her hair and pooling in the crevices between her shoulders.

Over the window was a canvas blind with the image of a tropical beach, the water pristine and the sun beaming. Liz pulled the shade down and for a moment tried to picture herself there. She and Andrew had taken a trip to Hawaii with a few friends over spring break of their senior year. It was all she could do to get her mind off her mom. The print looked comically out of place in her bathroom—dusty slipper prints on the blue tile, drain hole with silt in the center of the floor—about as out of place as Andrew would have been in rural China.

They hadn't ended things on bad terms, and just last week, Liz had called him out of the blue. She'd had an open beer next to her as she talked, and, at one point in the conversation, she'd seriously considered getting undressed in front of him. It had been so long since she'd felt seen by anyone, let alone as someone who possessed her own needs and desires. But just then, Andrew said something that surprised her.

"You know, I'd really love to come visit."

Despite Liz's misgivings about Qixian, she found herself resisting Andrew's offer. She didn't want him to take away any more of what was hers. Liz questioned whether Andrew could ever truly see her in the way she saw herself. How could he have loved the person she was when she was still figuring that person out?

Christmas blew in with little fanfare. Save for the tiny windowsill effigies of Santa and the handful of plastic trees adorning restaurant entranceways, there wasn't much to signal that the day was in any way unordinary. Liz missed the atmosphere of Northeast Ohio around the holidays: snowy wreaths pinned to doorframes, window displays downtown, the big Christmas tree in Lock 3 Park, with its tiers of gaudy gold and silver tinsel and frosted bulbs. It was her first Christmas away from home, and the first without her mom.

At home, her mom had delighted in Christmas. Even though they didn't have the blow-up lawn figures or pyrotechnics of some of their neighbors, Pearl insisted on driving out to Elyria every year to buy a tree. They decorated it together, unwrapping the ornaments packed in bubble wrap and cardboard at the back of the closet. It was her family at their happiest, even though each year, Phil had the honor of placing the angel at the top.

Liz's students surprised her by bringing gifts to class. Most were small, token things, often whatever they could find at the xiaomaibu or pinch from their dorm room that morning: stuffed animals, cards, Pocky, a bedazzled tape dispenser. Liz felt guilty taking them. Her sense of propriety in America dictated that there be some kind of exchange—on Christmas of all days—and that accepting anything from a student might raise red flags. She still had over a hundred grades to give out. A couple of Liz's students were failing outright, and Liz was sure that some of them were looking for every excuse to appeal to her better nature.

But she decided, in the end, that to reject the gifts would be an even worse offense. She was touched by the presents, if only just the thought of them. Even though most of the gifts had come unwrapped, Liz covered them in old newspaper and arranged them in front of the radiator nonetheless. In her room, she hung up string lights she rummaged from among handsaws and PVC piping at the hardware store. Beneath the dim glow, she called Phil, more out of obligation than anything else. He didn't pick up, and Liz ended up leaving an awkward, rambling message on his voicemail. She was careful to make no more mention of her desire to leave, inquiring instead about any plans he'd made to mark the occasion. "I miss Mom," she added, just before hanging up.

Liz asked Lin to join her for Christmas dinner. The snow had mostly melted, but on the way to South Yard, embankments were flooded, and the dirt roads bubbled over with mud. There was no drainage, so bricks were laid in the middle of the street to form a walking path, and people clustered under awnings to avoid the icy drip. With the wind at her back, Liz passed street stalls hawking bacon-wrapped scallions, tender, braided spirals of baked pastry, the young Chinese man peddling hot milk served fresh from a metal dairy container.

Liz must have passed the man a hundred times. But it occurred to her that she'd never really stopped to look. The way he dipped the ladle into the metal tank. The curve of his bicep straining beneath his apron. The sly, guileless smile he gave when he asked how much sugar to add. Liz imagined him slipping her the bag, bloated and warm, and the two of them sneaking away at night. At reception of the qinglu fandian, she would let him talk, her feet making tiny circles on the hard floor. Though quiet and reserved at his milk station, alone in the hotel room he'd be effusive, knowing when to apply pressure and when to relent.

Even Liz had to admit it was an absurd fantasy. A secret Chinese lover? Ridiculous. Liz enjoyed allowing herself these moments of small, fleeting joy when she could get them. But what she wouldn't give to have someone else thrill her for a change.

At the restaurant, Lin retrieved a box from her bag and set it down on the glass counter.

"But I'm not even your teacher," Liz protested, making her best attempt at exuberant Chinese refusal.

"Open it," Lin said. Liz undid the metallic ribbon. Inside was an apple, dipped in candied lacquer.

"I thought apples were only for Teacher's Day?" Liz asked.

"It's a Christmas tradition!"

"Not where I'm from," Liz replied, laughing.

"That's strange. We were always taught it came from America." Lin explained the word for Christmas Eve shared the same first character as the Chinese word for apple. "Anyway, it's the least I could do to show my thanks."

The food arrived: meat and vegetable buns served on a steaming tray.

"I did it, you know," Lin said, holding a bao between her chopsticks, little sesame seeds flecking off the blistered skin.

"Did what?"

"Broke up with Travis," she said, "exactly like you said." Liz edged forward in her seat, her eyes widening to the size of saucers.

"You did what?" Liz asked. She couldn't believe Lin had actually gone through with it. And yet, at the same time, Liz had coached her. Standing out in the middle of the big track, they role-played both parts, like it was an English skit Lin was practicing for class. It was necessary, Liz knew, for Lin to get the intonation right, the way the words were meant to sound, if she was really going to make him suffer.

"I told him I wouldn't come over anymore," Lin said, her words resolute. "Not if he was the last man on Earth."

Liz wished she could have seen it. All five foot nothing of her telling Travis off like that. Was she standing with her hands on her hips, really letting him have it? Chances, unfortunately, were slim. More likely, Liz thought, Lin had been pouting—crying even—unleashing soft blows against Travis's chest. Like the effete girls in serial dramas, who made their boyfriends hold their purses for them and then let out a thin, shrieking *wo taoyan ni* whenever something didn't go their way.

The poor girl. Liz remembered her first relationship in high school and quickly shirked it off. At the end of the day, Lin was better off for it. Even without Travis, Lin still had her mom in Yuci, the flock of animals who occupied her living room like squatters. That was more than Liz could say.

"I'm proud of you," she told Lin, "I couldn't have done it better myself."

The day before she left for winter break, Liz dropped off her grades with Headmistress Zong at the waishiban. Headmistress Zong spoke only Chinese, so it was a mystery to Liz how the foreign men were able to communicate anything to her. It was one of many quirks of the Foreign Affairs Office that Liz used to commiserate about with Travis. Calling the teachers at all hours. Stopping by unannounced. Requiring attendance at lavish banquets whenever some dignitary or another paid the school a visit. A part of her still missed that kinship, but whatever sympathy she had for Travis had long run dry.

Liz entered the squat brick office. Headmistress Zong was sitting with her back to the door, her gray hair cut in a bob. On the table was a hongbao stuffed with her holiday bonus, a gift from the office to all the foreign teachers. Liz already knew how she would spend the money. She'd decided on a solo trip to Vietnam over Spring Festival, a flight to Hanoi and then a winding bus ride with stops all the way down the coast. It would be a new country and a new experience for Liz, but, most importantly, it would be hundreds of miles away from Qixian.

"Chengjidan," the headmistress yawned, holding out her hand.

On Liz's final grade sheet, she'd given three students marks under sixty. Only one of them had ever come to class but all three never submitted a single assignment. She handed the grade sheet to Headmistress Zong, ready to turn and make her way back out, but the woman in the office circled the three names and called her back in.

"They failed," Liz said in Mandarin. "They didn't pass."

Headmistress Zong shook her head. "Bu keneng," she said. "There can only be one failing student."

Liz scrunched her face, not sure if she understood.

"It reflects badly on the school if there are too many," Headmistress Zong said, this time a little slower. She explained that failing students tarnish the university's reputation, an impediment to getting more funding at the end of the year. "At most we can have one failing student per class, as an example to the others." She used a phrase Liz recognized: sha ji jing hou. Kill the chicken to scare the monkey.

Liz evidently still looked confused, so the headmistress grabbed the grade sheets that had been left that morning from the other foreign teachers and foisted them at Liz.

"You see, all the other teachers passed their students." She paused over Travis's sheet. "All, except for one."

Liz rifled through the names on Travis's sheet until she saw a red dot by the name Lin He, with the number fifty-eight, the only failing grade on his roster.

"There must be some mistake," Liz piped up, pointing to the offending line. "Lin is the best English student at this school."

"These are the grades Travis laoshi submitted," the headmistress said, "and we must take them at his word." Liz couldn't believe it. She wanted to tear the paper into shreds.

"You don't understand," she told her. "This is unfair." And then, before she could stop herself: "Lin is refusing to have sex with him. That's why he's giving her a failing grade." She was shouting now, the sound of her voice reverberating against the stucco white walls. She'd used the profane cao—fuck—instead of the more euphemistic zuo ai—to make love. She didn't mean to say it that plainly, would probably have softened it if she could, but she'd meant what she said.

Headmistress Zong tipped her glasses back from the crook of her nose.

"We'll look into it," was the only response Liz heard back before pocketing the red envelope and leaving the office.

By the next evening, Liz had already boarded the sleeper train to Beijing, a month's worth of clothes and supplies in her backpack. She had all but forgotten the conversation with Headmistress Zong, elated just to be leaving, when she got a text from Lin.

I have two days to pack up my things, Lin wrote. *The dean just told me I've been expelled.*

5

"Explain it to me one more time," Qi Fei said, her hands folded on the floral tablecloth.

"You already know what happened."

"I want to hear you say it," her mother said. "In your own words."

Lin lifted her eyes from the center of the table. It had been weeks since she'd last boarded the public bus for home that departed from the campus gate. Lin had almost forgotten what it felt like to be surrounded by her childhood accolades—brass medals, awards, diplomas—all carefully framed and hung by her mother. There was a finality to it, a sense that, when distilled down like vinegar, this is what her life had amounted to.

"Wo fancuo le," Lin said. "I never should have trusted him."

"Admitting a mistake doesn't change the outcome," Qi Fei said. "How could you be so irresponsible?"

"I was the best student in class, Ma—" Lin started.

"Bullshit," Qi Fei yelled, pounding her hand so hard the table shook. "The top student doesn't get thrown out of school."

Less than a day ago, Lin had finished packing up her dorm and retrieving her pets from Liz's house. There was no ceremony and no goodbyes; Liz, like the rest of the teachers, had already left campus. Lin debated texting her at all. Her face flushed with shame every time she began a new message. But she didn't want Liz to worry when she came back to find all her pets—the ones Liz had promised to care for—filched from her home. The last thing Lin wanted was to make Liz feel like she'd done anything to let her down.

"Maybe Qixian wasn't the right place for you," Qi Fei continued. "Ever since you got to university, there's been something different about you."

If Lin had changed, she'd scarcely been aware of it. Only one thing was for sure: She'd been spending more time with Liz.

One afternoon not long after Christmas, Lin had confided in Liz that every decision in her life felt like it had been cast by divination blocks. From when Qi Fei pressured her into pursuing the sciences in middle school to getting assigned a major based on her gaokao even before she'd started university.

"That's insane," Liz had said. "In America, students are admitted to college on more than a single test score. You can try out lots of different subjects before choosing your major."

It wasn't a surprise to Lin. She'd seen enough American movies to understand the concept, but it was the first time she could ever trace its corollary: Liz, her presence so vivid that Lin could almost embody it herself. And yet, it was a world wholly unavailable to her. Other things Lin would have tolerated six months ago—rote learning in class, overcrowded dorm rooms, Party overreach—now felt unbearable. At home and in school, she'd only ever been taught to do what was asked of her. She'd never considered if any of it was what she wanted.

"Haven't you ever thought about what you'd like to do with your life?" Liz had asked. "Find out who you really are?"

The door to the kitchen popped open a crack and Boom squeezed in, the white spot on his nose shining against his black coat. He wound his way around the four legs of the table, nuzzling against Qi Fei's ankle.

"I never should have let you bring him home," Qi Fei yelled, kicking her leg up. "Do you know how humiliating this is for me? You've become just like him, you know, only ever thinking about yourself."

From the very beginning, Boom had watched the episode with Travis unfold. Lin felt the old shame rise in her chest. Her fascination with Travis had caused her to neglect him, and she'd scarcely been aware that Boom had moved on without her, too.

"Boom had nothing to do with it," Lin said.

"Then tell me why you were cutting class."

"I didn't cut class," Lin said. "Travis laoshi asked me not to come back." It was the first time she mentioned his name to Qi Fei, and she felt her lips burn, like she'd been holding back poison. She remembered how she'd gathered herself up from Travis's room the night she broke things off, the dull warning in his voice as she left. And yet she wanted to trust him, to believe in the innate goodness of the first friend she'd ever made.

"What did I tell you about laowai?" Qi Fei said. "They're not like us. They'll use us just to get ahead." She wrung her hands behind her neck. "If you didn't cut class, then how did you fail?"

But to tell her mother the reason for being expelled—for failing the final exam due to her absence—would have meant having to tell her everything else, too. Lin cast her eyes down, saying nothing.

"Buke zhixin," Qi Fei said. "I thought I raised you better than this."

Lin hadn't received any other explanation for her expulsion, but something didn't seem right. She couldn't understand why no one had tried to get in touch with her about the exam, or why she wouldn't have had the chance to make it up. The punishment was too severe, even by Chinese standards. She'd heard of other students who'd been given the option of taking remedial cram classes to make up the grade. It wasn't fair either, but it was a kind of injustice she'd come to learn. A system she could work within.

Lin knew it was pointless, but part of her wanted to get in touch with Travis. She was certain he couldn't have acted alone, that he'd gotten Meiying, or Cai Cai even, to carry out his bidding. She wanted desperately to know who'd been responsible. Lin remembered when she first took Travis shopping at the baihuodian on campus. She'd seen the washing machine in his kitchen filled to the top with black water and laughed. He'd been so helpless, unable to even wash his own clothes. And yet, right beneath her eyes, he'd gathered strength. And this was how he'd chosen to repay her.

Lin knew she was too smart for it, that she should have known better. The knowledge that she wouldn't be returning to school in the spring made her want to retch. But, most of all, she hated that her mother had been right.

"It won't happen again, Ma," Lin said.

"Again?" Qi Fei exclaimed. "Again?" She stood to leave. "Don't you get it, Lin? It can't happen again. You no longer have a future."

The next morning, when her mother went to work, Lin shook out a cup of dry pellets from an industrial sized bag. She smoothed the delicate fur behind her rabbits' ears, set out a frozen rat in the center of her snakes' tank. She tipped the shaker of flesh-colored flakes into the aquarium and watched them waft, slowly, toward the gravelly bottom.

Her mother still hadn't spoken to her, and Lin feared that the silence would linger like the smell of hot pot on her camisole. She didn't mind spending time with her pets, but she began to miss having an audience. The ability to ask instead of needing to intuit what someone thought or felt. She missed Liz most of all, the calm that came with her counsel. Surely she would know what to do. Lin had gotten used to texting Liz whenever she had something on her mind. But Liz was hundreds of miles away now, in Beijing waiting for a flight out, if not already in Hanoi.

The door opened with a creak and Boom stepped shyly into the bedroom, like edging around a puddle. He glided in figure eights around Lin's legs, but Lin stopped herself from reaching down to pet him. Instead, she unlatched the lock on the window and let Boom hop down to the ground level below. He'd gotten used to roaming, the freedom that came with the outdoors, and who was she to deny him?

Lin hadn't stopped caring about Boom. It was just that she couldn't help associating him with Travis, the terrible mess she'd made. Boom couldn't take back her decision to seduce Travis after class, nor could he charm the dean into getting her reenrolled at school. Staring out the window, Lin even begrudged Boom his small mobility, his ignorance about the disappointments of the world. A cat, like any pet, was a reflection of its human owner. Pity for Boom that he'd been taken in by one so flawed.

If Lin was honest with herself, she was also envious of Liz's free will, her ability to travel on a moment's notice. Lin wished she could leave her own predicament as easily. Her old fantasies about imagining a new life for herself somewhere else were no less prevalent now than at the start of the semester. Lin had never had to question her life before. Her mother was unwavering on the timeline: school, job, family. But now the future lay open and bloated as a puffed duck, waiting for a sign of what was to come.

The following evening, Lin was in bed, watching a video on her phone, when she heard the metal screech of the front door. Footsteps echoing down the narrow hall. Her mother back home from the accounting office. Lin braced herself for another haranguing at the dinner table, or worse, more silent treatment. But she was surprised to hear another voice.

"I'm sorry to come over announced," a demure voice chirped in Mandarin, polite as a schoolchild. "Are you sure it's all right to come in?"

"Of course," her mother replied, more jubilant than she'd sounded in days. And then, bellowing in her old tone: "Lin, someone's here to see you."

Lin never had any visitors. So when she entered the living room, she did so guardedly, like lowering into hot water. In the doorway, as unmistakable as she would be peering out from her flat in Qixian, there she was.

"Liz?" Lin asked, as if waking from a dream. "What are you doing here?"

"The Foreign Affairs Office gave me your address," Liz said, quickly switching to English. She slipped on a pair of gray slippers. "It was the least they could do."

"Qing zuo," Qi Fei said, shepherding Liz to a chair at the head of the table. She made a show of smiling, her voice chipper and bright, even though Lin knew her mother hated being caught unprepared.

"Kuai chi, kuai chi," Qi Fei said, presiding over a plate of orange wedges and a bowl of seedless grapes she strained in the sink.

"I thought you were going to Vietnam," Lin whispered.

"Change of plans," Liz said. She plucked a grape from the bowl and rolled it between her fingers. "Flights were all sold out."

"Xinxian de," Lin's mother urged, handing Liz a shrink-wrapped milk box with a plastic straw attached to the package. "Imported from New Zealand." It was the most expensive beverage they owned. Lin had seen the carton lodged in a cabinet for months, waiting for a worthy enough occasion.

"Much better than buying from Japan," she continued, "or, worse, America." The Minister of Commerce had recently pledged to spend more on US goods in exchange for a suspension of tariffs. It was supposed to represent progress in trade talks, a step in the right direction. But if Lin's experience with Travis was any indication, any supposed compromise seemed to result in Americans getting the better end of the bargain.

"Liz is from America," Lin said, trying to preempt any further critique.

"Is that true?" Qi Fei asked. "Nanguai your English is so good! I thought all foreign teachers were laowai, but this one doesn't even look American."

Lin could tell her mother was pleased. Even despite the expulsion, Lin had kept her promise: She'd made a friend.

"How do you like it here?" Qi Fei asked.

"It's great," Liz said.

"Yes, but which do you like better?"

Liz squirmed in her chair. "You bi you li," she said, equivocating. It seemed impossible to Lin that China and America would ever be anything but linked. Inextricable. Number one and number two. Though which was which was still a point of contention.

"What do Americans think about China?" she asked.

"I don't know," Liz said with a laugh, "I'm not most Americans." She'd confessed to Lin during one of their walks that she found the Chinese habit of speaking for an entire country absurd, as if any place could have one collective point of view.

"We Chinese think of the world as one big family," Qi Fei said, spreading her arms wide. "Any American teacher is welcome in our home."

Lin couldn't believe what she was hearing. Hadn't her mother just berated her for wrongly entrusting an American teacher? Why should Liz be any different?

"I want to give you something," Liz said. She pulled a plastic folder from her purse and placed it at the edge of the table.

"Lin told me the news about the expulsion," Liz said. "I thought it might be difficult for her to apply to another university in China."

Lin knew the only schools open to her now were the third-tier sanben that extorted money from the children of wealthy families who couldn't test into better universities. Even if her mother could somehow afford it, it devastated her to think she'd now have to join their lowly ranks.

"It's not much," Liz continued, "but it's a start. A path on the way to something bigger." Inside the folder were two sheets of paper on official letterhead and an envelope containing a stack of neatly wrapped red bills.

"What's all this?" Qi Fei asked.

"An acceptance letter from Cuyahoga Community College and a signed declaration from the consulate in Chicago. If you take them to the embassy in Beijing, they should be able to give you a student visa to America."

Lin was stunned. She'd never truly entertained the possibility of going abroad for school. An experience like that could change everything, expose her to an entire world she'd never envisioned. A surge of excitement flowed through her. And yet, Lin was also wary. She hadn't applied to school in America, had never even asked Liz about the prospect. She'd made the mistake of trusting a foreigner once and wasn't about to repeat it again.

"I appreciate whatever you're trying to do," Lin said, "but I can't accept this." She sensed her mother across the table. It was bad enough she'd brought a foreigner home. Lin didn't want to be a traitor by forsaking her country, too.

But when she turned to look, her mother had tears in her eyes.

"Thank you for looking after my daughter," Qi Fei said. "You know, Lin used to be such a good student. I hope that one day she can take after you."

Lin remembered the way her mother used to compare her to her cousins growing up, from their standardized test scores to the number of Tang dynasty poems they could recite from memory. Lin had always bested them. But now her mother's face was aglow with the kind of pride she'd once reserved only for Lin.

"You must stay for dinner," Qi Fei said to Liz. "What time do you have to leave in the morning? Don't pay for a hotel. Yes, of course you can stay here. Bu yao keqi. I'll take you to the train station on my way to work. It's no trouble at all."

"I don't want to be an inconvenience," Liz said. "I'm happy to sleep on a couch or—"

"You can stay in Lin's room," she said, without even glancing over. Qi Fei shooed Liz to the bedroom to set down her things and closed the door. It was only when Liz was safely out of earshot that Qi Fei returned to the table in the kitchen.

"It's all my fault," Qi Fei said suddenly, holding her head in her hands. "If not for me, maybe none of this would have happened."

Lin blinked her eyes. She'd been expecting the worst. That her mother wanted to disown her, or that she'd sooner trade up for Liz if given the chance.

"Bu mingbai," Lin replied.

"I didn't encourage you enough," her mother said. "Your whole life, I never wanted you to watch foreign shows. I couldn't afford to send you to cram school after class." She sighed. "I don't know the first thing about the West. It's no wonder you failed English."

Lin stared across the table, her mouth agape. She knew better than to let this opportunity pass.

"You never did help me with my homework," Lin said, hiding a smirk in the corner of her mouth.

"Liz is different from other laowai," her mother said. "She wants to give you an opportunity not a lot of people get. She sees your potential, like I see it, like I've known all along."

She scooted her chair next to Lin's and draped a hand over her shoulder.

"You can do anything in this world," Qi Fei said. "Don't let anyone tell you different. When I'm dead and gone, that's what I want you to remember."

It was the closest Qi Fei had ever come to expressing love, and Lin realized then that, no matter what, her mother would find a way to make it work. She would borrow from neighbors, work extra shifts, endure the absence of her only child. One look at her mother's face and Lin knew she'd accept Liz's offer. She couldn't bear to disappoint her again.

By the time Lin got to her room, Liz was already lying on top of the covers. Qi Fei had been slowly reappropriating parts of Lin's room for storage ever since she left for Qixian. There was a porcelain vase stuffed with fake geraniums, mismatched stationery covering her old desk, bookshelves bursting with magazines and old newspaper clippings.

"I'm sorry for prying," Liz said, her attention rapt, "it all just feels so familiar."

"What does?"

"This apartment," Liz said. She glanced over at the wallpaper warped from age. "My mom kept everything. It was probably a reaction to having to leave her whole life behind when she left China."

Lin had never considered whether anything about the cramped space she and her mother shared could resemble America. Balcony for storing bulky appliances. Boxes stacked floor to ceiling behind long fabric curtains.

The glimpses she'd seen from movies had been of garish homes with basements and front yards and two-car garages.

"She seemed to know she would never come back," Liz continued. "So she built an entirely new life for us in America instead."

Lin hopped into bed next to Liz, her legs propped up beside hers on the duvet.

"What's it really like in America?" she asked. Light was fading from the sky, the outline of her wardrobe barely visible across the room.

"Everyone is free to be themselves," Liz said.

"Like being able to say whatever you want?"

"It's the security of knowing you'll be accepted for who you are."

"But what if something goes wrong?"

"You'll be staying with my brother. He'll help with whatever you need. You'll never feel alone."

The whole time she spoke, Liz gazed at the ceiling, never meeting Lin's eyes. Her words felt strangely wooden, as trite and aspiring as a Party slogan.

"Oh, and don't worry about expenses. The envelope should get you through at least the first few weeks."

Lin understood, then, that the flights to Vietnam hadn't been sold out. Liz had canceled her trip and given her the money she would have used to travel instead.

"Why are you doing all this?"

"Because not all foreigners are assholes," Liz said. "The Travises of the world don't speak for all of us." And suddenly Lin remembered the reason she'd been so reluctant to end things with him in the first place.

"You're leaving for the winter, too, right?" Lin asked. "I don't have anyone I can leave my pets with." She sat up, her heart beating wildly in her chest.

"I have an idea," Liz said. "But you'll have to trust me."

They ate dinner that night, and in the morning, they slipped out of the apartment before dawn. On the back of Qi Fei's motorbike, Lin strapped the crate of gerbils, the snake tank, the small rabbit carrier. She popped the tricolored fish into plastic bags and knotted them tight at the top. Lin gripped the throttle and felt the cold sting her eyes, the roads blurry in the dark. Liz rode behind her, her arms clutching the narrow cushion beneath her seat.

At the pet store on Wukang Road, the sidewalks were deserted, cleared even of the kuaidi couriers, the baozi shops with their tower of wooden steamers, the smell of ginger and chives mixing with the vinegar in the air. Lin unloaded the array of enclosures and left them outside the shop's glass doors, a bicycle lock linking them to the handlebars. After all these years, she didn't want to have to see the owner's reaction when he arrived. She didn't deserve even his pity.

"It's better this way," Liz said, kicking at a tuft of grass snaking through the concrete. And though Lin wanted to believe her, she almost felt worse for these animals than the ones who died under her mother's watch. At least they didn't have to know I betrayed them, she thought, that I was responsible for their fate.

They drove another twenty minutes to Jiaocheng, the sun rising at their backs. By a tiny arched bridge that ran above a stream, Lin opened the final cage, and Boom slid out onto the pavement.

Boom looked around, dazed, and let out a nervous mew. He rubbed his head in the space between Lin's ankles. In her mind, she replayed what his former life had been, the one she was condemning her other pets to, and nearly called off the plan right then.

"Yu guo tian qing," her mother had once told her. There is no change without sacrifice. She would have to lose something without ever knowing what, if anything, she would gain in return. Lin had already abandoned Boom for Travis once already. He'll be better off without me, she reasoned. With time, he'll forget I ever existed.

Lin said this again and again in her head, each time with greater conviction, so that by the time she turned around and stepped speedily back on the motorbike, she felt like she was driving away not only from Boom, but from Travis and her roommates and all of Qixian, too. Like ripping out a part of herself that would forever remain in China.

A tear rolled down her cheek from beneath her helmet, but Lin quickly willed it away. She felt the weight of the embassy paper in her jacket pocket. The promise in her mother's face. The echo of Liz's words in her ears. She didn't look back.

6

"This is as far as we can go," the tour guide explained, speaking into a megaphone. She turned and pointed at the shadowy land mass behind her. "Back there is North Korea."

Liz stared out across the water. From the upper deck of the ferry, she stood gripping the exposed guardrails. The Yalu River, the strip of water separating China from North Korea, mostly frozen in January, looked narrow enough that Liz could imagine North Koreans trying to swim across it during the summer months. There were economic opportunities in China, the tour guide said, though it was unclear from her tone whether she believed China to be profiting off North Koreans' labor or doing a charity by not sending them back.

A relatively small price for freedom, Liz thought. She pictured the electrified fences in Northern Mexico, the savage deserts that stretched for miles along the Texas border. The lengths to which refugees fleeing war in Syria had to go to avoid capture or death. But, of course, everything was relative. Most immigrants were looking to settle in Europe or Canada or the states. Hardly anyone she'd grown up with in Akron—neither her mom nor her brother, certainly—would have dared utter the words "China" and "free" in the same breath.

The ferry stopped, and through the thick chunks of floating ice, Liz could see the thin channels the fleet of tour boats had carved from shuttling tourists from the shores of Dandong, on the Chinese side, out to the center of the river. A woman dressed in a red-checkered jacket and thick earmuffs had been selling fried crabs on the banks of the river right before Liz embarked. Liz had bought one—the crispy red like a pleasing shock against the gray—but still couldn't quite figure out how to eat it without removing her frozen hands from her gloves long enough to peel back the shell.

"Look, over there," a man said, pointing over Liz's shoulder. The voice was in English, and Liz would have been lying if she'd said it was the first time she noticed the person it belonged to. She'd seen him the minute he stepped on board: wavy brown hair, flannel shirt, boxy camera dangling from his neck. An otherwise generic-looking foreigner, Liz thought, had he not also been accompanied by a Chinese man of about the same height and build. His accent screamed American, even from afar, and Liz felt a chill run down her spine, imagining Travis or Jim or Collin traveling with her in that moment.

After visiting Lin in Yuci, Liz wanted to get as far away from Qixian as she could. Going abroad wasn't possible without her bonus, but she realized she could still afford a ticket heading east on the hardscrabble night train, past Beijing and Tianjin toward Dandong, the terminus of the line. She was drawn to it by its peculiar placement, a site of contested history. The border city had passed hands between China, Japan, and the US over the last hundred years, like a three-way tug-of-war. Everything from signs to street names was written in at least two languages. But more than that, Liz wanted to see the limits of China, how far she could go before the old rules she'd come to learn in Qixian stopped applying.

"It's getting closer," the man said. Liz stayed quiet, trying to blend in with the crowd of faces around her. She could tell that she and the man were the only two non-natives aboard, but she wasn't sure how he'd been able to spot her so easily.

For a moment, Liz couldn't tell what he was pointing at, but then it blinked into view: a small fishing boat with a one-stroke engine, no trowels, and rubber tires on either side. As it got closer to the ferry, Liz could make out the face of the sole man on board. He was wearing a puffy jacket over a pair of khaki pants, his hair matted down in a ski hat. In the narrow boat were cartons of cigarettes, grain alcohol, large plastic tubs labeled "Ginseng."

"This is a real North Korean trader," the tour guide announced.

The fishing boat slowed to a crawl and the other passengers on board quickly crowded around the mantle. They were shouting and holding up billfolds like they were at an auction, leaning precariously over the edge. But the man on the boat just shook his head at their questions, not saying a word. He held up his fingers to show the cost of each item before pressing each red-backed bill into his palm. Liz was about to head downstairs, uninterested in the ensuing melee, until she heard the voice—not of the American—but the Chinese man he was with, pipe up.

"That's the worst Chinese actor I've ever seen," he said. He looked about Liz's age, with a wisp of a mustache and a wide smile. He wore thick-rimmed glasses that perfectly complemented his cheekbones. The way he spoke English reminded Liz of how her old classmates used to mockingly address her, and it almost made her cringe. But he wasn't bad-looking, cute even, and what he said was so outlandish that Liz couldn't stop herself from responding.

"You think that guy's pretending to be North Korean?" she asked. "What good would that do?"

"Easy money," the man said. "Baijiu is nothing special, but say it's from North Korea and people will suddenly rush to buy it."

She laughed. It was true, of course. It wasn't unlike some of the scams she'd seen in Qixian: men posing as cab drivers, sex workers moonlighting as masseuses. Everyone pretending to be something they're not.

"I'm Stephen, by the way," the man said, holding out his hand.

"Liz," she said, "nice to meet you." In her other hand was the stick of fried crab she was now trying to distance from her body.

"This is my friend, Byron," he said, pointing to the American.

Liz nodded and did her best to stifle a laugh. The name Byron sounded like the Chinese word bairen: white person. Just as well, she thought. It made sense that Stephen was speaking English for his benefit, even if it still wasn't clear to her why they were traveling together.

Liz looked back at the man in the fishing boat. "How do you think it works?"

"He's an independent contractor," Stephen said. "He buys everything wholesale and splits the profits with the tour companies after."

"Smart," Liz said. "We should all be so resourceful."

From the middle of the river, Liz could see both sides. To the west were thirty-story apartment buildings and rows of luxury hotels. Directly facing them to the east were squat, one-story homes with pitched roofs, green-and-white guard towers, a rusted Ferris wheel that looked like a stopped clock.

It was as if the river had bifurcated a once-solitary land mass—privileging one side and condemning the other—relegating each to its own destiny.

Still, Liz didn't completely believe Stephen's story. Save for her president's deranged fondness for its dictator, Liz had little knowledge of North Korea, and no idea what life was like for actual people who lived there. If she looked hard enough, she thought she could see the man's narrow eyes pressed east, back toward his own shore. How helpless he must have felt, unable to make contact in even the most basic human way. She didn't blame the man on the fishing boat, whoever he really was. She felt sorry for him. She couldn't imagine why anyone would willingly choose to be an outsider when just trying to fit in was hard enough.

"And you," Byron said, picking a piece of seafoam out of his hair. "You don't do such a great acting job yourself." Liz whipped around, her face scrunched in mock anger.

"What do you mean?"

"I could tell you were American from a mile away."

Liz flinched. "What gave me away?"

"You're single," Stephen said, and then, blushing, continued: "I mean, you're not part of a tour group." Liz looked around and saw that everyone else on board was either wearing branded lanyards or following a tour leader's bright talisman. At least someone noticed me, Liz thought, as if, for the first time in two months, she was finally being seen.

"Do you have any plans for tonight?" Stephen asked suddenly.

"I'm not sure yet," she replied, not knowing how much she could trust two strangers she'd only just met.

"Don't worry about it," he said, "forget I asked."

"Trust me, there's nothing to do here," Byron cut in. "Dandong's entire cachet is in its proximity to the border."

"I guess that explains this," Liz said, gesturing at the ferry.

"If you want to go out, though, that's a different story," Byron continued. "Stephen says he knows a great spot."

Liz turned to look at Stephen again and caught his brown eyes blinking back. She searched his face for signs of a serial killer but saw only a shy grin and a flutter of nerves that seemed to mirror her own.

They agreed to meet for drinks later that night, but it was only at the entrance to the place that Liz realized she'd made a mistake. Stephen had texted her the name in Chinese, so she hadn't connected the meaning to its English translation—TRUE LOVE CLUB—emblazoned in all-caps technicolor on the establishment's marquee. The oversized doors were clouded in frosted glass. Wind gusts raked like stiff fingers across her face.

This was a stupid idea, Liz said to herself. Hadn't there been an exposé on the History channel about foreigners being kidnapped and forced to do hard labor in North Korea? Her eyes darted from the door to the streetlamp glowing at the end of the empty block. She mentally evaluated the swiftness of her feet.

But before she could finish the thought, the heavy door in front of her swung open.

"You made it," Stephen exclaimed. He was wearing a button-down shirt and navy jacket, his black bangs swept across his face. He smiled and stepped toward her, enveloping her with both arms.

"I couldn't miss the place."

Stepping into the building, Liz had the sensation of entering a Vegas casino: stout columns of glass bulbs, metallic paint, performers dressed head to toe in sequins. Liz joined Stephen and Byron in a booth away from the stage. She was wearing lace-up boots and a pair of skinny jeans, an upgrade from her teaching outfit in Qixian, but she still felt underdressed compared with the throng of Chinese women sitting cross-legged in miniskirts and heels.

"What brought you out here anyway?" Stephen asked.

"Vacation," Liz said.

"Not exactly the flashiest destination," Byron chimed in. Liz thought better than to mention what could have been: the white beaches of Doc Let or the boat ride to Halong Bay, hundreds of tiny islands twinkling in the night sky.

"It's just my first stop," Liz fibbed. "I'm on break through Chinese New Year."

"Six weeks off? Maybe I should've been a teacher," Byron said.

"People assume you're one already," Stephen laughed.

"Yeah, because I look like I have nothing better to do with my life. No offense," Byron said, turning to Liz.

"Some of us didn't have other options," Liz said. Qi Fei, Lin's mom, had seemed so admiring of her, the fact that she was from China and had come back here to teach. But Liz had become all too aware of the stigma of foreign English teachers.

"We're traveling too," Stephen said, as a waiter with a cordless earpiece ran three bottles of Tsingtao to the table. Stephen poured one into a slender glass and offered it to Liz. "Have you ever been to Shanghai?"

She shook her head. The only other picture of China she had was of the backwater town where she was now loath to show her face.

"It's great there," Stephen said. "From the outside, it can look really intimidating, but when you're on the ground it's such a close-knit community. We both work in tech, but there are plenty of jobs for English teachers."

"Or anything else," Byron snickered.

"Shanghai is a huge city," Stephen said. He brought the bottle of Tsingtao to his lips. "Over there, you're free to be anyone you want."

Without warning, "Beat It" thudded over the club's AV system, and a Chinese man dressed in Michael Jackson's signature leather jacket and fedora began moonwalking across the stage. Liz winced, imagining the backlash this bizarre scene would engender in the states, but she couldn't deny she was enjoying it a little, too. Just then, the earpieced waiter returned to the table.

"Excuse me," he said, in shaky English, "but will you please sing us a song?"

"Keyi," Byron replied, a smile pursing his lips.

"You speak Chinese?" the waiter asked. On stage, the Michael Jackson impersonator weaved his hands behind his head and over his crotch. "Your Chinese is very good," the waiter added, flashing a thumbs up.

"Na li, na li," Byron replied. It was what Liz said too whenever she received a compliment and wanted to be polite even if, secretly, she believed it was true.

After the waiter left, Liz turned to Byron. "You're not seriously going to sing, are you?" Byron gave a weak shrug.

"I guess *someone* forgot to mention the staff here like to pick on laowai." He glared across the table at Stephen.

Liz was used to the kind of foreigner who was wont to cause a scene, to be the center of attention. But she'd never considered the reverse: that along with celebrity comes a responsibility to entertain. Even Byron, Liz knew, would never, no matter how much he wanted, be seen as anything but an outsider. It surprised her that someone like him could experience what she'd known her whole life in the states. That being different was its own curse: an eternal oddity, forever being made a spectacle.

The Michael Jackson impersonator shuffled off stage and a voice boomed over the loudspeaker: "Please put your hands together for a very special guest."

"Cheer for me, would you?" Byron said, stretching his legs. "Make it seem like I'm someone important."

This should be entertaining, Liz muttered under her breath. The memory of the late-night train from Taiyuan with the other American teachers flared up in her mind, and she sunk further into her chair. But when Byron started singing, Liz's jaw nearly dropped. The song was familiar, a schmaltzy ballad she'd heard her mom play when she thought no one else was listening: "The Moon Represents My Heart." Liz pictured Pearl as a young girl, lying awake at night in Fujian, dreaming of the well-studied suitor who would eventually take her to see a moon halfway across the world. And yet, she couldn't connect the lyrics to the sound emanating from Byron's mouth.

"You seem surprised," Stephen said.

"I've never met a foreigner who could really speak Chinese."

"You mean a *white* foreigner. You don't give yourself enough credit," Stephen smiled. "Even if they hate it a little bit, deep down, every foreigner here wants to feel like they're the only one."

"What do you mean?"

"They want to be like Marco Polo. Like every experience is uniquely their own."

Liz considered her own reasons for coming to China: her search for self-discovery, her desire to interrogate her past.

"And you wouldn't?" she asked, a little defensive. "Wouldn't everyone rather be their own person if they had a choice?"

"We don't really think like that," Stephen said. "We have a saying. Shu da zhao feng. Tall trees attract the wind. Besides, wasn't that you trying to blend in on the ferry?"

Liz blinked back at Stephen. She couldn't believe he'd been able to glean something about her that she hadn't even admitted to herself. After getting the text from Lin about her expulsion, Liz had called Phil to explain the situation. She wasn't thrilled about the possibility of entrusting Lin to him, but she didn't see an alternative. Getting Lin into school in Ohio seemed imperative, the least she could do. Liz had practically begged Phil to ask his colleagues in Chicago for help with her visa and to let her stay with him at his apartment in Cleveland.

"Having you come back is one thing," Phil said, "but why should I stick my neck out for her? It's not like China's done anything for me lately."

Liz could hear the revulsion in his tone. She wondered if that's the way Pearl would have thought of her now, too. Undoing all the opportunities she'd given her. Rejecting her own Americanness. Doing everything in her power to resist going back.

A chorus of applause followed Byron as he exited the stage. People pointed and thrust their hands toward him like he was an alpaca at the state fair.

"That was actually pretty good," Liz said.

"Live here long enough and you learn a few tricks," Byron said. "You know, I really envy you. I wish I could still see China through fresh eyes."

They talked until the bar closed at dawn. Liz felt like she'd divulged her entire life story up until moving to China: her deadbeat father, the failed academic; her self-hating golden child of a brother; her immigrant mother who loved her new country so much it killed her. Once through the cloudy doors, Liz strained at the sun swelling in the sky and shaded her eyes. Byron ordered a taxi on his phone and he and Stephen piled into the back seat.

"Can we drop you off?" Stephen asked, but Liz waved them off. It wasn't that a part of her wanted to be with Stephen alone. But it was one thing to follow two strangers to a bar and another to go back to their hotel with them.

"Text me," she said, as the car peeled off down the street.

The air outside was still. Sunlight rankled the tops of trees, and Liz felt more alive than she had in months. She reveled in the intimacy of travel that was absent in her everyday life, when everyone was a stranger, and she could say anything because she'd never have to hear from them again. And yet, Liz also yearned for closeness in a context that wasn't so transient, which seemed to her much more difficult to find.

Liz headed east, toward the Yalu River, the steps leading down to the water's edge bathed in a yellow glow. The only people out were the occasional jogger and a few elderly men in dull-colored swim caps. They lined up on the banks of the river and took turns plunging into the freezing water only to emerge seconds later, their bodies downy with drip, born anew.

It looked both exhilarating and revolting. Pearl had once told her about the bathhouses in Fujian, how hot water opens the pores and cold water constricts them, the combination like yin-yang, two perfect halves of a whole. Liz heard the crash of another person diving off into the murky river and felt something stir inside her. She checked into a twenty-four-hour spa across from the Friendship Bridge, exchanged her passport for a purple electric wristband, and headed into the baths.

There were four kinds of baths in ascending order of temperature—some misty, others full of fragrance—and beyond that, a whole ecosystem of services that seemed as quaint and old-fashioned as a Medieval Times. Massages, haircuts, a restaurant with walk-up counters where patrons slurped breakfast noodles in identical cotton robes. There were no windows and no clocks. It seemed to function as its own underground society, oblivious to what was happening on the surface.

Liz tried to make sense of everything, but her head was spinning. The water had calmed her nerves but did little to provide any clarity. She couldn't deny her attraction to Stephen. And yet, it was in a context she'd never felt before. He was so unlike any of the men in her past that it both thrilled and terrified her, a tingling at the pit of her stomach.

Liz unspooled a mat on the carpeted floor and placed a pillow under her head. She slept until the sun had begun to set again, and when she rolled over to check her phone, she saw a message from Stephen.

Dinner tonight? it read next to a smiley face. *Byron found a great North Korean place. Very authentic.*

Inside the restaurant, the three of them sat around a wooden table. A translucent curtain of Hangul script partially separated them from two Chinese businessmen, the only other customers. In the corner, an ancient Hitachi monitor played sun-bleached North Korean propaganda films on loop. But the first thing Liz noticed was the waitress.

"You seem to really like her," Stephen said, teasing. He was wearing a collared shirt with the top button undone, the fabric snug against his arms. "You haven't stopped looking at her since we sat down."

It was a strange thing to admit, but every time the woman brushed past their table, Liz could almost taste her fragrance, like a pair of soft hands closing around her throat. The waitress was otherwise unremarkable: face as round and plain as a ceramic bowl, cheeks slightly sunken in, dark hair knotted in a bun. And yet, there was a sweetness to her that Liz recognized but couldn't quite place.

"I don't blame you," Byron interjected. "No one comes to Dandong and doesn't imagine what life is like *over there.*"

Liz stared at the lazy Susan. The lighting was dim, more dark than moody. On the TV screen, men and women were smiling the widest smiles she'd ever seen. They were dressed in plain clothes with muted colors, beiges and grays and corduroy browns. She couldn't understand anything they said, but the scenes seemed to play out as a series of reunions: wives running to the outstretched arms of their soldier husbands, families embracing across what appeared to be both sides of the Korean border.

"What will you have?" the waitress asked in Mandarin. It struck Liz that the waitress was the first North Korean she'd ever met. Their two countries had been feuding for decades, and how strange it felt that there they were, each speaking a language that was not their own, in a place neither of them could rightfully call home.

"You don't suppose she's acting, too?" Liz asked, when the waitress left the table. Stephen shook his head.

"Her accent's off," he said. "Plus, she's not wearing any makeup."

"What does that have to do with anything?"

"It's illegal to wear makeup," Stephen said. "The North Korean government banned all cosmetics as capitalist." Liz brought her hand to her own face: winged eyeliner, blush, mascara that made her eyes look stiff as a rosebush.

"Maybe we'd all be better off for it."

Byron leaned across the table, his beard bristling. "You do know how they come here, right?" Liz shook her head.

"The waitstaff, the cooks—everyone—they all live in the same block of company housing across the border. Every morning, a van arrives to pick them up and shuttle them into China. The windows are tinted so they can't see anything outside. Even the driver is separated from the passengers by a black partition."

"All to prevent any threat of escape?"

"Everyone wants to leave North Korea, even if it still means working for the government," Byron said. "Not just anyone can do it. There are extensive background checks, vetting."

"So it's a privilege to get to work here?" Liz asked. She wondered if just being at the restaurant was the closest thing to freedom the waitress experienced. That being trapped in this tedium, day in and day out, was what she might have looked forward to most each day.

"Even then there are no guarantees. The government will know if anything is amiss."

"And then what?"

"Consequences," he said, before slipping into silence.

"What is it that we're doing here then?" Liz asked. "I mean, where does our money go?"

"To be honest, Liz," Byron said, "we're most likely supporting the regime."

Liz turned the words over in her mind but still couldn't make them right. Even though she'd probably never encounter the waitress again, there was something wrong about seeing her in a set of shackles and not giving her the key.

"We shouldn't be here," Liz said suddenly, nearly clamoring to her feet. She hated Byron in that moment for suggesting the restaurant and herself for going along with it. The repercussions of her actions could hurt someone—*had* hurt someone already.

In Yuci, even after seeing Lin off, Liz couldn't bring herself to tell the full truth. That she'd been the one to tip off the waishiban, that her selfish desire to oust Travis had backfired. She'd even lied when she told Lin about life in America, as if the same prejudice she'd grown up with somehow wouldn't apply to her. For weeks, she'd railed against Travis and the other teachers, and yet, it was her own misguided sense of entitlement that had resulted in Lin's expulsion. If only she'd never met me, Liz thought, maybe then she wouldn't have to bear the guilt of forever ruining Lin's life.

"There are never easy choices," Stephen said. "Every decision has its own trade-offs."

Just then, the waitress arrived with the food. Stir-fry with cuttlefish and bell peppers, buckwheat noodles, dumplings dyed black from squid ink. Her voice was all kindness when she addressed them, and Liz was surprised by the lightness in it, nothing like the orderly bleakness she expected from someone living under a despot. The scent of her perfume hadn't diminished. If anything, it seemed heightened, exaggerated by the heat of the dishes.

"Why go through all this trouble at all?" Liz asked. She looked around the restaurant, and it was like the signs had been in plain sight all along. The lack of windows, the dismal outfits, the propaganda films on loop. It was all part of the facade that there was nothing else out there, that despite being in a different country, the waitress may just as well have never left home.

"Wouldn't you strive for a better life if you could," Stephen said, "no matter what it took?"

Before Liz could respond, the waitress came by a final time, to leave the check on a corner of the table, and Liz inhaled slowly, wanting it to last. The perfume, a small act of subversion. The things we all do to keep hope alive.

Liz hadn't cried in weeks, but she suddenly felt herself breaking down. That scent. It was her mom's. Every day, in the weeks Pearl had spent undergoing treatment before she died, she'd still put it on. Liz had stayed all night in the ER when Pearl was first admitted, enduring test after test until there were no more tests to take. She held her hand, in the round plastic chair by her mom's bedside, speaking to her and hearing only muddied fragments in return. On weekends from college, Liz did her homework on her lap, playing *The Big Bang Theory* and *Community* on repeat, like laughter was the only way to keep herself from crying.

"What's wrong?" Stephen asked, reaching a hand across the table.

"My mom," Liz started. "I never knew how alone she must have felt."

Pearl had always insisted that just making it to America was enough. And yet, she never felt at home. She'd come as an immigrant, and up until the day she died, she'd remained one. Pearl withheld every negative thing, no matter the circumstance, and confided in no one. Maybe deep down she feared that despite being born there, her children would grow up and still never be accepted as anything other than foreign, too.

"This is going to sound crazy," Stephen said. "But why don't you come to Shanghai with us?"

"You can't be serious," Lin said.

"That's a great idea," Byron chimed in. "We have a couch you can crash on and everything."

"Yeah, but what about my job?"

"Just tell them something came up and you had to go back to the states," Byron said. "I promise it won't be the first time they've heard it."

"But—" Liz paused, "I don't know the first thing about Shanghai."

"We'll show you around," Byron continued. "Plus, you can make triple your salary."

"No need to rush into anything," Stephen said, eyeing Byron. "Just come down for Chunjie and see how you like it. The rest we can figure out later."

We. Stephen had made a good point. Liz still had vacation time left and no plans to use it. But the truth was she'd already made up her mind. There was nothing for her back in Qixian—not the other teachers, not the administration—nothing save for a couple suitcases worth of belongings she could easily replace. Going back would only remind her of the past. Miles away from Travis and Lin, Liz could start over. Even if she couldn't be a new person, she could at least be a new version of herself.

"What time did you say your train was?" Liz asked. Byron checked his watch.

"In an hour. We'd better get going," he said, scanning the bill's QR code. "So, what'll it be?"

More than anything, Liz wished she could ask her mom what she would do. For all Liz's excitement, she knew it wouldn't be easy to make a new life somewhere else. There were so many other questions she would have wanted to ask Pearl, too: What was the village like where she grew up? What kinds of food did her parents make? What was the first thing she remembered about America?

Liz knew her mom's marriage to her dad had been arranged by family. He was a great catch: smart, successful, ambitious. He had an offer to study in the states, and Pearl would get married and go there with him, eventually starting her own family an ocean away. But had she ever wanted to leave? Her mom had had a whole life in China and needed to believe, in the end, that it would all be worth the trade-off. Why would anyone in her position have made that choice?

"You deserve the best, Lizzy," her mom had told her in the hospital, clear as day, the last words she'd spoken. "Remember the best parts, the most important parts, and leave the rest behind."

7

For fourteen hours, Lin couldn't sleep. She slumped against the hard armrest by the window, heaved the scratchy blue blanket up to her neck. The pressure in the cabin made her ears ache. She feared that if she ate or drank anything, it would upset her already iffy stomach. She was too embarrassed to ask to leave her seat, let alone attempt the taijiquan her mother insisted would promote proper blood circulation.

Whenever Lin closed her eyes, she saw visions play out on the underside of her eyelids: plane propeller malfunctioning, tail catching fire, crew and passengers strapping on oxygen masks like patients admitted to a ward.

But with her eyes open, Lin saw her surroundings in a different light. She sneaked glances through the plastic shutter, staring at the dark mass moving just beyond her reach. The sky looked as limitless as the ocean, clouds like tiny swells of tide covered in fog. For the first time in months, she was above something, charting her own path. Whatever had happened up until then wasn't the least bit important. She was moving to a place where no one knew the slightest thing about her past.

Lin transferred planes in Detroit, a city so free of her preconceptions that she initially mistook it for Cleveland. The baggage claim felt like a fever dream: carpeted floors and cinder-block columns in all directions until, finally, she was ushered into a great hall bathed in white. The man at customs stamped her passport after only barely glancing down, and—much to Lin's relief—let her pass without asking a single question.

Lin spotted Phil first. Outside of the baggage carousel, he was dressed in khaki pants, wool coat, a burgundy scarf. He was the male version of Liz—thin eyebrows, widow's peak—but with a heft to his midsection and high cheekbones that gave him the impression of someone perpetually pleased with himself.

"You must be Lin," he said, extending a stiff hand. "Welcome to the promised land."

Lin nodded weakly, still too overwhelmed to speak. She couldn't get over the shock of seeing hundreds of people around her and hearing only English come out.

"You must be starving," Phil said, as Lin stepped up into the cab of his station wagon. The air was so crisp it made Lin's eyes water. Phil switched on the ignition, and the car lurched to life like a startled animal. The lanes on the highway multiplied: two to four then eight, unfolding like a paper fan.

In the Costco parking lot in Avon, the grid of vehicles looked vast enough to be its own city. All her life, Lin was used to having just as much as she needed. She never wanted for warm clothing or school supplies or worried about going to sleep hungry. And yet, once inside, she found it hard to grasp the abundance. Aluminum cans as wide as her thigh. Prawns enough to have depleted an estuary. Aisles that she could lie lengthwise in and still not reach the ends of.

"Free samples are over there," Phil said, motioning with his finger. "Eat as much as you want."

Lin rubbed her eyes, staring dizzily at the rows of boxes and bottles lit with fluorescent lighting. She barely averted a couple pushing a shopping cart large enough to pilot. Compared to the markets back home, the scale of choice was paralyzing. Mounds of peppers were arranged in different-hued pyramids, lined up like purses in a luxury store.

Abundance was the wrong word; Lin couldn't get over the *excess*. No one, she was sure, needed this much. It was obscene, and yet there was a part of her that was taken by it, too. She wondered what it would be like to live that way, to be so full of sustenance that she could hardly breathe. To suffocate on extravagance.

"Ready?" Phil said, sounding impatient. Lin settled on a double-pack of bread, picking up and examining a half-dozen before putting them back on the shelf, trying to discern the difference between wheat and pumpernickel and multigrain.

At the cash register, Lin peeled back a twenty from the stack of fresh bills she'd exchanged at the airport. Phil looked at her and nodded, as if testing her loyalties. He handed the woman at the counter his membership card but didn't offer to pay.

The semester started later that week. Classes were held at Cuyahoga Community College's Metropolitan Campus near downtown Cleveland better known as Tri-C. It was much larger than her university in Qixian, full of wide concrete pathways and asphalt parking lots that seemed impossible to fill. The buildings, strewn with ivy and made of brick, were abutted by vast fields, where once a day a snowmobile came to plow. There was a fountain out front, devoid of water and Kenny G, too.

Lin had been used to the ebb and flow that dictated each day in Qixian: reciting "March of the Volunteers" every morning, group calisthenics at the big track, the blare of the noon bell to signal lunch. But it seemed as if everyone at Tri-C made their own schedule, lived off campus, went to classes on their own time. There was no gate that encircled the school grounds, no one at a dorm room reception who cared the slightest about her comings and goings. It was a kind of independence she'd never known before, a choice over every small decision that eschewed the very notion of a single path.

Lin registered for classes at the International Students Office. According to the visa that Phil had helped her procure, she was admitted on an F1, as a STEM student, under a government initiative called Community Colleges for International Development. The goal was to train international students in high-impact fields that would help grow the technical resources of their home countries.

"What brings you to Tri-C?" a freckled woman asked through a loudspeaker in the glass, like a bank teller. On her desk was a plush miniature of the school's mascot, a teal triceratops. Lin repeated what she'd told the consular officer at her visa interview in Beijing.

"I came to study at community college because Western knowledge will help strengthen China's morality." She had to bite her tongue to get it all out with a straight face, as if it hadn't been supposed *Western knowledge* that had sabotaged her own morality in the first place.

"I'm not seeing a TOEFL score here," the woman said, squinting her glasses at the screen.

"I didn't take it," Lin said. Liz had never mentioned anything about a test. It seemed bad enough that community colleges, much to Lin's shock, didn't even offer bachelor's degrees. If she wanted to become a veterinarian, she'd have to apply later and transfer to a four-year college.

"We'll have to enroll you in ESL, sweetheart," the woman said.

"ESL? But I—" Lin wanted to tell her about the twelve years she'd studied English in Yuci, her perfect grades in high school, even the tragedy of her tryst with Travis. But it was like she'd forgotten how to speak.

"It's all right, honey," the woman said, slowing her speech to a crawl. "Just know we communicate a little different here. You're in America now."

Lin's new English teacher looked, mercifully, nothing like Travis. Mr. Watkins was a slight, balding man, with thick hairs that covered his arms and hands. It took some time for Lin to find his classroom, and when she entered, she was surprised to see only about ten students, most out-aging her by at least a decade. Even more surprising was the sight of two Chinese girls sitting next to each other in the center of the row of seats. One was tall and dour with a square jaw, while the other was round-faced and thin, with skin that looked so much like porcelain it might crack. They were clearly friends, wearing the easy nonchalance of familiarity between them like a favorite sweater.

Back in Qixian, Lin would have sat up front and avoided those girls at all costs. Even though they were a long way from home, she was wary of whatever information they, like her roommates, might be able to expose about her. But Mr. Watkins had already begun his lesson and Lin, already rattled from being late, plopped down at a desk just barely out of the girls' earshot.

"When Americans ask you where you go to school, you'll want to be able to impress them," Mr. Watkins said. He pointed to a map of the Cuyahoga River Valley that he projected on the white board and ran a laser pointer up and down the blue squiggle in the center.

"Back in the 1960s, this river was so slick with oil that it famously set itself on fire." He advanced to a grainy still of the river, a trail of orange and smoke smoldering across the foreground.

The bigger of the two girls sitting next to Lin, pudgier and with broader shoulders, leaned over to the other.

"I don't know about you," she whispered, in Mandarin, "but China doesn't seem so polluted after all."

Lin stifled a laugh. In high school, her teachers had rarely drawn attention to the environmental costs of China's development. It was important to focus on the benefits—wealth, jobs, a first-world standard of living—instead of what was forsaken in order to get there. At least in America you could talk about these things, Lin reasoned. It would be everything her experience in China was not. After class, she smiled politely to the two girls and excused herself without sparing them a second thought.

The bus ride on the 63 to and from campus was blissfully quiet. Lin pulled her scarf down from around her nose and peered out the window, clearing a small circle of condensation from the glass. There were still remnants of Christmas, bright lights strung up between streetlamps and nativity displays assembled on lawns, inflatable likenesses of Jesus and his mother that sagged from rain and snow.

It hadn't only been Qi Fei; everyone in China was instructed to be wary of foreign influence. Even when Lin was out celebrating with Liz on Christmas, she was cognizant of the official rhetoric: to refrain from spiritual display, from false iconography. Was this what China would look like if people could celebrate so openly? Lin stared at the white clumps that clung to store awnings. On the ride from the airport, Phil had said that Cleveland got so much snow because of the lake effect—something about warm air mixing with cold—that Lin didn't quite follow. But just the idea of being close to water felt like a gift to Lin, its own kind of freedom.

For meals, Lin ate at restaurants where waitstaff visited her table without her having to yell. She struggled, at times, to decipher the contours of their speech, the pitch and speed. Lin was shocked the first time she was asked if she wanted water straight from the tap. In Yuci, Qi Fei had discouraged Lin from cooking. But gradually, her trips to IGA, a mile away on foot from Phil's apartment, took on a familiar pattern: instant noodles, raw vegetables, prepared food. Green beans were pre-washed with the ends trimmed. Spinach leaves were stored in clamp-shell tubs with none of the stems. It felt extravagant to Lin that so much of the edible parts went to waste.

At home, Lin rarely saw Phil who, despite calling in a favor to expedite her visa paperwork and putting her up in his second bedroom, otherwise ignored her. His civil servant job, reminiscent of China's long-shattered iron rice bowl, meant that his hours were consistent along with his post-work activities, which seemed to consist mainly of playing video games and lurking on online forums. Although he was four years older than Liz, he lacked her curiosity about the world. Lin missed the easy conversation that came with their shared heritage. The more she learned about Phil, the more she realized he wasn't at all connected to his.

At night, with the blinds drawn and the low hum of street traffic outside, Lin messaged Liz. She wrote to her often, hoping to hear some word from her, but Liz rarely responded. Lin had gotten used to texting her every day when they were on campus, back when there was hardly anything of intrigue to report. But now that she was in America—where the eddy of daily changes made her head spin—communication trickled to a crawl. She had barely heard at all from Liz since she landed at Phil's doorstep. In bed, her mind wandered, searching for what it was she'd done wrong.

Sitting alone at the round tables of the Tri-C cafeteria one afternoon, Lin noticed a flier printed on bright red paper. It was an advertisement for the college's Chinese American Alliance. Lin scrunched her face. The idea of Chinese and Americans working together on anything seemed futile, especially after the last few years, but not impossible. She thought about Liz and her old promise to her mother. It probably wouldn't hurt to meet more people willing to bridge the distance between her new home and the one she'd just left.

The meeting was held in a dim, windowless room inside the Student Union, with carpeted floors and upholstered chairs arranged in a semicircle. Lin sat on the far side, crossing and uncrossing her legs. She watched the handful of faces float in, all with similar eyes and skin tone, hair that had been dyed blond at the tips or shaved but still unmistakably her own.

"Let's start by welcoming our new guests," the club's president began. "Can you say your name, major, where you're from?"

A prospective EMT from Parma spoke first, but by the time he finished and Lin introduced herself, a silence filled the room.

"We get that you're *really from* China," the president said, eliciting a few laughs. "But where are you from in the states?"

"I'm from Yuci," Lin said, still not understanding. "I just arrived a week ago."

"I'm sorry," the president said again, "I think there must be a misunderstanding. This group is really for Chinese *Americans*."

Lin hadn't been aware that people in America organized themselves by ethnicity. Outside of the foreign men in Qixian, she'd never given much thought to race. Nearly all her classmates, like her, had been Han and even those who weren't did a remarkable job of assimilating.

"I think there's probably another group for students from China," a man in a beanie responded.

"It's bad enough being mistaken for them," another voice said. "We need people to know we have different viewpoints. We're not the Communist Party."

"I personally think it's fine if she joins," someone else offered.

"I don't know," a woman with a nose piercing called out. "My family worked their asses off so I could be here. Not like these new immigrants with their Gucci bags and Lamborghinis."

Some of the other members around the circle nodded. Lin realized then that they resembled her in just one way: face. Unlike Liz, most had never been to China and weren't interested in what life was like there. They couldn't fathom the idea of a Chinese student, an only child from the mainland, who wasn't just trying to spend her parents' money.

The woman raised her voice a notch. "And now teachers assume *we* can't speak English. Everything our parents fought for—poof—gone."

What was so tough about being huayi? There were no visa issues, no classes in a second language, no having to navigate a foreign culture. In Yuci, when her mother found out Liz was Chinese American, it only made her admire Liz more. It was inconceivable to Lin that anyone could feel so intent on changing their perception in America that they'd dissociate from their own homeland.

"But aren't we all at least Chinese?" Lin mouthed. "Don't we have that in common?"

"No," the same woman said, sounding offended. "Chinese Americans are just as American as anyone else in this country. What's so hard to understand about that?"

Before the meeting ended, Lin rushed out of the room, so upset she thought she might faint. She was so determined not to have to see any of the members again that she didn't look up as she charged across the hallway.

"Hey, watch out," a man said, holding out his arms.

"I'm sorry," Lin replied. She was newly conscious of how she pronounced every syllable, the particularly Chinese way she'd doubtless accosted this stranger.

"It's all right," the man said, looking at her. "You're in Mr. Watkins's class, aren't you?"

Lin blinked her eyes up to meet his. He had a mop of brown hair, the slightest wisp of a beard. In his self-introduction in class, he'd said that he was from Argentina, but Lin couldn't recall how he ended up in Ohio. How anyone had.

"Mateo," he said, extending a hand. He spoke with an accent that was of somewhere else, its own small comfort.

"Lin," she replied, offering her own.

"A couple of us are hosting a party on Saturday night," he continued, "you should come."

"That's tomorrow?" Lin asked.

Mateo nodded, naming the number of a street. "Things should get going by 11." It was already later than her dorm curfew would have been back in Qixian.

Before Lin could think to say otherwise, she was nodding and walking away, the assenting words already out of her mouth.

Lin could hear the music before she even approached the door. The house was a two-story walk-up with clapboard siding painted purple and a snow-trampled path that led to a backyard. People congregated on the landing with plastic cups in their hands, women in short dresses and cut-off shirts despite the weather. Lin ascended the stairs. She'd already had two beers before taking the bus over, if only to inure herself to the cold, barely glancing up long enough at the people guarding the door to gauge whether her presence alone would draw stares. She had come with no one, after all, and presumed she would hardly know anyone there either.

It was warm inside. At the entrance was a pile of coats, and Lin added her jacket to the heap. She was wearing a dress she'd bought at a department store in downtown Cleveland, red and sleeveless with ties that crossed beneath her chest. Looking at her reflection in the mirror, she was surprised by how well it fit, how the color complimented her complexion. Still, she'd imagined it was meant for someone else. Someone well-versed in social graces, confident in the strength of her conviction. Not at all like the girl she'd known in China.

A crowd had bottlenecked at the staircase to the basement. Downstairs, the room was thick with smoke—the smell like a hot pot restaurant in winter—tables and floors sticky with spilled liquor. Lin saw a laptop propped in one corner next to a set of speakers and, in another, a line for beer. She queued at the end, palms resting on her hips. Someone handed her a cup, and she drained it before reaching for a second. The bitter taste of baijiu from Travis's banquet had vanished, replaced by the cold, sudsy taste of possibility.

Out of the corner of her eye, she spotted the two Chinese girls from her ESL class. They were dressed in outfits Lin recognized from the mainland: fake sequins, ruffles, chintzy fabric meant to be worn once and quickly forsaken. They sipped quietly from their cups, a resigned yearning in their glances. How utterly out of place they looked. Was this how those huayi at the meeting had seen her, too?

"Now, Lin, that's a normal-sounding name," a voice said, clasping her around the waist. It was Mateo.

"My aunt is named Linda," he said, like they'd been midconversation. "That girl is Gua, I think," he continued, pointing over his shoulder. "And I don't even know what the other girl is called," he said, leaning in closer. "She never speaks." Lin was reminded of her own childhood, what her former classmates used to hiss about her in the hallways.

"I'll talk your ear off if you let me," she said. She hadn't noticed it before, but Mateo had the same faint beard, same freckles on his cheeks that Travis had. Lin knew the way the story sounded: that Travis had taken advantage of her, a naive freshman without a single friend. But she also knew it was she who'd first come on to Travis. That without him, she wouldn't have made it to America, to Ohio, to this crumbling house basement surrounded by corn fields.

"What brings you to Ohio?" Mateo asked, calling out over the music.

"I got kicked out of school," Lin said. Mateo gave her a look that suggested both concern and admiration. Lin remembered the conversation she'd had with the registrar days before, the textbook answer she'd given then. It was the thing she was most ashamed of, and yet here she was, shouting it with abandon.

"Fucking my teacher," Lin clarified, not waiting for Mateo to respond. She took another sip, circling her lips with her tongue. From over the brim of her cup, she thought she could see Mateo's expression change. She wondered then if she'd somehow gained a power, too, of being able to wield this other language as her own.

Lin laughed once, loudly, a stab in the night. She teetered on her heels, pressed a hand to Mateo's chest. She could feel the two Chinese girls lock eyes with her from across the room, and yet didn't feel the slightest obligation toward them.

"I'll drink to that," Mateo said, raising his cup to hers. The music was pounding, hardwood pulsing beneath her feet. People all around her were stomping and jumping, and it felt like the floor could cave in at any moment. Mateo held out his hand, and Lin took it, not the way she first went to shake it, but grabbed it, led him out to where the crowd surrounded them, whooping and clapping with such abandon that she let herself go, too.

Lin remembered what she'd first thought about Travis, that there would always be things about China that would never be enough. It was only now in America that she'd finally understood that feeling: the permission to do whatever she pleased, to be unapologetically herself.

The music picked up, the bass reaching a feverish pitch. Lin raised her arms to the ceiling. She closed her eyes. The room spun in prismatic circles around her. She felt a pair of lips, wet and searching, on her mouth. It was the last thing she remembered before it went dark.

8

Liz had never before seen a Chinese city. Her impression of the country had almost entirely been confined to Qixian: the wide fields for tilling sorghum, the school's polychrome front gate. The teaching building was so cold she had to wear her coat over her blouse when she taught. The bathrooms had no doors or partitions between the stalls, so when she squatted down to shit between classes, she had to avoid the shock of her students catching a glimpse of her in the mirror.

"I learned to skip oatmeal in the mornings after that," Liz told Byron on the train, laughing. Stephen sat beside her, their arms tingling at their sides but not quite touching.

The three of them had boarded the gaotie from Dandong to Shanghai, a distance that would have spanned nearly the entire West Coast in the states but took just over ten hours. It was a welcome respite from the train Liz had ridden back and forth to Golden Hans in Taiyuan with the other Americans and it was a far cry, too, from the overnight liupiche that Liz boarded from Qixian to Dandong. She'd had a hard seat on the jittery local train, which every few minutes blasted its overhead lights and blared the station name over the intercom for passengers to disembark.

Instead, Liz, Stephen, and Byron had their own horizontal bunks in a private cab, each latched into the metal dividers like rungs on a ladder. There was a set of sheets, a pillow, and a pair of shrink-wrapped slippers under each mattress. The window flashed alternating scenes of streetlights and dense sky as the train sped between platforms. In the morning, while Liz was still tucked into bed, a conductor rapped on the door to let her know they would soon be arriving in Shanghai. Liz bolted up, sheepish, like a child scolded for sleeping through her alarm.

"It's normal," Stephen said, emerging from his own bunk across the aisle. "There's always someone going around to make sure people get off in time." Liz enjoyed imagining a world where the worst possible fate was to miss her stop. Her only responsibility was over herself and her own sleep, which, given her middling track record, seemed like responsibility enough.

On her first day in Shanghai, Liz walked along Jingmei Road, gawking at neon-lit convenience stores, restaurants with awnings in French, department stores so tall they blotted out the clouds. It was almost Spring Festival, and the cold that Liz had grown accustomed to in Qixian and Dandong had been replaced with a pleasant warmth. No longer did the streets choke with dust. The avenues were lined with large streamers in reds and yellows. Bright paper lanterns swelled from storefronts, framing statuettes of ceramic dragons clenching gold coins in their snarled mouths.

Stephen and Byron lived above a highway, a six-lane tarmac that sometimes made the seventeenth-story windows rattle. The building had a front reception and a doorman who greeted them by name, a gym, and a spa with complementary mineral water. The elevator in the lobby shot straight up, skipping the fourth and thirteenth floors for luck.

"Your apartment is beautiful," Liz said, still remembering how the rats scurried in the ceiling of her red-brick flat, or the way the toilet paper in her bathroom got sprayed whenever she turned on the shower.

"The view could be better," Byron said, motioning toward the sill. Liz stared at the trail of headlights below, a wild, snaking creature moving as one.

"They're building an even taller apartment building near Pudong," Stephen said. Liz looked in the direction of the water but couldn't distinguish between the phalanxes of cranes and steel in the distance.

"I can really see myself living here," she said. Liz suddenly felt certain that everything she'd come to China to do was riding on this: finding an apartment in the French Concession, commuting on the ditie, going to shows, making friends who loved the city as much as she did. She would do whatever it took, even if it meant scouring classified listings for tutoring jobs.

"How can you know where to live if you've barely seen the city yet?" Stephen asked.

"Are you volunteering to be my tour guide, too?"

That night, they went out for drinks in the Hole. Liz had assumed it was the name of a bar, so she was confused when they reached a grassy park on Julu Road with what appeared to be an enormous sinkhole formed in the center.

"I prefer 'food and beverage crater,'" Byron said, lifting his pinky in the air. "The bars around here used to get noise complaints all the time, so the government shut them down and moved them here instead."

From where they stood, it was impossible to tell what was below the surface of beech trees and stone benches. But as they descended the lighted staircase, Liz could see the concrete oval emerge like a subterranean skate park, white-columned porticoes that gave it the air of a Roman market. Nightclubs and lounges were cloaked in gauzy red. A maze of restaurants touted everything from German sausages to falafel. There were several times more expats than Liz had seen in all her time in China. It could have been Paris or Morocco or Spain. If she blinked, she could have forgotten she was in China at all.

"They say all of Shanghai's foreigners can fit inside here," Byron said, smiling. Liz imagined a bazaar—a mini Epcot—with hundreds of representatives standing in genteel outfits, selling wares, calling out to passersby in their native languages. It seemed astounding that foreigners had been given a space within the confines of the city where they could carve out their own community.

Stephen settled on an outdoor bar with a patio table and chairs, and Byron ordered the first round.

"Where did you two meet anyway?" Liz asked.

"Here, actually," Stephen said. "A meetup group for people working in tech."

"Both our leases were expiring," Byron explained, "and I thought it would be fun to move in with a local guy." He took a large swig. "Not that he lets me practice my Chinese at all."

Stephen gave Liz a pleading look. "I go out of my way to make things easier for him, and this is the thanks I get."

Liz laughed, bringing the glass to her lips. She liked the feeling of sitting out there with them. It couldn't have felt more different from dinners with Travis and the other foreign men in Qixian. The three of them fit together in a strange way. Liz could align herself with Stephen, another

Chinese face, as easily as she could Byron, an American. She'd become used to the openness that seemed required of expat friendships, the casual references to the body: sweating, fucking, la duzi. But there was a sense of acceptance that came from being with them too, a community that Travis, or even Lin, could never quite provide.

The next morning, Liz felt the sun peek through the blinds in the living room. Byron was asleep and Liz's backpack lay split open next to her on the couch. Liz had fallen asleep in the same outfit she'd worn, barely managing to wash her face. She could hear Stephen running water in the kitchen, his feet padding toward her in house slippers.

"Just in case," he whispered, setting a steaming mug on the coffee table.

"What time is it?" Liz asked.

"Lunchtime," Stephen said. "I want to show you something."

Downstairs at a street stall near the apartment, Stephen ordered two plastic-sealed cups of doujiang and shengjianbao blackened with sesame seeds.

"Make sure to bite a tiny hole and blow so the liquid doesn't burn your mouth," Stephen said.

"These are delicious," Liz exclaimed. "Perfect hangover cure."

"I thought you might appreciate a more authentic experience."

Liz was entranced at how the city stirred to life. Shanghai seemed to represent everything Qixian wasn't—dense, polished, cosmopolitan—like stepping foot on foreign soil. And yet, there was something familiar about it too. Her mom and dad had passed through Shanghai on their way to America nearly thirty years before. She was part of this city, even if it was only a hint of a memory traced over her subconscious.

Walking around, Liz tried to imagine her parents there, two faces hardly distinguishable in a crowd. She wondered if they knew then that they would never return to China. That whatever life was awaiting them in America would seize them in its clutches—A-frame home in the suburbs, wide asphalt cul-de-sacs, beige SUV—and refuse to let go.

Liz and Stephen arrived at a park where on either side of the cobblestone path lay rows of umbrellas, opened as if newly touched by rain. Affixed to the front of each was a sheet of paper. Some were typed and others were handwritten, embroidered on stationary, the characters hard to make out without stooping down for a closer look. Liz thought they might be a reference to the protests in Hong Kong, a subversive form of solidarity to the object that gave the movement its name.

"Brave," Liz said, keeping her voice low. There were a handful of chairs and canvas stools spread out every three or four umbrellas. Liz eyed the dissidents carefully: a pair of grandparents in plain clothes, a forty-something man hunched over his phone, a huddle of ayis in windbreakers and down coats.

"The word I'd use is desperate," Stephen said, stifling a laugh.

"How can you say that?" Liz asked. "These people are risking their lives." Liz assumed Shanghai was more liberal than the north, a luxury afforded by its distance from Beijing. And yet, Liz realized she knew almost nothing about the umbrella movement itself, which took place when she was still in high school, the substance of the protestors' demands or what they hoped to gain.

"I think a few middle-aged bachelors will survive," Stephen said. Liz shot him a look, and then, annoyed that she'd have to investigate herself, crouched down in front of an umbrella and pierced through the dense script. Nianling, gaodu, jiaoyu shuiping.

"It looks like a personals ad," Liz said. The sheets of paper read like a laundry list of physical traits, followed by things like education level and job. Some had a small thumbnail photo affixed to the corner. Others looked like they'd been laminated several times, capable of weathering months or even years.

"I thought you might mistake it," Stephen said.

"You can't be serious," Liz replied, giving Stephen a shove. "Why don't people just use a dating app?"

"Parents are old-school," Stephen said. "Besides, most of the people in the ads aren't even aware their parents are doing this."

Liz stood in the center of the path as traffic milled lazily around her. Occasionally, she saw an interested party walk over to the umbrella's proprietor to exchange pleasantries, maybe even a phone number. But, for the most part, people barely seemed to notice them. Even despite their bright colors—bold patterns of plaids and pastels—Liz knew they could never serve as a real proxy for attraction.

"What would yours say?" Liz asked.

"No house, no car, no PhD," Stephen started, before stopping himself. "Let me try again." He collected his breath. "Twenty-five years old, apartment in Shanghai, software engineer," then added, "devastatingly handsome."

"Sure," Liz said, smiling, warmth spreading across her cheeks. "I don't think I even asked you. Where do you work again? Microsoft? Apple?" It would have made sense given his ease with English, his comfort with foreigners. But Stephen shook his head.

"Local company," he said. "One you've probably never heard of."

Liz looked back at the umbrellas. She balked at the thought of her own profile being posted like that in broad daylight, peddled like a hocked purse. What the prospective advertisements seemed to be missing felt like the most obvious requirement of all: love. Or at least the capacity for it. These parents were just trying to be helpful, but the energy felt misplaced. Their sons and daughters weren't shopping for a new TV or a rice cooker: they were looking for a life companion.

"Would your parents do that for you?" Liz asked.

"I've begged them already, believe me," Stephen said. He rounded a flower bed and flashed her a smile. "But they said I'll have to do the dating myself."

They came back to the apartment to change before taking a taxi to dinner: Stephen, into dark jeans and a button-down shirt, and Liz, donning boots and a black dress. She stepped out of the cab onto a sidewalk bursting with people. It reminded her of the first time she attended a majority-Asian event in college, where she'd tried to place the feeling of being surrounded by people who looked like her but shared no relation. It took all of college and even her first months in Qixian to identify that experience as a tiny part of her relaxing. There was an ease Liz would have felt even if she weren't there with Stephen, its own kind of safety.

The restaurant had a view overlooking the Bund with blown-glass light fixtures and floor-to-ceiling murals. Schools of live sea bass and crustaceans floated in crowded tanks. The waitstaff guided them from the foyer to the balustrade outside. From Liz's seat, she could make out both sides of the Huangpu River, ferries and cargo boats glinting in the water. The Shanghai skyline danced in front of her in undulating waves of light.

"You know you didn't have to take me here," Liz said. "I would have been perfectly happy with more dumplings."

Stephen waved a hand. "Trust me, you're doing me a favor," he said, "I love seafood."

"Shanghai's probably a great place for it."

"It is. But when I was a kid, all I wanted was Western food. You're probably going to laugh, but hamburgers used to be considered sophisticated."

Liz did laugh. "I bet you must have eaten a ton then."

"Yeah, but every time I did, I threw up. I guess my body knew it wasn't for me."

Stephen was wearing cologne, a cross between a hearth and an alpine grove, that Liz found pleasing without being overpowering. When the waiter came around, he ordered without looking at the menu.

"Around that time, I started getting interested in other things outside China too," Stephen continued. "My parents took me to Windows of the World in Shenzhen on our first family vacation."

Windows of the World was a theme park, he explained, but unlike Cedar Point or Worlds of Fun, its main draw was scaled-down versions of famous world monuments: Dutch windmills, a mock Eiffel Tower, Egyptian hieroglyphics below a bust of Mount Rushmore.

"Back then, we didn't have money to travel, and most ordinary Chinese still weren't going abroad. Windows of the World was an opportunity to see all the world's treasures in a single place." He ran his hands over the white tablecloth. "It opened up a portal in my mind," he said. "I knew that one day I would see the world for myself."

Stephen's reasoning struck Liz as similar to the way her father might have thought when he decided to leave China. What she remembered most about Ron was his stubbornness and conviction, the hard and fast rules that governed their household.

"And did you?" Liz asked. "See the world?"

"I've traveled a little," Stephen said. "But I regret not studying abroad. So after I graduated, I did the next best thing. I made foreign friends here.

A whole community. I'm still learning a lot from them." Liz suddenly considered whether any of the foreign teachers—whether she—might be doing anything worthwhile by being there.

"One of my students is in America now."

"One of your students?" Stephen asked. "From Qixian?" Liz gritted her teeth, immediately regretting having brought it up.

"And it's her first time there?" Stephen asked. "What does she think?"

Liz didn't know how to respond. Ever since she'd left Lin's house in Yuci, Liz had barely kept in touch. Lin had texted often, even suggested a call, but Liz ignored her messages. Instead, she thought about how hard it must have been when her mom first went to the states. Culture shock and confusion, the struggle to grasp her new environment.

But Lin, unlike her mother, spoke English. And it wasn't as if she was alone. She had Phil, who had already communicated her arrival in his typically effusive style: *She's here. All good.* No, Lin would find things to love about America. Liz was sure of it. More and more, she tried to convince herself it was actually for the best. But the more time she spent thinking about Lin, the worse she felt.

"It's a once-in-a-lifetime opportunity," Liz said, more biting than she intended. "How do you think she feels?"

Just then, a four-piece jazz band began to play. Out of the corner of her eye, Liz noticed the couples at the other tables surrounding them. Tall and assertive women with bold eyes and elegant reserve. Liz felt pedestrian by comparison. She was newly jobless, with hardly any savings to her name. She seemed incapable of getting to the heart of her connection to China, the one thing she'd set out to do. All around her was a universe woven from silk and velvet she felt she hadn't earned.

"For the record," Liz said, twirling a finger in the air, "my version of America is nothing like this."

"How do you mean?" Stephen asked.

"I've never lived in a big city," Liz said. Growing up, her mom was careful never to order more than they could eat. She never allowed her or Phil to buy outside food at venues, always sneaking in her own. Now, Liz was sitting at a table full of dishes she'd never seen, much less tasted.

Stephen peeled a crayfish between his fingers. "All I know is that Shanghai was modeled on the West."

"I'm just not sure how much longer any of this will last," Liz said.

"Any of what?"

"Cooperation. Mutual interest," Liz said. "It's one thing for you to be sympathetic to Americans, but you can't tell me you don't feel the tension."

Ever since the trade war began, relations between the two countries had soured. Suspicions were magnified, lines drawn. Some of the taxi drivers in Qixian had even refused service to the other foreign teachers, when previously they might have been thrilled just to share a car with one.

"People are always going to like foreign things," Stephen said. "That's one thing that will never change." He stopped and looked at Liz, stretching his hand across the table.

"No matter how bad things get," Stephen said, "just know that you belong here."

The gesture caught Liz off guard. His hand felt warm clasped around hers, their fingers intertwined. She felt her own breath quicken. Beneath their table were dozens of tiny red shells teeming between their feet.

When she got back to the apartment, Liz followed Stephen to his room. Stephen ran his hand from Liz's shoulders to her hips, undoing the buttons on her dress one-by-one. He motioned for her arms and drew the fabric over her head. Liz took off Stephen's shirt with considerably less finesse, removing his belt and then unspooling the pant legs from his feet. They both stood facing each other, stark and chilly in the moonlight, before Liz laughed and hauled him under the sheets.

It had been months since she'd been with anyone and some part of her was eager to prove that all her mechanics still worked. She hadn't slept with Andrew, her ex, until a month into dating him, not wanting to give him the wrong impression. But that life with Andrew in Ohio felt like an eternity ago, a great *before* compared with her life in China now, like the two could scarcely be held to the same standards.

Stephen moved slowly, traveling from the nape of her neck to her navel. Liz kept a hand on his back, the smooth arch of his shoulders, the way they tensed and glided. She felt her body becoming lighter, her heart rise in her chest. She delighted in the rush that had been off-limits to her in Qixian. The flood of exhilaration at ceding desire. But there was something else too. She'd always hidden away a part of herself that she feared no one would truly understand without explanation. Liz let out a breath, long and deep. She could be as open as she wanted.

"You awake?" a voice boomed from the other side of the door. It was Byron's. Liz pulled the covers up over her head. She dreaded the thought of him barging in, saying something snarky about how he'd seen this coming from day one and wondering why it had taken them so long.

But when Byron opened the door, he looked somber and grave.

"Haven't you guys seen the news?" he asked. Liz and Stephen shook their heads. If Byron had registered that the two of them were sharing the same bed, he didn't let on.

"There's been a virus outbreak in a city 500 miles west of here. Doctors are worried that it's something really major."

"What kind of virus?" Stephen asked.

"No one's really sure," Byron said. "People are saying it's like pneumonia, but the symptoms are all over the place."

"What does that have to do with us?"

"Officials are shutting down transportation into and out of the city," he said. "They're even talking about barring people from leaving their homes."

Liz stifled a laugh. "That's impossible," she said. "It's almost Chunjie. Everyone's getting ready to travel."

"Look downstairs for yourself."

Liz craned her head by the window. The steady stream of traffic she'd seen mere days before had trickled to a crawl. A makeshift barricade had been erected and tiny figures outside the building were bottlenecked at the front entrance.

"I didn't see you guys at all yesterday or I would have mentioned it," he started. "But I bought a flight home. Kind of last-minute, but everything was starting to sell out."

"Doesn't that seem extreme?" Liz asked. Byron shrugged.

"I won't be gone long," he said, "just until all this blows over."

Byron left the room, and Liz and Stephen got dressed. They helped him pack in the afternoon and by the evening, saw him off by the elevator.

He texted them with a selfie from the airport. *Last meal*, he wrote, alongside a take-out container of xiaolongbao. Before they knew it, he was gone.

Later that night, with the lights dim and the shades drawn, Liz and Stephen crept lopsidedly into bed. Liz turned a deaf ear to the reported casualties, to the people trapped in sub-par hospitals, to the smell of not-quite-burning-trash that peppered the air with black streaks. She didn't ask about Stephen's other expat friends in Shanghai, the ones who had chosen to go home like Byron or those who were hunkered down like them. She ignored the increasingly ominous warnings she received over text:

> *The Department of State Urges Americans Not to Delay Travel Home.*
> *Transportation Options May Soon Be Unavailable.*
> *US Citizens Should Make Plans to Return Home NOW.*

"If it's anything like SARS," Stephen said, "it might be a while." His voice sounded serious, but his face betrayed a certain softness. "I'm all for you being here," he said, "but are you sure you want to stay?"

He could have said almost anything then and it wouldn't have mattered. Liz tugged at the blankets between them, wrapping her legs around his. She joked about the two women from 1708 with permed hair, the old man from the park blasting Beijing opera from a pocket radio. Liz made plans for the next day, and the next day, and the day after that: what foods they would order in, the shows they would watch on TV. None of the future math troubled Liz in that moment. She felt as if she and Stephen could go on forever.

Liz turned toward him, feeling the warmth of his breath on her cheek. She pressed her lips to his, the spell of heat and dampness like the answer to a question she hadn't known she'd asked. Stephen drew his hands higher, cradling his thumbs against her chin, his lips the taste of spring rain. Liz shut off the lights, and in the dull glow of moonlight, draped herself in Stephen's arms, imagining the front gates to the building open, the cool wind wafting through its metal bars.

9

In the kitchen in Phil's apartment, Lin spread out the ingredients on the counter. Two cloves of garlic minced into thin ovals. Limbs of ginger pureed into a think pulp. Stalks of green onion finely sliced, the green leaves coiling from their white stalks. She coated a wok with oil, tossed the ingredients in, and waited until they began to sizzle, for the rich scent to reach her nose. Just before taking the heat off, she added a few shakes of salt, a dash of huajiao, and a dollop of chili pepper.

In China, good food was cheap and plentiful, nearly impossible to avoid. But most of what Lin encountered in Cleveland was bland and overpriced. After weeks of eating American take-out, she yearned for the tastes of home. The monthly stipend her mother gave her was quickly depleting, and Lin realized she would risk starving if she didn't try cooking herself.

She pored over recipe blogs, substituting what she couldn't find at the supermarket with their closest equivalents: the longer Asian eggplant for the stouter Italian, cooking wine for sherry, fresh red chilies for a plastic-wrapped package written in Spanish. Each dish—strips of eggplant and squash, scrambled eggs and sweet onion, cubed pork and diced potatoes—took on an almost mythic quality, harkening her back to Yuci. She wasn't ready to return, and yet there was a reassurance to it, a calm eye of familiarity in the hurricane of her new life.

"Something smells good," a voice beckoned from the living room. Phil was sitting on the couch, a soft gray sinkhole adorned with two dull-colored Browns cushions. He had his feet propped on the coffee table. The TV droned with the same channel of primetime news Phil watched religiously each night.

"Thanks," Lin said, "almost ready." She cleared a space on the coffee table amid the mail-order catalogs and grocery circulars and set down two bowls and chopsticks.

"What's for dinner?" Phil asked.

"Yuxiang rousi."

For all her newfound excitement about Chinese food, Lin realized she'd begun to miss speaking Chinese, too. Increasingly, Lin was frustrated that there was so much she wanted to say in English but couldn't, like trying to squeeze icing through a faulty nozzle. She knew Phil could understand some basic words and phrases in Mandarin, even if he was too embarrassed to speak it himself.

"What?" Phil asked. Lin sighed, resigned to typing the characters into her phone.

"Shredded pork with garlic shoots."

"What's a garlic shoot?" Phil asked, lifting the stout green tube between his chopsticks. "It looks like a pipe cleaner." He brought it to his lips. "Ugh, tastes like one too. People really eat this stuff?"

Lin questioned why she'd decided to start making extra food for Phil in the first place. Partly it was to repay him, in some small way, for helping her get to America. Phil lamented that he was too busy to cook, his fridge stocked almost exclusively with microwaveable meals and bulbous vats of supplements. Lin had to buy her own rice and vegetable oil from IGA, even soy sauce. But it was also because she felt a little bad for him, this life he seemed to share with no one but himself.

"I should have said this before but do me a favor and don't make anything too Chinese for me," Phil said, picking out the slivers of pork. "The only vegetables I eat are either fried or wrapped in bacon."

The words BREAKING flashed in all-caps across the TV screen. The news program abruptly cut to a video feed of a market—tanks of fish, caged birds, hides of duck hanging from wire rafters—but the volume was turned low enough that Lin couldn't hear what they were saying.

"You probably eat all that stuff too, huh?" Phil asked, pointing at the screen. It had been months since Lin had seen a market with produce arranged on green tarps or hunks of meat in a cold display case, and she longed for even a bad imitation of it in Cleveland.

"What did your mother used to cook?" Lin asked.

"She made a lot of Chinese food when we were little," Phil said. "Dumplings and soups and sweet buns for the holidays. She once braised a whole pig in sections in our oven." He laughed. "And to think we only ever wanted to eat lasagna and meatloaf."

"We?" Lin asked.

"Me and my sister. And we got our wish. Mom pretty much stopped cooking anything Chinese after Dad left." The old dishes at least helped to explain the cast-iron wok in Phil's kitchen, the metal blackened and perfectly seasoned.

"Why's that?"

"Too many bad memories probably," Phil said. "After he finished his PhD, Dad taught at the university for a little while, but then things really fell apart." He took a bite from his chopsticks, and Lin thought better than to ask him to elaborate.

"To raise you and Liz alone must not have been easy," Lin said, thinking of her own mother. "Your mom must have wanted the best for you."

"Maybe. The only problem was she never really learned the language. She'd say things like, '*Phirrup*, you need to speak better *Engrish!*' It was humiliating. At school, I pretended not to know her. I wanted nothing to do with it." Lin felt her throat tighten.

"You know what she made us promise?" Phil asked, his eyes far away. "That we wouldn't ever go to China."

"I don't understand," Lin said. "Why would she have said that?"

"She told us that she gave up everything so we could have a life here. There was nothing for us to try and go back."

It was a different time: China was poorer then, with fewer opportunities. And yet, it still stung to hear Phil say it. Lin wondered what it meant for Phil to have obeyed his mother's wish but for Liz to fly in the face of it. Perhaps she'd read her mother's words a different way, like a challenge.

Lin turned back toward the TV. She thought she recognized the location on the screen but still couldn't place where exactly in China it was.

"Mom raised us as Americans," Phil said, following Lin's eyes to the flashing news. "I still get frustrated by them sometimes," he said, "the people who come to this country with their hands out, without ever bothering to learn the first thing about it." Lin looked down, picking at her last bites of garlic shoot.

"I didn't mean you," Phil said, quick to interject. "You're different." He tried for a softer tone. "You speak English. At least you can pretend you belong."

The bus to IGA was delayed again. Snow had been falling for four days straight, reducing mailboxes and street signs to shapeless blobs. Bus times were already irregular, and in the mornings on the way to campus, Lin tried to arrive early so she could wait under the shelter of the bus awning or, if she was lucky, on the grated bench, where she kept her mittened hands wedged underneath her thighs for warmth.

Most times, though, she was resigned to standing, trying to avoid the man bundled in a thin fleece blanket on the bench, who greeted her with a curt hello and an appeal for change. When she first saw him, she simply apologized and averted her eyes. Since then, he'd stopped asking her for money, but he still liked to engage her in conversation, as if playing host to a television audience. She saw the way others at the bus stop simply ignored him: older women wrapped in dark headscarves, men with long curls of hair tucked behind their ears like ribbons.

And yet, Lin couldn't help but feel sorry for the man, trapped within the closed-circuit loop of his own subconscious. Lin missed her pets more with each passing day, but even she found it strange that most Americans felt more sympathy for a limping dog than a person living on the street. She was amazed that, even in the richest country in the world, ambivalence seemed to be the only acceptable response.

"Bie zou," Gua crowed over the phone.

"I can walk," Lin said, "it's no big deal." She'd already made it halfway to IGA.

"Only poor people walk anywhere," Gua replied. "Stay where you are. We'll pick you up."

Driving was Gua's favorite American thing. She owned a light blue Prius—the fuel cover ripped clean off and the back bumper slightly dented—and she drove fast, down empty freeways before rush hour, burning through Lakewood, her dyed hair blowing like a lion's mane.

"Why else come to America if you can't speed?" she asked, barreling down with Lin in the back seat as the car veered toward AsiaTown.

Gua refused to let Lin shop at IGA, with the same fervor and all-knowing that she'd plucked Lin from the dance floor at Mateo's house party and rushed her to the bathroom. By the time Lin could speak again, Gua handed her a wad of toilet paper and a breath mint and calmly escorted her out of the basement to her car.

"Call me Gua," she'd said, her features looming large in the dim light, head the shape and size of a cantaloupe. She spoke with the blithe indifference of someone insisting on using her real name regardless of whether Americans found it too difficult to pronounce.

"And this is Xiao Bai," she'd said. Even with her head buzzing, Lin could plainly tell how Xiao Bai had earned her nickname. She was from Tianjin, a satellite city bordering Beijing, and her parents were real estate dalao who'd struck rich in the flight to the suburbs. Her skin glowed so white Lin was sure she'd been bathed in lightning cream as a baby. Xiao Bai greeted her with a nod, her parted shoulder-length hair a perfect contrast with its heavy, dark gloss.

The three of them arrived in front of Asia Plaza, each letter in the awning red and jagged, like it had been shot through with electricity. The green-tiled pagoda was half-covered in snow. Inside, there was an aging forklift in the back of the foyer next to a jiu-jitsu studio. The fountain had been switched off, the round basin dry and calcifying against a border of fake rocks.

"This is really better than IGA?" Lin asked, raising an eyebrow. Crumpled streamers and paper lanterns were swaying from the metal rafters. They claimed a rusting cart from the vestibule and edged it toward the sliding doors.

"If you don't eat right, your body isn't shufu," Gua said, wearing a sweatshirt tented over a blue tracksuit. And, once again, she was right. Lin felt like she hadn't truly been full in weeks. Each aisle revealed a half-forgotten memory, a new object of desire. Lin marveled at the shrink-wrapped jerky, freeze-dried scallion pancakes, tangyuan floating in sweet syrup. An oasis in the frozen desert.

"Buke siyi," she said. Mr. Watkins had boasted in class that Ohio was a big state. And though it was still smaller than some Chinese cities, Lin had wondered where all the Chinese people were hiding. She'd started to take comfort in the mere presence of them whenever she could. Back home, pecking at her nightly meals, Phil may have looked the part, but he barely counted.

"Hope you're not still bothering with what's-his-name," Gua said, over the hum of the grocery loudspeaker. It had already been a week since Mateo's party, but Gua still wouldn't let it go.

"I haven't talked to him," Lin said, trying her best to sound repentant. Lin had already thanked Gua and Xiao Bai for rescuing her, as if from a sinking ship, stressing that, without them, shei zhidao what might have happened. But on the inside, she felt the whole thing was overblown. It wasn't like she couldn't take care of herself.

"Boys like him aren't really the kind you want to impress," Gua said. "I had to beat plenty off with a stick my first year."

"Some guys will wait outside Chinese American Alliance meetings just to paoniu," Xiao Bai added.

"Those meetings are a waste of time," Gua said. Lin nodded. She was tempted to tell them about Liz but was afraid they'd just dismiss her as another huayi who secretly disdained them.

They threw their groceries into the trunk and got back into Gua's car. Despite the minor concessions, it was easy for Lin to gravitate toward Gua and Xiao Bai. She found herself going to AsiaTown with them a few times a week, hanging out after class anytime their schedules overlapped. The house where Gua and Xiao Bai lived was the basement unit of a white duplex in a neighborhood with shady trees and buildings barely taller than the power lines. Their unit was comprised entirely of furniture that looked like it had once been flat-packed: pine bookshelf, gray sectional, dining room table that folded to half its size.

"All here when we moved in," Xiao Bai explained. Lin looked around the room for any trace of them, some proof of their presence. She found a couple of Bawang cosmetic bottles in the bathroom, but the rest of the place looked anonymous, like anyone could have lived there.

"It's not like we're staying," Gua said, catching Lin's eyes. "Why invest any more than we need?"

"You came here alone?" Lin asked.

"Same as you," Gua said. Surely, she'd taken the same gamble for the chance to earn her degree, traveling halfway around the world to live in a town where she didn't know a soul. Gua was a second year, a few months from graduation. It was imperceptible to anyone from the outside, but Lin yearned to know someone who understood that adjustment in quite the same way.

They made hot pot together with a packet of chili spices from Asia Plaza and a large basin divided in half like a yin-yang. After dinner, they played poker, using watermelon seeds for chips, until eventually Gua got salty at losing and took a handful of them in her mouth.

"It's getting late," Lin said. It would have been enough to take the bus home—what Lin always said as she donned her jacket by the door, trying to be polite—but Gua shook her head.

"Just get in," she said, a steely expression on her face.

Lin never had to think twice about walking alone at night in Yuci, where violent crime was almost nonexistent, and police weren't even allowed to carry weapons. But in Ohio, there were stories nearly every day on the evening news about someone or other getting killed. Lin passed a shooting supply store every day on her way to and from campus.

"Watch out for them," Gua said, jutting her chin across the street at the colony of dull-colored tarps sprouting underneath the highway overpass that bifurcated Gua's street.

"They track your movements," she continued. "They know when you're home and when you're out. I had to start sending things to school because I kept getting my packages stolen."

Lin nodded without saying a word. She knew she was meant to disparage the people who lived in tents, just as she was supposed to admire Gua's shrewdness. Though Lin's English was better, Gua was more street smart, more attuned to the realities of living in this country. But Lin found something enviable about strength in numbers, a group of people who looked out for each other in times of need, like all that individual effort could be channeled into a collective good. It was a feeling Lin hadn't felt since she left China, one she didn't even know she missed. Perhaps, she reasoned, it was something she could harness, too.

Gua's car pulled up in front of Phil's building, and Lin stepped out.

"Your mom's in Shanxi, right?" Gua called after her.

"Yeah, why?"

"You should call her," she said. "Haven't you seen the news?"

She got the text a day later. *Guai bu de*, Lin thought. She'd forgotten all about the start of the new year. Nearly all the messages she'd exchanged with her mother since arriving in Ohio had been in the form of stickers: animated GIFs that basically confirmed she was still breathing, and little more. Lin felt it was better for them both if Qi Fei knew less about the specifics of her new life. It helped that she only ever appeared interested in the same basic questions: *Are you eating enough? How cold is it compared to Yuci? Are you being nice enough to Phil?*

So when Lin got her mother's message, she barely glanced down, expecting to thumb back a peppy cartoon rat with the character for fortune dangling from its teeth. But she was surprised to receive a string of texts that started with a jolt: *You should stay inside.*

There were a rash of deaths occurring in Hubei, her mother explained, about twelve hours south of Yuci. Xinhua and CCTV were reporting on people going into hospitals with minor symptoms like coughing and chest pains and leaving in body bags. It all looked like the normal flu—breathing trouble and fevers—but the difference was that patients weren't getting better. Even after all the standard precautions, casualties were mounting in large numbers, and hospitals were powerless to contain the surge.

It's pretty isolated now, her mother wrote, *but cases are expected to increase. Make sure to take care of yourself and be vigilant.* The words themselves were not alarming, but Lin could sense her mother's worry behind them. She imagined her standing in the kitchen, immobilized, while state media blared on television.

Haohao baozhong, Lin read over and over again, but the words rang hollow. There didn't seem to be much she could do except wait, especially since she wasn't even the one in China.

You should be careful! Lin wrote back. She wondered if this was how Liz felt when she was taking care of her own mother near the end, their roles reversed, suddenly needing to be more parent than child.

Lin considered texting Liz, too, but then remembered the string of unopened messages and thought better of it. If she was being honest with herself, she was frustrated at Liz. There was so much Liz hadn't adequately prepared her for, enough for Lin to feel like she was running around blind in a new country. Hadn't Lin done everything she could to make sure Liz felt settled in Qixian? Perhaps Liz had imagined that Phil would be her surrogate in America. Or maybe it was Lin who had found her own replacements in Gua and Xiao Bai. Either way, she resolved to try and get in touch with Liz, just as soon as she figured out how bad things really were.

For dinner that night, Lin looked up how to cook linguini in a meat sauce, using some of the canned tomatoes she bought from Asia Plaza. She'd tried pasta, once, at an overpriced café in Qixian with Travis but hadn't been impressed. The interpretation was different this time—angel hair instead of daoxiaomian—but she didn't find the authentic version any more inspired.

She handed the bowl to Phil, thinking he'd at least have a more positive reaction to her cooking, but his eyes were fixed on the screen. One of the TV anchors—a bloated man with swollen jowls—was talking about the deaths in Hubei.

"I just don't know why people are overreacting," he said to a guest sitting across the table. "We've got modern medicine. Nothing like that would happen here."

"It's China's problem," the guest said. "They really ought to start calling it the China Virus."

Lin thought of the grieving people she'd seen in photos and video reels from the hospital, their faces and skin like her own. It reminded her of when the two men from the meikuang came home with news about her father, the injustice of not comprehending this sudden loss. How could the reaction in this country be so indifferent? She realized her own food on the table had gone cold, but by then she'd already lost her appetite.

On the commute to Tri-C the next morning, Lin arrived late, and the man in the bus shelter had already begun his rant. He raised and lowered his hands like an orchestra conductor, the other passengers forming a semi-circle of distance around him. Only when Lin approached, the passengers edged away from her, too. Lin didn't understand. Perhaps it had been a mistake to engage the man in the first place. Or maybe things really had been simpler back when she spoke to no one.

There was a light rain coming down and Lin took a step closer toward the shelter, coughing into her mittened hands. A woman near her reared back, like she'd glimpsed the head of a cobra. Another twisted her mouth into a scowl. Her whole life, Lin had been looked at differently or not been looked at at all. That was nothing new. But she'd never felt like she'd been spurned for the very fact of her existence.

By the time she got to campus, class had already let out, and Lin rushed into the lobby to wait for Gua and Xiao Bai, as had become their custom. But when she arrived, she noticed that Gua had come alone.

"Did you see the police tape around the building?"

Lin shook her head, explaining that her bus was late, and that she'd barely had time to notice anything. Gua pulled out her phone and showed Lin a photo. It was the Advanced Technology Training Center, where their ESL class was held, and on the front limestone was a message scrawled in paint: *Go home chinks and take your dirty disease with you.*

"I don't understand," Lin said.

"It means us," Gua said, sensing Lin's confusion. "It's a slur for Chinese people."

"What happened? I thought this was only going on in China."

"The first case was reported here this morning."

"But who would even write that?" Lin asked. "There can't even be that many of us on campus."

"Exactly," Gua said. "Someone wants us gone." Lin looked around, registering the absence for a second time.

"Where's Xiao Bai?"

"She flew back to China this morning," Gua said. "The tickets cost a fortune, but her parents were afraid they would suspend flights any day now." Things were moving so fast that Lin couldn't keep up. It seemed rash to her, unnecessary.

"It's just a misunderstanding," she said. "I'm sure all of this will pass."

Later that week, Lin went shopping with Phil at IGA. Gua told her she was laying low for a while, and Lin finally heeded her warning about not traveling on foot. In the parking lot on the way back to the car, Lin had a grocery bag in each arm. Phil held a jug of detergent in one hand while staring at his phone in the other.

"Watch where you're going," a man's voice called out, colliding with Phil's shoulder. The encounter knocked the detergent to the ground, where a puddle of blue liquid was pooling on the asphalt.

"What the fuck," Phil said, regaining his balance. "You ran into me."

"Are you calling me a liar?" the man asked. He was taller than Phil with a thick beard that ringed his face and a tattoo under his right eye.

"Forget about it," Phil said, backtracking. He stooped down to pick up the detergent. Lin was standing a few steps behind, the two grocery bags limp at her sides. She wished that the man would keep walking now, but his pace slowed to a halt.

"Forget about what?" he said. "That you brought the kung flu here?"

"The kung who?" Phil asked.

"Don't play dumb with me," the man said, shoving Phil in the chest. "You brought the kung flu here. Now *you're* going to die for it."

The blows came hard and swiftly. The man swung two fists which Phil was able to dodge, but he connected with crosses that clipped Phil's nose and jaw. Phil had his hands up, taking swings of his own, until the man landed a punch to the side of Phil's head, the force of which caused him to fall backwards and slam against the bumper of a parked car.

Lin wanted to run or call for help, but her entire body was frozen. She was watching the scene as if in slow motion, her mind still disbelieving what was unfolding before her. Phil's body was crumpled on the ground, and the man was standing above him, kicking and stomping with his feet.

Suddenly, an employee from IGA marshaling shopping carts rushed over to break it up. He grabbed the man in a bear hug and threatened to call the police before the man finally turned and hurried to his car.

"Are you OK?" the employee asked Phil. Phil had blood dripping from his lip and his face was as soft and bruised as a persimmon. He rubbed his hand against the back of his head where he'd collided with the car's bumper.

Phil nodded weakly, still dazed, his usual confidence gone. He and Lin made their way back to the car, Phil's gait slow and measured.

They drove home in silence. The whole way, Lin remembered the first questions she asked Phil when she arrived from the airport over a month ago: *How do you open a checking account? Which is the best cell phone provider? Do the public buses accept cash?* She marveled at how those slight, insignificant inquiries had until only recently been the most pressing questions she'd faced. She wished she could go back to that time, when mundane things were so hard there was no ability to consider anything more fraught.

"Should we go to the hospital?" Lin asked, when they arrived at Phil's apartment.

"Forget it."

"We should at least file a report with the police. Imagine if the guy had a gun, or if he hurt someone else—"

"I said forget it," Phil said, raising his voice. When Lin bent over to take off her shoes by the door, she realized her hands were still shaking.

"You—we—had nothing to do with this," Lin said. She felt closer to Phil than she'd thought possible. Even if she might never be accepted as one of their own, she knew that huayi would forever be mixed up with China, whether they wanted to or not.

Phil walked to the kitchen and raked a hand over his forehead.

"You know, I'm not the kind of guy who believes in special privileges," he said, "in certain people getting to game the system." He ran a towel under cold water. "Everyone who makes something of themselves should do it the honest way."

Lin blinked back, not understanding the connection.

"I wasn't going to say anything, but she really forced my hand on this," Phil said, breathing in. "My sister feels really guilty for what she did."

Lin cocked an eyebrow. "Liz? Guilty about what?"

"Getting you expelled."

Lin tried to speak, but the words got caught in her throat. She was stunned. For so long she had assumed it was one of her roommates or another classmate or Travis himself. Never would she have imagined it was the one person she considered her friend.

"I don't understand," Lin said.

"It was an accident," Phil continued. "Liz never meant to mention the guy, but it just came out."

Phil didn't have to say anymore. Deep down, Lin had known that she'd been expelled not simply for failing a class. And yet, at no point had she ever been asked to make sure Travis's story checked out.

"I didn't want to ask for an expedited visa," Phil continued, "but Liz practically begged me to help, so I did." He looked up at Lin for the first time. "But I can't help you anymore. I can't take that chance."

Lin looked around the room, not sure she understood what she was being told.

"What do you want me to do?"

"I don't know," Phil said. "But you can't stay here."

Lin knew that Phil had only ever tolerated her presence, but this felt beyond reproach. The outbreak was spreading quickly—that much she understood—but his spite was clearly misplaced.

"I came over weeks ago," she said. "I didn't—"

"Look, innocent people are getting blamed for this," he said. "*I'm* getting blamed for this. I wanted to work in government to enforce the rules, not be a victim. I really hope you understand."

"But I couldn't have brought this here," Lin said, raising her voice. "Do you know how ridiculous that is? Wuhan is as far from my hometown as Mississippi." She was screaming now, remembering Mr. Watkins's worthless geography lesson. She was sick of people assuming they knew the first thing about where she came from.

"All I know is that China started all this," Phil said, matching her tone. "It's not safe here anymore. I think it would be best if you left."

Lin felt a rush of blood to her face. "Not safe for who?" she snapped back. She thought again of the gun store near campus and felt her arms go limp. "Where will I even go?"

"I don't know," he said. "Back home? Things were fine before people like you showed up."

Lin wondered if Phil could hear the hypocrisy in his own words, how his parents, a generation removed, had arrived to this country the same way she did. When had things truly ever been fine? She knew it then as clearly as when she broke up with Travis. She was destined to be punished by a man for something she couldn't control. In the end, a man's word would always be worth more than her own.

Lin was standing outside Gua's duplex at the side door just above the basement. Across the street, she saw the tents, a powder dusting of snow flattening the tops. Her mind raced to the people living inside. *They track your movements.* Yes, but would they recognize her as being any different? Were all of them—Xiao Bai, Gua, Phil—now just one and the same?

She thought about the other reported attacks: a woman burned with acid outside her apartment, another stabbed, an elderly man beaten into a coma. In a different time, she would have found safety in what she knew. Her pets. Liz. But Lin couldn't bring herself to say her name. Worse than Liz getting her expelled was the shame of being deceived to spare her feelings, like she was too fragile to have been told the truth.

She didn't have the slightest idea how to navigate this. Liz had gone on and on to Lin about Midwestern hospitality. "You won't find friendlier people anywhere," she'd said. And yet, Lin had done everything right—learned the language, kept her head down, followed the rules—and had still been met with cruelty. If Americans saw Chinese as the enemy, what choice did she have? She would have to become American, too. She would love this country that hated her.

The door in front of her swung open.

"I'm scared," Lin said, a pair of suitcases trailing behind her.

"Come in," Gua replied, her eyes scanning the tents across the street, before quickly closing the door.

10

Living together was meant to be temporary. A stop gap for a week, maybe two, just long enough for Liz to get a sense of the city, stretch her legs down its wide boulevards and narrow alleys—the curbs quietly possessed by bikes or parked cars or the metal hull of an off-duty sanlunche—and start anew.

Waking up in Stephen's apartment in Shanghai, Liz was amazed how little prepared she was. She replayed the train journey from Dandong in her head, trying to picture the way each of the empty stations looked at night. Or how each new city might look, illuminated by the crackling glow of dawn. She wanted to feel the rush of landing in a new place. It wouldn't have mattered where they were. Each time—grabbing Stephen by the hand, their bodies rushing through space—she would have wished only that they'd decided to go farther.

"Day twenty-three," Liz droned, scrolling through her phone in bed.

"I don't know why you're still keeping track," Stephen said. He rolled onto his side. "Without an end date, what does the counting even mean?"

"I don't know," Liz sighed. "A reminder that I'm still alive?"

Unbeknownst to Liz, she and Stephen had taken one of the last trains to Shanghai before the lockdown. At first, there was hardly any information at all. And then, like reception returning to a radio tower, it was all anyone could talk about. There were only about a hundred cases in the city, clustered in arterial pockets, but local authorities didn't want to take any chances. An official edict was made to limit movement to only essential trips: grocery stores, factories, hospitals.

But within days, other freedoms started to disappear. A man in the building across the street from Stephen's had tested positive and, almost immediately, the whole complex was partitioned off like a construction site. Tall cranes came in to blanket the building in a fine mesh netting before wrapping it in plastic. Crews dressed in bio-hazard suits delivered shrink-wrapped food and water to the apartments' occupants. Ambulances were parked outside, their sirens splitting the air.

A team of security guards monitored the flow of traffic into and out of the gates, each armed with a black, handheld thermometer. Travel between buildings was strictly forbidden, to say nothing of trying to get across town. City officials had suspended entry for anyone who didn't have a place of residence in Shanghai. In order to leave, occupants had to validate their ID and residency permit with the guards—once when leaving and again when coming back—to prove that they lived on the premises.

Stephen was allowed to go out during the designated window allotted to his floor, but because Liz was still registered in Shanxi, she couldn't so much as leave the building. In three weeks, Liz had gone as far as the balcony of Stephen's apartment. Every day, she measured the plants with her fingers. She looked down at the vacant street, hoping for rain. She imagined an older version of herself, an IV protruding from her spidery veins, being wheeled outside so she could see the world below her seventeenth-story window. A world she barely remembered was real.

Stephen sat up, his body dappled by the light peeking through the blinds. He smoothed a hand over Liz's hip, guiding it back and forth between her ribcage and her thigh. His touch was gentle but firm, familiar enough that her body didn't resist it, but still so novel that Liz could momentarily forget where she was. His phone buzzed.

"Shit, I'm late."

Liz groaned. Stephen's mom lived across town, near Pudong, but insisted on calling almost daily to check in on him since the lockdown.

"Wei," his mom said, her voice sharp and insistent. "Neng ting de jian?" Stephen hopped out of bed. He threaded a shirt over his head with one hand while keeping the phone muted in the other. Seeing Liz still lying under the covers, he shot her a quick shooing motion with his eyes.

"Sorry," he mouthed, as he straightened the pillows and smoothed the sheets up over them. Liz threw on a sweater and a pair of shorts. She coiled her phone charger around her wrist and made it to the doorway before seeing Stephen's video flicker on.

"Zhongyu lai le," she heard his mom exclaim. "Now, how's my only son?"

Liz rolled her eyes. It was the same cloying tone Pearl used to employ whenever she called Phil at college. *I'm right here, you know*, Liz used to think, listening to her mom's animated voice, her promises of sending a care package to St. Louis like she wished she could deliver it by hand. Stephen had barely mentioned her to his mom. He'd said only that an American friend had been visiting and got stuck in Shanghai when the borders closed. Byron had gone home, he explained, and she was temporarily staying in his room.

Liz opened the door to Byron's room and flopped down on the bed. She acknowledged that the situation had snuck up on her, too, but was still annoyed by the pretense. Were she and Stephen hooking up? Dating? Was this just one long one-night stand?

On the nightstand was a mug of cold coffee. A paperback with its spine cracked. Liz recalled the bedroom in her former house in Akron. "This is just temporary," her mom had told her and Phil the morning after her dad hadn't come home. Weeks, even months later, when it was clear he'd left for good, Pearl still never said anything more. It was strange how a sting of disappointment was so easy to relive, but how other memories felt like they could have happened in a previous life. Byron's room already looked like it had the stale quality of absence. How long did he expect to be gone?

Liz heard a voice approach the door. "You want to meet her?" Stephen asked. A tremor shot through the doorknob, and Liz sprang to her feet.

"She's right here," he said, motioning the phone toward Liz. Liz shot him a withering look before putting on her brightest smile.

Chunxia Zhu was sitting at a table, her phone framing a backdrop of lily bulbs in tall vases. Her hair was pinned in a neat bun. Bright red lipstick. A shawl draped over a red and gold blouse. Stephen had described his mom as someone who only ever wanted to eat Shanghainese food. Who thought people from the north were barbaric, and that southerners had bad taste. Whenever they went out to eat with family, she always opted to split the bill, never fought to pay. She had a passion for gossip, Dior, and good deals. Liz stiffened. He was right to worry how Chunxia would react.

"You didn't say she was Chinese," Chunxia said, peering into the camera as if she could reach the other side. "Can she speak too?"

"Hui," Liz said, nodding, though careful not to say too much.

"But surely not Shanghainese," she said, smirking. "Laojia zai nali?" she asked, this time directed at Liz.

"Fujian," Liz replied.

"Fujian?" Chunxia exclaimed. It was common knowledge that Fujian was full of pianzi: telephone scammers, con-artists, women surely out to catfish her son. Liz was nonplussed. Not everyone could have a hukou from a first-tier city.

She handed the phone back to Stephen.

"Xia yici, bai bai," Stephen said, before hanging up. He looked up to find Liz sulking.

"What's wrong?" he asked. "I thought you'd be excited I finally told her about us."

"You could've given me a heads up," Liz said. "I would've at least put on a bra. Plus, I'm pretty sure she hates me anyway."

"That's just her way," Stephen said. "Ma may sound mean, but she's just," he paused, "calculating. It's hard for her to trust outsiders."

Liz flinched. She knew he didn't mean it that way, but it only confirmed what she already knew: she would never be considered truly Chinese.

"Don't you think her calling every day is a bit much?" Liz asked. Stephen gave a blank stare, as if he hadn't considered another option. Liz tallied another cultural difference to her mental list.

"You know how Chinese mothers are," he said, and immediately froze. "I'm so sorry, Liz, I didn't mean—"

"It's fine," Liz said, waving him off.

"You know I wouldn't have answered if I thought it would upset you." As much as Liz wanted to fight him on it, he had a point.

"You haven't eaten," Stephen continued, "let me make us some breakfast."

Spring Festival had come and gone. There were no fireworks, no extravagant CCTV special. The streets were barred with red tape and the trains moored. Away from their families and with no ability to travel, everyone was told to enjoy a different kind of holiday. *Sacrifice to stay home and keep fellow citizens safe*, official communications went. Liz guessed that part of the reason Stephen probably told his mom about her was because he would have been questioned at Chuxi dinner anyway.

Do you have a girlfriend now? some obscure great-uncle would ask, sucking fish scales between his teeth. Liz didn't know how Stephen would have answered. He did genuinely seem to appreciate her. Stephen did all the shopping, ferried take-out orders from beyond the gate. Liz was grateful that Stephen tolerated how she lingered in bed, streamed shows on Netflix until her VPN gave out, obsessively tracked news from home. Despite her displeasure at being trapped in his apartment, she knew it was a far better alternative to being stranded outside.

Liz thought back to the night she had with Stephen and Byron in the Hole, the last big gathering of them anywhere. How Byron had said that all of Shanghai's foreigners could fit inside. She bristled at the idea of being rounded up with other non-residents and brought there. *For safety.* She remembered her own country's history, how Japanese Americans had been forced to relocate to a place where most had never heard of or set foot. If her parents had been alive in the US then, would they have been lumped into that category? Would she?

Liz had heard Byron complain once that he would never be accepted as Chinese in China, and Stephen had surprised her by retorting: "What did you expect? This isn't America." Liz had never envisaged her own country as a bastion of acceptance. She pictured foreigners of all ilk—leery single men, families with children—carrying hiking packs and wheeling suitcases, all gathered inside the park on Julu Road. It was hard to imagine any government having the authority to orchestrate something like that now. And yet, the swiftness that Chinese officials had moved to build camps for Uyghurs in Xinjiang, how seemingly normal life had resumed since, gave Liz pause.

Stephen was at the stove cracking eggs into a frying pan. It had become their routine in the mornings: Liz put on the kettle for coffee, which Stephen didn't drink, and Stephen made breakfast. Liz's phone buzzed.

"They're talking about testing people at airports in America now," she said.

"You mean like the temperature checks we have here?"

"More basic than that," Liz said, sighing. "They're just asking people where they've traveled in the last two weeks."

Like all the residents in the building, Stephen was required to take his temperature readings three times a day and report to the authorities if they were abnormal. Liz had heard that people were wary of revealing if they were sick, even to family members, because of fear of being turned in. The only recourse to the illness had been, as far as Liz was aware, indefinite hospitalization at an over-crowded state-run hospital, with cots lined up like traffic cones for sports drills on a gymnasium floor. It was a fate, if not worse than death, then at least quickly approaching it.

"Can you imagine any of this happening in the states?" she asked. "People forced to shelter in their suburban ranch homes?"

Liz could already picture the riots that would ensue in Akron. Town hall parking lots overflowing with pickups. Guns belted in holsters. State and local government facing threats. No, back home, things were proceeding as normal. Concerts, basketball games, even the simple act of going to a restaurant for dinner. She thought about Byron on one of the last flights out of the country and wondered why she hadn't decided to go, too.

"It's all for good measure," Stephen said, "a necessary precaution." She couldn't understand how Stephen maintained such a chipper attitude.

"But don't you think there's something devious about all this," she asked.

"What do you mean?"

"All it takes is for one person to get sick and the rest of us—" She made a slashing motion across her throat. "The whole building gets condemned. The government traps us with no regard for the people inside."

"I think you're overreacting," Stephen said.

"I am not," Liz insisted. "Why does everyone here seem to accept their role without any outward objection? Can't they see it's only a matter of time before some other liberty gets snatched up under the guise of 'collective wellbeing?'"

"We're out of eggs," Stephen said. "I'll go buy some this afternoon. I get an hour—"

"I feel like I'm not pulling my weight," Liz interrupted, trying her best to sound both serious and pathetic. "Just let me try to go."

"We've been over this," Stephen said. "It's too risky. They'll ask for your permit, and when you don't have it, they'll have you on record. Who knows what will happen to you after that."

Liz had no reason to believe it wasn't true and that Stephen had her best interests at heart. But she couldn't help feeling like it was partly selfish, too. That, deep down, Stephen was afraid of being associated with a rule breaker.

"Some of us don't get the luxury of humid air on our skin," Liz said, throwing up her arms. "Better enjoy it while you can."

From the living room, Liz heard Stephen's footsteps echo down the hall. She stared at her own shoes by the entryway and wondered what use they'd ever served.

Outside, the sky was overcast and gray. Across the highway, Liz could see a grid of symmetrical windows framed by air conditioners. Over the last three weeks, she'd watched lives play out in those tiny rectangles—appearing and reappearing, getting up early or staying up late—each halogen bulb alighting its own tiny prison. One neighbor did yoga every morning. Another had a cat that lazed around all day. A woman in curlers and fleece pajamas paced the balcony while taking calls, her voice reverberating like a stage actor in an amphitheater.

Liz came to relish those short breaks away from Stephen, when she didn't have to be self-conscious about no longer wearing makeup to impress him or the fact that he knew her bowel movements as well as his own. Those trips were the only times they were apart in the month since they'd left Dandong. It would have been unthinkable in her last relationship with Andrew, where she prioritized her independence over nearly everything else. It's not that Liz wasn't happy with Stephen. There just weren't that many bright spots to be had. Things were going well between them. She didn't dare imagine a scenario where they weren't. She couldn't leave him now even if she wanted.

And yet, ever since the lockdown, Liz had noticed a change in Stephen. A certain severity, like the only way of combating the dread outside was to undertake his own internal penance. He threw himself into work. After breakfast, he retreated to his office and hardly emerged before dinner. Liz thought that part of it was retaliation, wanting to assert a modicum of control over his personal time. She figured that whatever he was doing was akin to her own coping mechanisms: counting out her belongings, prattling around the apartment, obsessively checking her phone. She wanted the illusion of choice, even if it just led to greater unhappiness.

Stephen never talked very much about what he did, and Liz couldn't help wondering what he was trying to hide. All that time on the other side of a locked door made Liz start to question other things, too. Why did Stephen only seem to hang out with foreigners? Why did he insist on using an English name? She found herself getting annoyed at him for still only speaking with her in English, even now that Byron was gone.

They didn't talk about Byron or Stephen's other friends in Shanghai who he hadn't seen or heard from in weeks. The waishiban in Qixian had called Liz to see if she wanted to teach remotely, and although part of her questioned her decision not to return, she never answered. When the office stopped trying, Liz figured they assumed she'd left the country, too. Liz felt it as acutely with Travis as she did now herself: expats always had one foot out the door. You never knew when your last visa run would turn up empty or if something unexpected forced you to move back home. You had to be ready to leave at a moment's notice.

On her worst days, Liz wondered what was in it for Stephen. Dating an American meant accepting all the messiness that transnational relationships demanded. She thought back to True Love Club in Dandong and all the doll-faced Chinese girls with their impossibly thin legs. Were Americans just easier? Stephen did seem to have a distorted view of America, and it wouldn't have surprised Liz if his expectations around dating were similarly naive.

Liz had started to catch herself getting short with him, responding with the same judgment Pearl used to heap on her dad. Her initial aversion to dating Chinese guys began to crystallize. She feared she was doomed to only ever be attracted to men like her father: emotionally unavailable or never satisfied. She couldn't help wondering whether Stephen was just using her for a chance to leave the country. Why else go through the trouble when the real thing was all around him?

If Liz had other room left for worry, she might have felt bad for Stephen's elderly neighbors. Or her students, who were doubtless in a worse predicament than she was. Or Lin, still having to share an apartment with her brother. She was afraid even to call Phil, dreading his I-told-you-so insistence, now that flights between China and the US had ground to a halt, that she should have been the one to come back home and not Lin. Even if Liz had wanted to call someone, she couldn't bring herself to. Things were grim enough without her going and making them worse. She was oblivious to them like she was to the world outside her four walls.

Liz plopped down on the couch. Assembled on tall shelves against the walls was Stephen's collection of books, accumulated everywhere from Tibet to Hong Kong. He was fastidious about his belongings and would have noticed if anything was out of place, but Liz could hardly be bothered anymore to hide the fact that she was looking. She'd pored over the titles as many times as she'd rooted through the contents of his cabinets, for research. But somehow, as her eyes moved across the spines, she realized she'd missed three volumes protruding from the end, thick as a doorstop:

尽职调查与安全 Due Diligence & Security
情报研究 Intelligence Research
风险分析与筛查 Risk Analysis & Screening

The door creaked open, teeming with the smell of cigarettes and disinfectant.

"You're back," Liz said. It felt like Stephen had both been gone for hours and had only just left. "Did they have eggs?"

"No eggs," Stephen replied. "The store looked like bandits had rifled through it. There were still cartons left, but all the eggs inside had been taken out." Liz imagined a going out of business sale for everything including the shelves and fixtures.

"I did manage to find something else though," Stephen said. He plucked from the bag a bouquet of flowers, wrapped in a cylindrical cone, and a bar of Dove chocolate.

"This isn't exactly how I imagined it," he said, "but happy one-month anniversary." Liz unwrapped the bar and took a bite. Chalky and much too sweet, it was the best chocolate she'd ever tasted.

"How did you—" she started, when Stephen swooped in to kiss her, flecks of chocolate still ringing her lips.

"Look inside," Stephen instructed. Wedged between the rose stems was a crinkly plastic wrapper. Liz tugged on it and out came an N95 mask, complete with high-microfiber air filter.

"This was the last one anywhere," Stephen said, like a proud collector at a convention. "It was lodged on a top shelf with no box. Someone must have stashed it up there and forgot to pick it back up." Liz looked cock-eyed at the package.

"When I was checking out, an ayi saw me with this and tried to fight me for it. Lots of stores won't even let you inside now if you're not wearing a mask."

Liz unwrapped the package as gingerly as handling fine china. She folded out the cloth vents that expanded like gills and slipped the elastic over her ears, feeling both silly and a little lightheaded.

"Hold on a minute," Stephen said. "I've got an idea." He gave Liz a conspiratorial look. "But we don't have much time."

The weather outside had changed from light to dark, like lowering a dimmer switch. The rain started slowly, but by the time Liz put on her shoes and tiptoed down the hallway, it was bleating against the windows. Just pressing the L button inside the elevator made her giddy. She heard the faint saxophone of Kenny G, the same song that played in loop on subway platforms to signal the end of the day, like she—everyone—was stuck in the perpetual purgatory between leaving work and returning home.

"Act normal," Stephen said, standing an arms-length away. "Pretend you don't know me at all." He was as stern as Liz had ever seen him, careful not to make any special show of gesturing to her in light of the security cameras. With their masks on and a hoodie pulled over their heads, they looked like two bank robbers about to pull off a heist.

"I've seen a woman check out here in line before me. Her name is Li Jin, apartment 1705. With a mask on and your hair up you two could be twins." They reached the landing and Stephen stopped just short of the glass vestibule that opened onto the street.

"You just have to tell them you forgot your ID," he said. "The mask will help with your voice too."

"What are you trying to say about my accent?" Liz asked, suppressing a grin, but Stephen didn't budge. He pointed at the security guards in charge of registration perched under umbrellas at a fold-out table.

"Wait five minutes once I'm past the gate and meet me around the corner." And with that, Stephen disappeared, leaving Liz alone in the lobby.

Liz's knees were shaking. Her calves felt tight from non-use. Each minute she counted down felt like several days. She stared at the rows of cubby-hole mailboxes where delivery drivers were instructed to drop off food and packages. Outside, past the guards, were the two giant stone lions Liz remembered from her first trip from the train station to Stephen's apartment. "If you ever need to leave the apartment without me," Stephen had told her, "you'll never get lost coming back." As if she was in any danger of that now. In the distance, Liz could just make out a red banner adorned with yellow characters:

Contribute to the Motherland.
Be Patriotic.
Have a Second Baby!

The security guards posted by the entrance were collecting documents, writing information down. From the back of the queue, Liz couldn't stop staring. Real humans, doing real human things. It felt both utterly mundane and exhilarating.

"Shenfenzheng," the guard barked, holding out his hand.

"Duibuqi," Liz said, giving her best startled impression. She dug around in her purse. "I must have left it upstairs." The guard shook his head.

"Ms. Li, you're going to have to go back and get it." He was dressed in black camo with a nightstick at his side. Liz might have been intimidated if she were back in Qixian, past curfew and standing on the other side of the iron gate. But she felt emboldened suddenly, wondering what all there was she had to lose. She knew the only thing more threatening than a crying woman was a woman inciting her own sex.

"I'm buying a goddamn tampon," she shouted in Mandarin, shoving past the guard. "It's a fucking emergency."

Out past the gate and around the corner, the few people on the street were scurrying along, their faces covered with masks and clear plastic goggles, arms weighed down by groceries.

"I think the longer I'm stuck at home, the more I feel afraid of strangers," Liz said. The rain was cascading down her umbrella. Across from them were two older Chinese women, their hair dyed auburn, one with a tiny Shih Tzu poking out from her red handbag.

"What makes you afraid?" Stephen asked.

"It's like only being able to trust yourself," Liz said, "you against the world." She remembered as a kid being jeered at while driving with her mom and thinking, *if only he'd heard that I didn't have an accent, that I wasn't one of them, he'd realize his mistake.* All her life she'd been told it was still fine to laugh at Asian names, to make fun of Asian people, those weird foreigners who all looked the same and spoke with ridiculous accents. She'd done it too, if only to exonerate herself, however briefly, from the same cruelty of others.

"When you don't know who's been infected, everyone is a threat. And when there are only Chinese people, when that's literally all you can see—" Liz's voice trailed off. No longer did she view the people around her as part of herself. They represented something different to her now: an affliction, a crisis in need of being managed.

"But you see me, too, don't you?" Stephen asked, holding out his hand. "Am I that dangerous?"

Turning to look at him, Liz was reminded again of Stephen's kindness, his good nature. She was ashamed of her own self-absorption, the lengths she went to instigate drama. Surely, she'd been overreacting. It didn't matter that there were parts of Stephen she didn't fully understand. Maybe that's what a partnership was: never having to explain who you are.

"If everyone else is a threat," Stephen asked, "what does that make you?"

"Me? I'm an American," Liz said, puffing up her chest for emphasis. "Can't you tell?" Stephen shook his head and smiled.

"Each of us copes in different ways," he said. "But at least we have each other."

They'd reached the end of the block. Nearly everything was closed, so they did a loop around Stephen's compound, taking the opposite side of the street back.

"Look," Stephen said. In front of them was a stationary supply store. Inside, a family was sitting on stools in the middle of the room. The son was scooping out rice and fatty pork with a cup measure from a communal steamer. A newborn was sleeping in a makeshift crib made from old copy paper boxes.

"Life goes on," he said.

There was an expression Stephen had taught her: qing cheng zhi lian. Finding love in a fallen city. Back home, Liz didn't care what other people thought of her love life. The world was crazy, along with everyone else in it. Relationships were just about finding someone who was largely amused and slightly endeared to your particular version of it. It was most important to care about a person in the moment and not worry too much about the future.

But Liz found herself thinking more and more about the future—what lay beyond the miserable present—and not just when she'd be able to leave the apartment again. In Chinese, the word weilai meant "that which has not yet come." It seemed more enticing, somehow, when Stephen talked about them that way.

"Almost time," Stephen said, pointing at the two stone lions in front of the building, and the guard table just beyond it.

Liz wanted to scream. Instead, she slid off her mask and breathed deeply at the sky, the rain falling like tiny amulets against her face.

"We're surely past the worst of it," Stephen said, shaking the water from his hair. "It can only get better from here."

11

Gua's car was acting up again, so Lin had to stop. She jerked on the steering wheel and pulled off at the nearest exit, rumbling over the slick asphalt. She wasn't sure if it was real, or if she'd just been staring at the sun glowing over the horizon so long that she'd fried her retinas. But the roads looked pink, a deep fuchsia like the images of salmon roe or flamingo plumes that she'd only ever seen in nature documentaries.

Other sights were unfamiliar, too. Lin marveled at drive-up liquor stores, motorized irrigation turbines, towering wooden telephone poles that resembled church crosses. Tumbleweeds spun out onto the road, large as tractor tires. Post offices announced town populations in the hundreds. Aging metal oil rigs appeared every few miles, teetering up and down like ostriches dipping their beaks into water.

At the gas station, Lin didn't park on an incline, but when she shifted gears and turned the key from the ignition, she pulled up on the parking brake instinctively, as if it would provide a modicum more protection. Lin's mother didn't own a car in Yuci and Lin had never taken a single driving class. Just sitting in the passenger seat made her anxious, but Gua had insisted they share responsibilities. It was one of the preconditions for the trip.

"Don't you care that I've never driven before?" Lin had asked her, walking from the Commons to the cafeteria, the day before campus shut down.

"Couldn't be any worse than me," Gua said, pointing her nose toward the sky. "I learned to drive in Shandong. It doesn't get more diandao than that."

Gua had done most of the driving since they'd left Cleveland. She didn't drive confidently, like someone drawing from a deep well of experience, but, rather, like a person hell-bent on having something to prove. If she was driving too slowly in the left lane, it wasn't uncommon for another driver to speed alongside and honk, even shout something through their open window. But Gua wasn't afraid to reciprocate. Lin didn't mention it to Gua, but she was secretly scared for her, never knowing if one of the people she told off had a weapon warming in the glove compartment, ready to talk back.

Lin was worried for herself, too. Her first time behind the wheel, she sweated clean through three layers of clothing. She drove with her back arched, seat scooted up front, her hands locked in a steel grip. As a kid, Lin used to roll her eyes at the thought of being careful. Her mother had used it for all manner of xiao shi: drinking hot liquids, slipping on ice in the winter, walking outside with wet hair. But, more recently, she'd had to concede: people like her had been made to be vigilant in America for much less.

"What do you think's wrong with it?" Gua asked, standing at the gas pump.

"Bu zhidao. The car feels like it's floating," Lin said, "a gaotie without the tracks. Maybe we should have taken the train."

"We'd never even left Ohio if we waited on Amtrak," Gua quipped. "Besides, it's not like they don't have accidents either." It felt like everything in America was a calculated risk. No matter which choice Lin made, there was always something more malignant ready to take its place.

"Every time I go over seventy-five, I'm afraid the whole car might explode."

"Good luck finding anyone to help with that," Gua said, throwing her arms out wide. "This place is like a ghost town." She took a credit card from her purse and fed it into the machine. "It's a miracle we can even get gas."

The gas station felt like each new town on the drive: a shadow of its former splendor. Lin wished she'd had a chance to see who had populated the wide curves of Lake Michigan, the ornate Chicago buildings they'd driven past before all the businesses inside were vacated and boarded up.

"I'd be amazed if any restaurants were open either," Gua said.

They had, the previous evening, exhausted the cache of tuna fish and Wonder bread sandwiches they'd packed in Ziploc bags. They'd intended to buy more groceries at the ALDI off I-90 in Austin. But when they got out of the car, the line stretched around the side of the building, everyone spaced out like chunks of lamb on a stick of chuan. The outskirts of the Tri-C campus had acres of corn stalks that were taller than Lin. It didn't seem possible that there could be any shortage of food.

"Suan le," Lin said, closing the lid to the gas tank. "We've got to get back on the road."

It had, after all, been Lin's idea to go. When Tri-C made the announcement that campus was temporarily shutting down and classes were moving online, she welcomed the chance to leave. Her classes were easy enough that she could afford to skip them from the road, doing homework between driving shifts and submitting assignments by siphoning the weak Wi-Fi from fast-food drive-thrus.

Lin had lined the back of Gua's car with cardboard asparagus crates filled with non-perishables and as much of what Gua and Xiao Bai had accrued at Tri-C as she could. Anything that didn't fit she left out front, despite Gua's complaints that she was only abetting the proliferation of the tent city she so despised across the street. Lin had thrown a duvet cover over the lumpy conglomeration, a pitiful deterrent against a potential break-in, like a magician trying to make an elephant disappear.

She felt confident they could outrun it, this invisible force that had immobilized Tri-C, Cleveland, then all of Ohio, to say nothing of what it was doing back home. She couldn't decide which was worse, the situation there, with its rising death tolls and panic in the hospitals, or the way it was all talked about here: mismanagement, pointing fingers, denial. And while she would have preferred to go to California or New York, determined to see the great beaches and glitzy skyscrapers she'd only ever glimpsed in photographs, she knew the situations there were even worse.

No, she needed to go somewhere with fewer people, where the money from her mother could last longer. If the coasts had been hit the hardest, they were going to the best place still habitable: farther inland, toward the wide flat middle of the country that Mr. Watkins had called the Heartland, though it seemed no more loving—not any warmer or more beating—than the city she had just left.

"How much more driving do we have?" Gua asked from the passenger's seat, breaking the silence. Lin had insisted on a no-news policy ever since they left Ohio; the voices on TV could hardly be trusted, much less the radio. They sped past a sign announcing their arrival in South Dakota.

"We can get there by tomorrow," Lin said, "if we can make it through the state tonight."

Lin was hoping to go all the way to Yellowstone. It was still early for spring, and she wasn't entirely sure if the park would be open, but she figured they could stay as long as it took until things got safe enough to return to campus. Lin had managed to check out a tent from Tri-C's Outdoors Club despite not knowing the first thing about camping. The few nature preserves she visited as a child were mobbed with thousands of tourists meandering up a trellised path, with food vendors staked every fifty meters. The idea of pitching a tent outdoors was almost unimaginable.

"And what happens after we get there?"

"We'll figure it out," Lin said. "But mostly we just have to blend in."

Out the window, billboards advertised a six-ton prairie dog made of limestone. Helicopter tours over petrified rock fields. A gas station with a live tiger exhibit. One sign boasted of the chance to see an authentic Western town where visitors could pay to wrangle horses with a lasso.

"Do you ever wonder who lives here?" Lin asked.

"No, why?"

"It reminds me of the minzu villages in Inner Mongolia. People dressing-up in traditional clothes and reenacting tribal life for tourists."

"Well, you probably won't find many minorities here."

It wasn't the first time Lin thought about the people who called this place home, this vast expanse of America blanketed with little more than barren rock and yellow-hued scrubland waiting to reveal itself like a secret.

"I just feel like some things are so backwards in this country," Gua said.

"Backwards?"

"Like a lot of ideas are still stuck in the past."

Lin laughed. She'd gotten used to hearing her own country described that way by Americans. *Why don't you just use forks? Do people still eat dogs? Does everyone travel by bicycle?* But until Gua said it, Lin had never heard the term used to refer to anywhere in America, the great plains that brimmed over with civility, the land that beckoned with the force of manifest destiny.

"And yet, here we are," Lin said.

"Not for long."

"What do you mean?"

"I came here for school," Gua said. "To get my diploma and go home." Gua and Xiao Bai were both graduating in May, though Lin didn't know what would happen now that Xiao Bai had already returned to China. She knew as well as Gua that a foreign diploma used to be the difference between getting a job interview and not. But now Gua would be one of thousands of haigui who had studied abroad, whose knowledge of the West might no longer be received so warmly.

"You won't miss the good things?" Lin joked. "Life, liberty, the pursuit of happiness?"

"Maybe for some," Gua said. "But America is hostile to foreigners. They will always view us as outsiders."

"It can't be all bad," Lin said, motioning at the road. "This has got to count for something, right?" In America, there were no limits on out-of-province licenses, no regulations on driving due to pollution. The difference seemed especially stark: China was under lockdown, and here Lin was, on the open road, in a landscape devoid of people.

Gua shook her head. "You forget that when you're a foreigner in China, people want to help you. Strangers will offer directions if you're lost. Call a taxi. Give you food." She paused. "In America, they'll barely recognize you."

It was like what Qi Fei had first warned her about befriending laowai. Lin had trusted them, believed that they'd had her best interests at heart. And look how far that got her.

"You need to have a tough skin if you're going to make it," Gua continued. She seemed to view America as both an escape and a trap, a place full of lazy people who had somehow become rich, and where all the hardworking ones had to fight over the scraps.

Lin knew that coming here was the kind of opportunity bestowed only upon the very privileged or the very lucky. But it would have only truly been a gift if Lin had known what it would take to survive once she landed. In Qixian, when Lin asked Liz if she ever missed home, Liz told her that homesickness was for people who couldn't assimilate. Lin was surprised. She knew that Liz had felt adrift in Qixian. Then again, maybe it was easy for her to say. It was people like Liz and Travis whose passports allowed them to move between places. It wasn't hard to assimilate, after all, as long as you could find somewhere you were accepted.

"Would you stay?" Lin asked her. "I mean, if you could?"

Gua shook her head. "I'm here for the same reason you are. That's why we have to stick together."

Lin felt like there were gerbils scurrying in the pit of her stomach. Even if she questioned the dichotomy, she felt complicit in what Gua was implying. *You're either with us or you're with them.*

"You could spend your whole life here and never claim legitimacy," Gua said. "Honestly, wouldn't you leave too?"

By the evening, Lin thought that she and Gua had escaped it. There were no closures, no spacing out in queues. No one, save for Lin and Gua, seemed to be taking any precautions at all. Lin was going eighty, just barely above the speed limit, while Gua slept in the passenger seat, the silence in the car punctuated only by the dull rumbling over a rough patch of asphalt or the lopsided heap of belongings trying vainly to find peace.

Even if she still didn't exactly enjoy driving, Lin was starting to get more comfortable behind the wheel. With all her attention focused on staying alive, she could block everything else out. In the car, the miles seemed to retreat faster as they burned through the state. Lin wasn't sure if they were making fewer stops or if there were fewer things worth seeing.

Still, Lin was worried they might never make it to Yellowstone. She felt more and more like they were hurtling toward enemy territory. Over the last two days, she'd noticed a steady rise in red, white, and blue banners that blanketed highway overpasses and dwarfed roadside farmhouses. But even more troubling was the frequency of billboards bearing a different flag, crossed with blue stripes and studded with thirteen stars like sharp points of barbed wire.

Lin knew just how much she and Gua stood out. But how obvious was it to everyone else? There was something disconcerting about the way people had been looking at her with her nose and mouth concealed, the glares she got whenever she moved or sneezed or brought a hand to her face. Like they were itching to pick a fight.

The town they stopped in at night to eat was small and unimpressive, about as scenic as the Cuyahoga outpost they'd fled. They got out of the car, and Lin noticed a sign—*Welcome to Deadwood*—strung between two trees. There were two rifle barrels overlaid in the shape of a cross and, next to it, the bare skull of an ox. Lin pushed down a lump in her throat.

"This was the best you could do?" Gua asked, rubbing sleep from her eyes.

The street was quiet and cold enough that Lin zipped up the purple windbreaker underneath her coat. She felt the condensation of her breath gather inside her mask. Hotels were showing no-vacancy signs in their windows and Lin immediately wondered if the neon glow was meant only for her and Gua's kind: a pox against foreign born.

A shop called Miss Kitty's had its doors locked, but through the window Lin could see decorations brandishing those same wrong flags. Lin gazed past them to the wooden BB guns and fake gemstones with Made in China stickers affixed to the bottom. If she didn't know any better, she might have easily mistaken them for being sold at any one of hundreds of tourist towns in China. She felt a perverse sense of pride swell in her body, a strange lightness, though it wasn't the kind she'd expected.

Light was emanating from a single bar and restaurant. Its square Plexiglas windows were covered in Budweiser decals, and a large inflatable whiskey bottle was strapped to the roof, like the nativity displays Lin had seen in Cleveland after Christmas. Just outside, near where they stood, was a row of motorcycles. It was as if these bikes had evolved to be bigger—taller seat, louder engine, wider handlebars—capable of swallowing their Chinese counterparts whole.

"I'm not going in," Lin said, when she and Gua were facing the door.

"You said it yourself," Gua replied, "this is the only place that's open."

"I'm not hungry." The rumbling of her stomach gave her away. Lin had only eaten a stick of dried beef and a bag of M&Ms all day. Gua peered at the doors, opaque with bumper stickers, and then turned back to Lin.

"What are you afraid of?"

"Do I have to remind you what happened to Phil?" Lin asked. But Gua, with a huff, moved in front of her.

"Take off your mask!" Lin shouted, grabbing her arm.

"What are you saying?"

"It makes us a target," Lin said, pointing at her own face.

"In China, we're chastised for not wearing a mask. We think you're being selfish." Gua paused. "Or have you just been away too long?"

"We're not in China," Lin snapped back. "We have a right to be selfish." But she realized then that it wasn't the mask people had been looking at. It was her eyes, her skin, her hair. Things that were much harder to hide or explain away.

"This hasn't changed anything," Gua said. "We were a target before this, and we'll be one after this passes, too." She brushed off Lin's hand and pushed open the double doors, leaving Lin out on the street.

A cold wind blew down the empty block and Lin shivered. Suddenly, she felt like her skin was being rubbed raw. She was ashamed for letting Gua go in alone. What if something happened to her too, and she'd been standing outside, like a coward, the whole time?

The walls of the restaurant are covered in expired license plates. The bathrooms are labeled "Cowboys" and "Cowgirls," and there are plastic trout dangling from the light fixtures. The waitstaff are clad in pencil skirts and white blouses that match the clientele: single men, biker couples, families with small kids. Affixed to the wooden beams are bull skulls, bleached photos of ranch hands, a neon Bud Light sign with a blond country singer twirling a lasso.

The swinging front doors squeak when she enters, and every head in the place turns to look. Gua goes up to the counter and eyes the menu. Two burgers, fries, sodas. It's the most basic order, so simple that nothing can go wrong, but the waiter mishears, or pretends to mishear, makes some joke at Gua's expense. It's harmless enough, what at a different time might have simply been ignored. But too much has changed. Someone needs to pay.

A disagreement ensues. Gua, in her clumsy English, is quick to talk back. The waiter motions to the kitchen and a group suddenly appears wearing studded leather jackets, bright red caps, bare heads tied with bandannas. The biggest, meanest one has a gravelly voice and smells like ash. *I'll explain in a language she might understand.* He brandishes a few of his teeth. There's an altercation. They all pile on. There are customers in the restaurant, enough to do something to stop it, but, like Lin, no one does.

"All set," Gua said as she sauntered past Lin, two carry-out bags in tow. They were heading back toward the car. The only light was from the headlamp of a motorcycle across the street. Lin was quiet, her body still buzzing.
"What did they say?" she asked finally, snapping out of her trance.
"They asked me if I wanted ketchup," Gua said. "I hate ketchup, so I told them no, so we don't have any now." She turned back toward Lin. "Hope that's OK."
Lin couldn't explain what she was feeling. She didn't think it was normal to have this strange discomfort, this creeping paranoia. It wasn't being the target of hate as much as it was the anticipation of it. It became a survival instinct, to curl herself inward, small enough that there was no surface area left to attack.
Lin wanted to believe in that most quintessential thing about America: that everyone was entitled to their own beliefs. She couldn't blame people for wanting to keep things the way they were, for turning away the outsiders, the people who came in with their own unfounded opinions about a country they barely understood. It was a country founded on aggression, where in order to be right, someone else had to be wrong. But thinking about the people who lived here, who had to endure injustices like that every day, made Lin feel like her grief was small and petty by comparison.
Lin walked back to the car gingerly, the ground like a pane of glass she had to prevent from cracking. Liz had said that homesickness was for people who couldn't assimilate. "It's only when you don't feel like you fit in that you start to miss the things that are familiar." No matter what she was experiencing, Lin knew one thing for sure: No one could relate to it more than Liz. To be accepted, and not, by your own kind. Never truly knowing where you belong. With the two countries jockeying over her loyalties, Lin wondered what it would be like not to pick either side. She decided to embrace her foreigner status: a person who belonged nowhere.

Once inside the car, Gua started the engine and heat gushed out of the vents. They ate their burgers in silence. Curly fries. A straw-lodged sip of Coke. It tasted like every trip to Dico's with Travis in Qixian, and every fast-food drive-thru she'd stopped at since she'd been in America. It tasted nothing, and exactly, like home.

12

Liz squinted at the floodlights lining the steel beams overhead. It was impossible to avoid their gaze: hundreds of flashbulbs that bore into her like a paparazzo's flash. The orange glow, like the outline of a sun on the horizon, marked her inner eyelid like a scar. She never saw one break, but she worried—in the dead of night, whenever she couldn't sleep—if any of the bulbs ever came crashing down. In the four days since she'd been admitted, the lights never so much as dimmed. They never went out.

"Is it possible to turn these off?" Liz called out to the phalanx of women in full-body hazmat suits who looked more like astronauts than nurses.

"It's for your protection," said a woman whose name, Wang Rui, was written in black sharpie across her arm sleeve. "Our guests sleep at irregular times. The lights make it possible to use the bathroom or go outside to make a call."

Her voice was so calm and melodic it belied the rest of their surroundings. Wang Rui, like all the other nurses, was dressed entirely in white Tyvek. Her sneakers were wrapped in plastic, her calves and shins lined with rubber gaiters like she was wading into a swamp. She wore a hood over her head, fastened in place with a thick plastic face shield, goggles, blue surgeon's gloves, and a mask. No part of her was left exposed.

"Do you at least have an eye mask I can use?" Liz asked. It was strange for Liz to hear herself and the other patients referred to as guests, as though they were all just weary travelers checking in at a hotel. Liz was not a guest, and she had not come by choice. It was bad enough that she didn't have any privacy, but did she have to be watched in blinding daylight while she slept too?

"I'm sorry," Nurse Wang said, casting her shielded eyes downward. "We only have essential supplies available for our guests."

The convention center turned shelter hospital where Liz was interred had been cordoned off into ten zones, each housing about a hundred people in cots on wooden bed frames. The sheer scale felt like being in an airplane hangar. Liz's possessions had been winnowed down to a small nightstand for taking meals, hooks for hanging clothes, and a trash can where waste was hauled off and incinerated in an industrial facility located outside the city.

Her cot was in section H, row 37, her back to a wall of fresh plywood and sheetrock that was erected as a temporary divider. For the first several days, sleep was the least of her problems. Day and night, Liz shivered in bed despite wrapping herself in as many blankets as she was allotted, routinely running a fever over what she was told was an acceptable range. She had temperature checks performed three times a day by Nurse Wang; once daily, she also had the insides of her nostrils parried and prodded with long cotton swabs that seemed to be jousting.

"Maybe just a cloth or a piece of fabric then," Liz said reluctantly. "Is that so much to ask?"

The next morning, Nurse Wang returned to Liz's bedside.

"I made this during my off shift," she said, holding out a band fastened with an elastic strap. "All our materials are running low." She lowered her head as if to apologize for the quality. Liz took it in her outstretched hands.

"Thank you," she said, too spent for sympathy.

But even with the eye mask on, Liz had to bury her face at night. The fangcang reverberated with the sharp howl of hundreds of human captives. Liz's nightly attempts at sleep—just as her routine of washing her hair and feet in an outhouse wash station in the morning—became the only way of marking time in a world without windows or sunlight.

"How are you feeling?" Stephen blurted out over the phone. "I've been so worried about you."

"Hao yidian," Liz said, staring into the camera. Stephen had insisted on calling over video to prove it was really her responding to his messages. That she was still alive. Liz was trying to put on a brave face to ease his fears, but it was impossible not to look like shit given the terrible lighting and the surgical mask and days without a proper shower.

"My temperature's back to normal," she told him. "The nurses say I can leave in ten days if my symptoms don't get worse."

Liz was speaking in Mandarin, not wanting to draw any extra attention from the ayis in her zone, from whom she was trying to keep her nationality secret. She was dressed in the same fleece-lined shirt-and-pants set that came standard issue, like prison dressing, to distinguish patients from staff. Liz would have scoffed at the notion back home, but here it instilled a sense of oneness, a feeling that they were all in it together.

"That's great news," Stephen said, breathing an audible sigh. His eyes were bright, if not for the bags underneath, his hair in its usual perfect coif despite his not seeming to expend the slightest effort. Stephen had called Liz twice a day since she'd been inside—more frequent than his mother—a fact that, for Liz, hadn't gone unnoticed.

"Are you sleeping enough?"

"No screaming babies here," Liz said, "so that helps." Children over five were held at a separate facility—*for safety*—but whether Liz felt worse for the mothers or the children who might never again see their parents was hard to say.

"What about the food?"

"Nurses used to have us line up at the door for meals," Liz said, "but the people who slept farthest from the entryway got angry about preferential treatment, so they started bringing us individual boxes instead."

"And are they edible?"

"Mama huhu," she said. Even on good days, Liz's appetite didn't allow for much more than a few bites.

"Are the nurses nice to you?" Stephen asked. Liz hadn't given the question much thought. She couldn't help vacillating between the feeling that death was imminent and that this was all just an appallingly elaborate prank. She couldn't process the reports she'd heard in other parts of the ward, where nurses held up the phones of dying patients so they could say their final words to loved ones on the other line.

"They better be treating you well," Stephen said, raising his voice. "Otherwise, I'll go over there and really give them a piece of my mind." Liz laughed. His tone seemed half composed of relief at her prognosis, and half enragement at her plight. She was glad that Stephen's concern for her could verge on vengeance. But if anyone had a right to feel spiteful, it was Liz.

Three days before she was admitted to the fangcang, Liz started to feel an itch in the back of her throat. It became hard to take full breaths without her heart beating wildly in her chest. But Liz tried to downplay the symptoms, not letting on to Stephen that her dry cough was anything more than a function of the stale air on the seventeenth floor of an airtight building.

One afternoon, while Stephen was working in his office, Liz watched a rerun of the 2008 Beijing Olympics on TV. There were no new sports matches anywhere and CCTV 5 was the only channel that broadcast in English, which gave it the conspiratorial lure of a guilty pleasure. They were showing the synchronized swimming portion, where two divers parroted each other's movements underwater. Liz listened to an interview with one of the Canadian divers who insisted that humans could train to have a diving capacity like fish.

"Your heart rate slows to a crawl and blood stops flowing to the outer extremities," he explained, body glistening. "I practice staying underwater for eight minutes at a time."

It reminded Liz of the campus pool in Qixian. Ice-cold water. Indolent lifeguards. First-years splashing around in the shallow end. Her own brief stint cheating death.

Wheezing on the dry land of Stephen's mattress, Liz had marveled at the idea. To never have to breathe again. To live free of breath. A dull pressure had developed on her lungs like a pair of depressed bellows. Then, waves of fever and chills, fatigue and muscle aches. It felt like each of her internal organs was being meticulously stabbed, a small, invisible monster taking up residence in her chest.

Liz dreamed of being underwater, of submerging in a hot spring, and smelled the sulfur on her skin when she woke up. The walls of Stephen's bedroom dripped with creamy reds and yellows that blistered and morphed into a thick meringue. Hallucinations. By then, Stephen had already confined her to his bedroom. Whenever he had to leave a tray of food at the foot of her bed, he did so in a hazmat suit of his own devising: blue hospital gloves, face mask, a plastic raincoat and hood that he zipped up and cinched tight over his head.

Eventually, Stephen had no choice but to turn her in. "What if things get worse?" he said. "I'd feel so guilty that I didn't do something sooner." But no decision was ever truly selfless. Guards were going door-to-door to search residences and perform screenings. Liz had no memory of what information he gave them, only that he stood idly by as three officials in matching spacesuits pushed open the door to his bedroom and ferreted her out on a stretcher. Liz wanted to make Stephen responsible for the outcome, good or bad, even if it was what he truly believed to be right. She was all too aware of that affliction, and the lengths a person might go to correct it.

"I'm just glad you'll be home soon," Stephen said. "Cases are going down. Things feel like they're getting back to normal."

Liz leaned against the sheetrock headboard. Every day, she saw the women who were allowed to leave, their beds disinfected and sterilized, and only occasionally saw a new body come to fill it. Still, she held the phone at arm's length, as if the infection could be transmitted through the wireless airwaves, too.

"I hope they are," Liz said, smiling, "for your sake." She was ready to leave the hospital but, more than that, she was excited to see Stephen again. The life she'd made with him in Shanghai—full of TikTok yoga videos, midnight cup ramen, and bad reality TV—was still better than any she'd had since coming to China.

"Haohao baozhong," she said, the refrain she'd come to use with Stephen before hanging up.

A few days later, the nurses led the women in Liz's zone in a stretch. It seemed silly for grown women to be doing a synchronized routine, but everyone else stood up, and Liz, not wanting to be singled out as the lone truant, reluctantly moved in line, stretching one arm over her head and then the other, swinging her hips in concentric circles.

"You're too young for this," Nurse Wang said when she came over to Liz's cot for her midmorning health check. "Most of our guests are three times your age."

"Daomei," Liz replied, like turning in her chips after a bad night of poker. The health check was the worst part of Liz's day, and Nurse Wang seemed to know it implicitly. She always paired her visit with snacks—white snow-sugar crackers, sweet biscuits made with rice flour—that filled Liz with an unexpected joy.

"Poor thing, you probably just graduated college," she said as she prepared to shove a swab up Liz's nostril. "Did you go to school in Shanghai?"

"I studied in America," Liz replied, wincing from the momentary pain. It wasn't a lie exactly, but part of her felt guilty for withholding the whole truth.

"Meiguo," Nurse Wang repeated. But instead of the full-throated awe Liz was used to the word eliciting, Nurse Wang said the word flatly, as if mourning some once great king.

"You should be careful with the foreigners living here," she said, casting a glare so acute it was visible even through her face shield. Watching CCTV over the lip of her plastic lianpen before bed, Liz had seen many of the same news reports. China had quarantined whole cities, built field hospitals in mere days, all to spare its citizens from the worst. Meanwhile, people in the West were still going out to stadiums and concert halls, thinking only of themselves.

"They're a threat to our wellbeing," Nurse Wang continued. Photos were circulating of foreigners in China brazenly flouting the quarantine rules: crowding in public spaces, hoarding groceries, not wearing masks.

Liz nodded, used to Nurse Wang's particular brand of unsolicited advice. Thinking of Travis, she had no trouble imagining the kind of foreign entitlement on display. But she was also aware of the reports from Western outlets that painted a very different picture: restaurants only open to Chinese nationals, foreigners barred from entering their own apartment buildings. Would Liz have even been admitted to the fangcang if she were seen as a foreigner with similar symptoms? If Nurse Wang associated Liz with such a danger, she would surely want nothing to do with her too.

"Your parents must have missed you," Nurse Wang said, "being so far away for school."

"My mom's dead," Liz replied, the words arriving more bluntly than they would have in English.

"I'm sorry," Nurse Wang said. "Ni de Ba ne?"

"Dead, too," Liz said, lying. Better to be an orphan, she thought, than a daughter whose father didn't love enough to keep.

"That really is bad luck," Nurse Wang said, sorting the testing supplies on her tray. Liz was surprised she didn't have a stronger reaction, but it was hard to muster any special pity when death was so present.

"Nonreactive," Nurse Wang said, "keep up the good work."

Liz thought about the other patients in her ward, how some congratulated or consoled each other when the test results were announced each day. But Liz preferred to keep her distance. She was afraid of getting too close with the other women, never sure whether their circumstances were more or less miserable than her own. The last thing Liz wanted was to make another situation worse by intervening.

"Are they buried here?" Nurse Wang asked suddenly.

"Buried?"

"Your parents. Did they die in Shanghai?"

"No, not here," Liz said. "They're from Fujian." She straightened up in her seat. "Wo de laojia."

"And you didn't go back?"

Never mind that the trains had stopped running for Chunjie or that whole cities in China had been locked down. Liz knew that as a Chinese daughter, she would have somehow been expected to go.

"It's a small town," Liz said, before correcting herself. "A village." Her family was from Meihua, a few hours east of Fuzhou. And even though Liz had never stepped foot there, it would have been wrong not to say she was from there, too. Lineage trickled down like a long, unbroken chain, surpassing any physical definition of home.

"I wouldn't even know how—" Liz started, before Nurse Wang interrupted.

"The first chance you get," she said, "you should visit." She looked as stern as Liz had ever seen her. "To your family, it would mean everything."

That night, Liz woke up to the memory of her mom's final moments in the hospital—the linen stiff and pressed over her limp body—and couldn't go back to sleep. Her chills were getting better, but the air inside the convention center felt stifling, like an anvil in her throat. She filled up her bottle at the water tower, the brushed metal and rust reminiscent of the cafeteria in Qixian, and then, rather than return to bed, exited through the thick plastic curtains.

Outside was quiet and still. Liz rubbed her shoes on a bleach-soaked mat and disinfected her hands. In the distance beyond the high fencing, she could see the windmill palm trees lining the highway, their tops stiff and bristly. Growing up, she'd associated palm trees with foreign destinations too remote to visit. She and Phil would crouch in the knee-high slush outside their apartment building with plastic shovels and pails, pretending the snow was actually sand.

"You're embarrassing me," her mom would yell in Mandarin, standing in her highwater sweatpants. "Do you want all our neighbors to know we're too poor to travel, too?"

Liz had always found a way to disappoint her. Nothing she did was ever good enough. It didn't help that neither Pearl nor Phil had ever made Liz proud of being Chinese. Pearl was willing to trade every piece of herself for her new country. So when Liz stepped off the plane from Cleveland, she'd wanted to wrest her mother from the one place she'd always been told to forsake.

And yet, Liz was no closer to understanding Pearl's connection to China than she was her own. What was she doing there? The whole enterprise smacked of vanity. Her reliance on Lin in Qixian, then Stephen in Shanghai. She'd done nothing to pay them back, this ungrateful American, this wolf in sheep's clothes. The braver, more selfless decision, Liz realized, would have just been to stay home. At least there she would have made all her mom's sacrifices seem worthwhile.

Dawn was beginning to break. The other patients would soon be up, the fangcang full of the familiar shuffle and chatter of the day. Liz felt like crying. She wished, more than anything, that she could call her mom and apologize for the mess she'd made. She let her hand linger on the phone in her pocket. Before she could stop herself, she dialed.

It felt like an eternity before a voice answered.

"Liz?"

"Hi, Lin," she said.

"Where are you?"

"I'm in Shanghai," Liz said, pointing the camera behind her at the dull outline of the convention center and the skyline beyond that.

"I thought the spring semester already started. How did you end up there?"

"I left Qixian after I saw you," Liz said. "I— I couldn't go back. I took the train down to Shanghai and got stuck during the lockdown." The last thing Liz wanted to admit to Lin was that she'd followed a man she barely knew to a new city and then promptly moved in with him.

"I'm sorry I didn't call sooner," she continued. "Things have been… unexpected."

Lin shrieked. "You're sick!" she said, pointing to where the camera had dipped to reveal Liz's hospital gown. "I can't believe it got you too."

"I'm OK," Liz said. "I'll be out of here soon."

"Is it really as bad as they say?"

Liz wasn't sure if she was referring to the fangcang or the illness. "Things are getting better," Liz replied, remembering her conversation with Stephen. "What about you? How's school? The situation in the states sounds even worse than here."

There was a pause on the other line. Lin's voice sounded as faint as if it was being spoken from a well.

"I left," Lin said. "The semester moved online, so I decided to travel."

"Sounds fun," Liz said, resenting her own ability to go anywhere. "You should totally see the country while you can." But the moment the words left her mouth, Liz was wary.

"Where are you now?" she asked, a tremor in her voice.

"We just got to Wyoming."

"We?"

"I'm traveling with a friend," Lin said. "A classmate from Shandong."

"That's great," Liz replied, visibly relieved. "I thought something bad had happened." She laughed to herself. "Like you and Phil had had a fight."

There was another silence until finally Lin replied.

"He threw me out."

"He did what?"

"There was an attack," Lin said. "He thought it had something to do with me."

"With you?"

"With people from China. That I was making it unsafe for him by being there."

Liz held the phone to the sky. She realized it had been weeks since she'd texted Phil to ask how things were going. As much as she'd hoped that Phil might be different with Lin, she knew it was risky to ever count on him to help her. And now that risk had turned to danger.

"Please tell me you're safe."

"Yes," Lin said, a little too quickly, and Liz couldn't help feeling that there was something more Lin was holding back.

"This is all my fault," Liz said, looking away from the camera.

"What do you mean?"

"I never should have trusted him with you," Liz said. "You shouldn't have to be out there at all."

"I had to go," Lin said. "I wouldn't have been able to stay in Cleveland, not with the school closed and no way to support—"

"I don't mean Tri-C," Liz interrupted, "I mean being in the states to begin with." She took a deep breath.

"It was my fault you got expelled," Liz said. "I'm sorry, Lin, I didn't mean for it to happen. I only wanted Travis to pay for what he did to you. I thought I was doing the right thing by helping you go abroad, but I didn't expect all of this to happen." She felt something catch in her throat. "I was selfish to want Travis gone, and I know it wasn't right to lie to you. But all this time I've been too ashamed to admit it."

The sun had come up, filling the sky with light. Liz was now angling around the other patients, holding back tears. She was waiting for Lin to hang up on her or tell her to fuck off or vow never to speak to her again.

"You did what you thought was best."

"What?" Liz said, disbelieving what she heard.

"It was the right thing to do," Lin said. "Even if Travis was never held responsible."

"You don't need to make excuses for me," Liz said. "I was wrong. And I was wrong about coming to China, too." This all could have been avoided if she'd just listened to Pearl. She'd come to China without the slightest idea of the consequences of her actions on the people around her.

"That's not true," Lin said. "There's so much I would never have known if not for you." Liz blinked into the camera at Lin's expression, which seemed to hold neither resentment nor judgment.

"Who would have guessed there was a whole fucked-up world beyond that miserable campus," Lin said.

Liz couldn't help but laugh. It was as if each of them was groping around after a bomb blast, trying to piece back together the fragments of their former lives.

"I forgive you," Lin said. "And I'm sorry, too."

Liz shot her a confused look. "Sorry for what?"

"That I couldn't make more of the opportunity you gave me." She paused. "I couldn't stop people from hating us."

Liz considered the anger she'd harbored against the other residents in Stephen's apartment complex, the people she felt responsible for her suffering. But now she was one of them herself—they were one and the same.

"It's an impossible task," Liz said finally. "You just being there—and being who you are—is doing more than you can possibly know."

"You too, Liz," she said. Her face floated on the screen for another moment before signing off. "I know your mother would be proud."

On the morning of her fifteenth day, Liz was preparing for her release. Her tests had all come back negative. Still, she felt it necessary to probe her body, trace her tongue around the inside of her mouth, flare her nostrils, feel the saliva pool in the back of her throat. Any minuscule change in her physiology could revoke her discharge. She didn't want to take any chances.

Liz used the last of her earnings from Qixian for the residency fee. Every patient had to pay for their own treatment and lodging, the Chinese equivalent, Liz thought, of going to rehab. Now that she was getting out, she dreaded how long she'd have to rely on Stephen again to get by until she could expect to find a new job.

"One last thing," Nurse Wang said, coming to Liz's bedside for her final check. "I haven't been able to leave Shanghai since before the holiday started." She reached into her gown and pulled out an envelope, thick and red. "Consider this a late New Year's present."

Liz remembered how her mom stood before the rust-metal stove in their apartment tossing shrimp chips into a wok of bubbling oil on Chinese New Year. At breakfast, Pearl would hand her and Phil a similar envelope. It was the one Chinese tradition her mom kept up in all the years since Ron left. Liz assumed it was because her relatives in China insisted on sending hongbao every year, and her mom would have felt too guilty if she didn't at least do the same. Pearl always withheld a portion of the money, like a bookie taking a cut of a gambling haul.

"If it weren't for me, you'd get nothing!" Pearl used to say, counting the fresh bank bills between her fingers. "How do you think I can afford to send money to all your qinqi?"

Liz had never met these relatives, nor did she have any way of getting in touch with them, so the origin of the money felt wholly contrived. Still, like so many things about her mom's life, Liz never questioned it. Regardless of who her relatives were or where they lived, all Liz knew was that the money was meant to fill an absence: a substitute for human connection. She never dreamed about one day being able to meet them, unless there was some way to go back to where her mom—where she, too—had come from.

"I can't accept this," Liz said, her cheeks blushing beneath her mask.

"Take it," Nurse Wang said, pushing the hongbao back into Liz's hand. "You'll need it for the train fare."

"Train fare?" Liz asked.

"To visit your laojia."

Suddenly, everything came into focus. Qiuting Chen. Liz had remembered her name scribbled across the tops of red envelopes. She was a great-aunt on her mom's side whose name translated as "graceful autumn," a seeming impossibility in Northeast Ohio. Grace was a ballerina twirling on pointed toe, not shoveling your front steps out from under a foot of snow in October. Liz had surely seen photos of her when she was young but wouldn't be able to identify her now.

Nurse Wang crouched down beside Liz's bed. "China may be a long way from America," she said. "But no matter how long the borders stay closed, we're your family here."

Liz nodded, her eyes slick with tears. Of course, Nurse Wang had known all along. She'd seen right through the flimsy cover of Liz's convoluted national identity story, saw her foreign registration status the moment she'd checked in. But she never made Liz feel any different for it. Nurse Wang had been impeccably—irrationally—kind, and Liz wished she could properly thank her in return. But even now, with all but her eyes concealed, Liz would never truly know who she was.

"Thank you," Liz said, a mix of surprise and gratitude in her voice.

"You know, you're still holding onto a lot of her energy," Nurse Wang replied.

"Who?"

"Your mother," she said. "It will be good for you to make peace—for both of you."

Outside of the convention center, Liz saw Stephen waving just beyond the front gate. She ambled slowly, still not entirely believing she'd be let free, tiptoeing past the security guards and the nurses and the rows of security cameras. When she reached Stephen, she embraced him with both arms. He was wearing a mask over his mouth, but underneath, Liz knew he was smiling.

"I was thinking about trying to find my family," Liz said.

"I can help," Stephen said. "It's the least I can do for getting you locked up."

Liz shook her head. "You've already given me too much." It was yet one more act of generosity she felt she couldn't repay. "I need to do this on my own."

But at the same time, Liz knew it was going to be a long road to Meihua. There would be a self-monitoring period and then, if she tested positive again, another two weeks of quarantine. What's more, she didn't know the first thing about how she would get in touch with her relatives once she got there.

"This is different," Stephen said. He flashed a grin, both shrewd and severe. "You'll see. With what I've developed, I can do more than just find them."

13

For weeks, they lived on the road. A Lueders Food Center in Spearfish. Dollar General in Moorcroft. Flying J in Gillette, where Lin broke down and ponied up the cost of dinner for a hot shower. Lin hated the stiff back of the driver's seat, the wheel pressed against her abdomen when she slept, like she possessed someone else's more robust, better-resourced stomach. They passed through the town of Ten Sleep, population 250, the name itself electrifying.

"Ten feels like more sleep than I've had in weeks," Gua said, embittered.

"I thought we agreed on no more motels," Lin said. They'd stayed at a Days Inn near Hazelton with walls the color of mustard and a stuck window. Even with a discount for the low season, the cost had gorged their savings. The night was so quiet it spooked her, and Lin feared that they would return in the morning to a car with a broken window, the meager sum of their belongings picked clean. They couldn't afford to lose anything. Lin and Gua rarely left the car, unsure that, even in the best of times in this country, they would be any safer.

But once in Ten Sleep, the name returned to taunt them. There was no lodging available, and each of the three restaurants had plywood shunts over their front doors and windows. Heaps of scrap metal and old farm equipment idled across abandoned yards. A gun supply shop bore the lone open sign, advertising bulk rounds of ammunition.

The virus was taking thousands of new lives every day, but Asians were being targeted irrespective of preexisting conditions. If Lin could be grateful for anything, it was that she and Gua were in the least-populated state in the country. They kept out of view, rarely stayed more than a night in a single place, and trusted no one but themselves.

They'd been biding their time in Wyoming until Yellowstone opened for the season. But when they arrived in Cody, they learned that the access road to the park was closed due to inclement weather. It was the first time it had snowed since they'd started driving, though it had been plenty cold, with temperatures routinely below freezing at night. They parked the car and waited for the blizzard to pass, staying clear of felled trees.

"Gou shi," Gua said. "Now what?"

"We'll keep waiting," Lin said.

For several nights, they slept in the parking lot at Walmart. Lin had abandoned the idea of trying to complete her schoolwork given the circumstances, but Qi Fei—once Tri-C passed along the news of her withdrawal—promptly stopped sending her monthly room and board stipend, certain that Lin was squandering yet another opportunity she'd labored to provide. Lin used the last of the money on instant oatmeal, Maggi noodles, mushy bags of Indian curry. By then, Lin had become inured to the extravagance of department stores she'd once found unimaginable. America had grown on her like a mold.

She and Gua boiled water on a metal camp stove latched to a can of propane, both borrowed from the Student Union, where they were increasingly dubious they'd ever return. In the evenings, they did loops until it got late enough that the Walmart closed, and they could slip into employee parking to loiter until morning. One night, when two guards with guns strapped to their holsters knocked on the glass and shouted for them to leave, Lin swore off parking lots for good. They took turns sleeping by the high brush that ran along the feeder road to the highway, fearful of surveillance.

Lin wasn't sure what dropping out of Tri-C would mean for her ability to stay lawfully in the country, but she didn't want to find out. It was enough for Lin to worry about being deported, but the idea of spending the night in jail—inside, even if on a cot bolted to the floor—would have almost been reason to tempt arrest.

Gua began talking about a distant cousin who might be able to help them. She lived in a city called Seattle, made famous to Lin because of a popular aiqing xiju, where a woman trying to give birth to her daughter in America meets a Chinese doctor in a maternity ward and eventually falls in love. Lin wouldn't have been able to place Seattle on a map—home to the two richest men on the planet—where, a century and a half earlier, hundreds of refugees fleeing China were recruited to work in lodging camps and salmon canneries. It felt as distant and unknowable to her as it must have been to her kinsmen then. A place akin to fantasy.

But now the city was notable for another reason: as ground zero in America, the place where the virus first took hold and was transmitted. It was subject to the same containment measures cropping up in other major American cities. As much as Lin pined for an end to her roaming with as much fervor as she might have, in bygone days, for a longhaired poodle, there was no going there now. There may be no going there ever.

The night they finally arrived in Yellowstone, the sky sulked. A shock of thunder startled Lin awake, and she rolled over, burying her face in her sweatshirt. It was still dark—the neon seams of her tent shone against the dull bluntness like stars—and Lin hated to get up in the middle of the night if she could help it. She made a habit of curling herself into a ball so small that her body might be mistaken as a ghostly trick of the fabric if she were ever discovered by marauders, or bears.

Lin heard what she thought were raindrops on the nylon fabric, slow at first, and then quickly gathering speed and strength. Soon, the noise began to sound more like tiny firecrackers, the fourteen days between Chunjie and Yuanxiao when the streets vibrated with what could pass for heavy artillery fire. When Lin angled her head toward the pitched roof, she felt a splash of water and wasn't sure how long the puddle by her face had been accumulating.

"Wake up," Lin said, giving Gua a shove with her arm. It was incredulous to her how Gua managed to sleep through anything, languorous as a cat.

But Gua waved a limp hand in Lin's direction before turning around in her sleeping bag, the mattress pad squishing under her. Lin knew that Gua was getting sick of her seemingly apocryphal stories of calamity. Each night, there was some new danger to contend with. Even when they were sleeping in Gua's car a half mile from Yellowstone, Lin had woken up constantly, startled by the sound of wind whistling through the tree branches or car tires screeching across the nearby interstate.

"We're going to drown," Lin said, raising her voice to be heard over the hail. "Or worse—be buried alive."

It was late by the time they arrived at the campsite and registered, and when Lin unpacked the tent to the ground in the dark, the stakes had fallen out before she'd had a chance to count them. Gua had chided her—*You never even checked the pouch?*—but Lin knew well enough that Gua hadn't thought to do so either. Gua was increasingly getting on Lin's nerves. She acted like a spiritual incarnate of her mother, someone who always seemed to know the right course of action only after the answer had already been made painfully obvious.

"It's just rain," Gua said. "Mei banfa. Nothing we can do until morning."

More than anything, Lin didn't want it on her conscience. God forbid the tent flooded and Gua died from hypothermia. How would she explain it to Gua's family in Jinan? With great effort, Lin slid the sleeping bag to her waist, crawled into her jacket, and unzipped the portal to the great beyond.

The tent flap was drenched. Lin found the culprit immediately, two of the stakes limp and exposed next to the holes that were dug into the muddy soil. The tent was positioned at an angle, so rainwater collected downstream, pooling in the folds of the fabric like a cupped hand. Her sneakers were soaked too, wedged into where the tent had gained separation from the ground.

Lin wiped off the fabric and looped the tent end into the stake, shoving it down into the soft earth. She debated whether she should get back in. The notion of camping as a hobby, something willfully sought beyond mere survival, had never seemed more absurd to Lin. Even though she was repulsed by the thought of another night with her spine curved and aching from the peeling leather seat, she found herself beelining for the car.

It was only when she was sitting inside the musty hull that she realized it was the first time in as many weeks since they'd left Cleveland that she wasn't sleeping next to Gua. She was beginning to feel like they had become as co-dependent as qingren, sleeping in such proximity they were nearly touching. Lin had always relished being alone. She felt like she should've welcomed the safe distance, the lack of contact with other people.

But something in her had changed. It wasn't loneliness, exactly, that she felt in America. It was that for weeks, she'd been made to feel less than human. Gua, as headstrong a person as she knew, was the only one who had accepted her. More and more, Lin found herself craving connection. Ten feet from Gua, she almost missed her heavy breathing, her erratic nighttime movements. She threw on a blanket and eased into the car seat as best as she could, the hail against the windshield threatening at any moment to pierce through.

By the morning, the snow on the ground had already melted. Lin hadn't seen the campsite in the daylight and was surprised at the number of cars that lined the grounds. Some of the RVs and camper vans were so tall they cast a shadow, their owners arriving with more than Lin had to her name: hammocks, tarps, tables, dirt bikes. Not far from their campsite was a communal bathroom, and Lin had never been so excited to see a shower. She poked her head into the tent, which was nearly flattened by the evening's weather, and pulled out the bag of toiletries that she kept stowed in the overhead pocket.

"It's fucking soaked!" Gua shouted, loud enough to startle the neighboring campsite.

"I tried to tell you—"

"You didn't tell me shit," Gua said. "It's your fault you lost the goddamn stake."

"Like you knew how to set up a tent?" Lin found herself barking back.

"You had one job," Gua sneered, her face so close to Lin's that she could see the pores. "I went out of my way to get you here, and this is the thanks I get? Abandoning me in the middle of the night?" They'd drawn stares from the other campers by now, people more interested in listening to nature than a language that already sounded as charged as a lit match.

"We each have to make our own choices," Lin said. "It's not my job to take care of you." It went against the idea of harmony, mutual struggle in the face of adversity. But Lin felt she needed to assert the barest wisp of her independence.

"We're like locusts tied to a rope," Gua said. "We sink or swim together. That's how we've made it this far."

They spent every waking moment together, and yet lived in their own worlds. At the heart of every argument with Gua was the same tension: Lin was too ungrateful, and Gua was so homesick she'd give almost anything to be back in China.

"You call this making it?" Lin screamed. "To have traveled a thousand miles, to have given up our only reason for being in this country, to become homeless—and for what?" The minute she said it, she knew she'd crossed a line. They were both aware that, without really knowing how, they'd become the people living in encampments that Gua used to despise.

"You think this was my choice?" Gua asked, bringing her hands to her face. "This is a nightmare. I would leave tomorrow if I could."

For the first time, Lin could see a change come over Gua. Sitting up in the sodden tent, her sleeping bag soaked around her midsection, she looked like a child too old to have wet the bed. Lin felt suddenly sorry for her, no longer the stalwart big sister she'd always been.

"I need your help," Gua continued, between tears. "I can't do this alone." Lin wished she could hold out her arms to her, to tell her that everything was going to be fine.

"I'm sorry I can't be more useful," Lin said instead. "I wish I could disappear too." She was crying now, not from shock or grief, but from a rage that wouldn't relent. When Lin remembered her birthplace a continent away, she realized that her anger all along had been misplaced. It wasn't Liz she was angry with, or her mother, or even Gua. It was Travis she was still fuming about, all these months later. It was his fault that she'd been made to fit into a life she didn't ask for, with only the blunt tools of her captors to rebuild it.

That afternoon, Lin decided to take a walk. She hadn't been more than one hundred meters from the car in weeks but now that they were inside the park—the dozens of campsites around them more garish by comparison—it seemed worth the risk. It was an illusion of safety, if not the real thing, in a world where nothing was certain anymore.

Lin had read about the prismatic hot springs at Yellowstone, the fauna that sprung forth as if from a fairy tale. But she'd so rarely been in nature, and never on her own, that the initial feeling of hiking scared her. The cold air pierced her lungs. Stubby grass clung to her feet. Her knees shook with each step, legs heavy from nonuse. Nearly as soon as she started walking, she felt out of breath. For weeks, she'd been living off freeze-dried food and sodium that coursed through her body like a sieve. To conserve the meager strength she had, she'd barely had any reason to move.

Gaining elevation, she began to feel her stride. She wound up a dozen switchbacks that ran alongside a frozen ravine with tall spruce trees that dotted the clay-colored cliffs. The path was quiet, the only sound for miles the swaying of tree limbs in the wind. By then, Lin was used to silence. She and Gua had run out of things to say. At their most hopeful, they would talk about Seattle, like it was some promised land. Flights to China were routinely getting canceled at the last minute, and the few that remained were going for exorbitant prices. Even if they somehow could afford it, they'd have to make it to a city before they could even dream of flying. But there was still the question of how they would make it there unscathed and how they could possibly afford to stay.

Lin didn't feel any desire to return to her life in Qixian, but more and more she yearned for a stability she'd only ever experienced in China. She missed the easy candor she'd had with Liz. She was ashamed that she hadn't known about her admittance to the fangcang before she called. That she'd let her anger at the betrayal eclipse everything else. She'd heard about the converted facilities and the emergency shelter hospitals that had been built. Though she admired the alacrity of the roll out—the single-minded focus on containment—it was also the Chinese way to never admit fault, to resist help until it was too late.

Lin took a deep breath, bereaved at what living in her native country had done to Liz, too. She was glad Liz was recovering; they'd both been through enough. Whatever grievances Lin still had felt minor, if not entirely pointless, in the shadow of a situation like this.

Lin looked out at the top of the ridge, her sightline just crowning the trees. Rain was coming down in fits and starts. She could feel the gravelly slab beneath her feet, smell the peat moss and sulfur. A butterfly, so pale it was nearly translucent, fluttered past her like a gust of pollen. She felt a paradoxical connection to nature, to the creatures she'd once claimed as her own, but whom she'd since doomed to abandon.

Qi Fei was right when she'd warned Lin not to waste her time with pets. She was destined to be alone. She'd disappointed Liz, done nothing to repay Gua. Her mother had practically disowned her. Who did she have left? At that moment, there wasn't anyone in the world who knew where she was. Lin closed her eyes. If she were pushed, she would almost certainly tumble to her death. But she could also be kidnapped or tortured or killed. Pain and suffering seemed to be all that was left in the world.

It was only when she opened her eyes that she saw it. A bear hunched over in the meadow below her, no more than fifty meters away. The bear had its face down, picking at something in the damp thicket. Its fur was the color of pine cones, thick tufts that rippled from its spine all the way to its jaw. Lin saw the remains of a carcass beneath it, the bones gleaming white, before the bear lifted its head and looked directly at her.

Lin froze, her heart lodged in her throat. She didn't know whether to run or yell for help. Was there any place more isolated than the wilderness? Her mother's voice echoed in her head, the early and insistent warnings from growing up an only daughter. Didn't she know that single women were vulnerable? That going it alone was tempting fate? Like so many of her bad decisions, she'd brought this upon herself. Lin waited to be devoured, for her body to return to loam and earth.

But just as quickly as she'd spotted the bear, it turned and stalked off deeper into the woods. Lin set off back down the trail at once, her heart racing. The encounter terrified her, but it was also thrilling. Everything she'd been fearful of in the world—her classmates in Qixian, the dean, her mother, the policemen who'd tapped on her car window at night—seemed to pale in comparison with nature. A chill hung in the air. If the world was ending, as it had seemed, there should be no reason to hold back. Lin had nothing to fear. If she was going to make it, she would have to survive like an animal, too.

Lin showered back at the campsite. The bathrooms were gender segregated, with a communal mirror and faucet in the center. She stepped onto the concrete floor, ignoring the mud that had been tracked in. When she turned on the spigot, it felt like the water was cauterizing her body, remaking it anew.

Lin looked at her reflection in the partitioned divider. Dripping hair, towel looped around her midsection, shoulders bare. She lamented the creases in her face, the parts that sagged in new places, spots that were puffy or dull from lack of sleep. But in the mirror, she also noticed a man standing on the opposing side. He had short black hair, cropped at the nape, and his face was matted in a thin beard that dotted his cheeks like acupuncture needles.

"Cold?" the man asked, in an accent she couldn't place. Lin's face was red, not with cold, but from the heat that rose in her stomach.

"I have an extra sweatshirt," he said, pointing at a pickup truck with a larger camper on its back idling on the other side of the lot from where Lin had set up her tent. She was listening, but the whole time, Lin was also watching the way his lips moved, the lilt of his voice like wood crackling in a fire.

"You're joking," she said. A man talking to her in a health emergency was unnerving enough, much less that he'd offered to show Lin inside.

"Suit yourself." He smoothed back his hair that ended in stiff, bristly peaks.

"No," she said, "no thank you." It was important for her to emphasize. She didn't want to intrude, was only minding her own business. But, at the same time, Lin felt a surge of desire so consuming that it nearly crushed her. Ever since she'd left Travis, she'd been holding onto a burning energy. That it might manifest in something beyond caring for a pet or completing her schoolwork frankly terrified her. Never did Lin think she would miss the rush she had of exerting power over something.

"Don't wait up for me," she told Gua later that night, when she crossed her way past their campsite. Her irritation seemed to absolve her of any guilt over perceived lack of responsibility.

"Where are you going?" Gua asked. Lin remembered the lie Liz had used about her expulsion, the half-truths friends tell when the whole truth would otherwise be too difficult to bear.

"If a doorway opens in front of you," she said, "there's no reason not to enter."

The man unlatched the door to the camper and Lin stepped inside. She marveled at the accommodations: sink, refrigerator, toilet, mattress strapped atop a slab of plywood. They passed through the cargo stowage into the rest of the trailer, silence rushing between them.

"I have some whiskey," the man said. "Do you want a drink?"

Lin nodded. She accepted the stout glass offered to her with a single ice cube, the brown liquid pooling around the sides. She took a sip, thick as tree sap, and knocked the rest down in a single gulp.

The man turned the knob to a stereo and the low hum of a trumpet sprung to life. "Do you like it?" he asked.

"Sure," she said. The music was dull and inoffensive. The man stood in the center of the room, his arms like two long machetes at his sides. Lin had resisted touching anyone—even Gua—all these weeks, had balked at the sight of bare skin as a blight. But before she could stop herself, she rolled onto her feet. She danced with the man for the length of the song and, when it ended, she found herself unfastening his pants.

Something broke inside her. She understood, then, that her experience in Qixian had only scratched the surface. In China, Lin would forever be pushing up against something large and intractable. What her country allowed for people like her, the limits on embodying her own worth. Her yearning to be back home—the duty and familiarity—had turned to revulsion. She'd always been seen by store clerks, her old classmates, even Gua, as something small and insignificant in need of saving. She wanted to claim now all that she'd been too afraid to demand before.

It wasn't until the man was naked, standing before her in the dappled glow of the trailer, that she let him pull off her shirt, its starched, mottled fabric bunching in his palms. She went toward him with her hands, her mouth, with a desperation borne from something held back. She wasn't thinking about the danger. Gone was the preoccupation she felt in the tent with Gua, her mind buzzing with fear and inhibition.

Lin wasn't sure the origin of such repression, whether it was the society she came from or the one she was reborn into, so that when he led her to the bed, it was both comforting and disturbing to feel the weight of the wood warp and buck with each movement, the way it had with Travis. She felt like she was seeing herself from afar, each motion divorced from her own intentions. When she came to, feeling the sensation of the man's spry legs as they slid in between hers, she cried out in a voice she hardly recognized as her own.

Lin held the man's hand outside the gleaming truck as the minutes dripped past like rain. She felt woozy, the drink sitting on an empty stomach. She left with a pair of thermal pants, a sweatshirt, and a paper bag of dehydrated food. When she arrived back at the campsite, Gua was sitting in the passenger seat of the car.

"What took you so long?" she asked, not looking up from her phone, and then, seeing the bag swaying at Lin's side, widened her eyes. "I was worried. It was getting late."

Lin tossed the bag to Gua.

"Where did you get this?" she asked.

"I'm providing," Lin said. "That's what duixiang do for each other."

She thought that it might be the only time she'd have to explain it. But for days after, Lin climbed into the silver camper of the Chevy Silverado to see the man who smelled of woodsmoke and kerosene. There were some nights she stayed away, to test the limits of their endurance, and others where she let herself be surprised—by pain or pleasure, it didn't matter—carrying all the tactile memories of him throughout the day.

She never even asked his name. She liked that she didn't have to explain herself, could let him draw her own conclusions about her, as if her backstory was just another part of her body to be discovered. Waking up with the windows slightly ajar, the smell of coffee wafting in the cool air, it felt to Lin like floating in a space capsule far away from Earth.

How many days passed like that at the campsite? Lin wished she could count them the way, as a child, she metered out individual grains of rice. It was getting warmer. Lin declined heavier clothing in favor of other supplies: food, money, things that would serve them when eventually they planned their escape. It was what she'd been taught all along: sacrificing self for the greater good. She suspected Gua knew full well what she was doing but knew better than to ask. Hers was a small price to pay, for watching over the car, in exchange for staying alive.

"You're going to hell," someone yelled at her once when she was coming out of the man's trailer.

But by then, she'd heard everything there was to be said. She wasn't scared of hollow, toneless words. There was no use trying to take her down in a foreigner's tongue. *Let me decide how I get spoken for*, she thought. *Let me control the narrative to my own story.*

"It's opening up," Gua told her, scrolling through news on her phone.

"What is?"

"Seattle."

The word caught Lin off guard. For so long, she'd toiled in the confines of the present, hardly able to consider even one step beyond.

"It's this man or me," Gua said, shooting Lin a cutting look. "You choose. I'm leaving with or without you."

Lin knew that Gua was true to her word. And Lin, having once put a man before her, was never more certain of what she had to do.

14

The bus pulled up to the station depot in Meihua. It was a winding six-hour journey from Shanghai, slicing through a ruffled sheet of low mountains into the flatness of central Fujian. Liz bought a bag of peanuts flecked with chili flakes and ma peppers from a hawker working the aisles to stave off her hunger. It was the spiciest thing she could find, which, south of Shanghai, was a greater challenge than she'd envisioned. The taste still felt dulled somehow, a pale shadow of its former self, and Liz, unable to tell how much ma it took to make her lips go numb, ate until the bag was finished and her stomach lurched.

When they got off the bus, Liz held her hand to her midsection.

"I'm ready for this to be over," she said. "The nurses swore I'd get my smell back."

The heat in the air made her hair sour like curdled milk. She and Stephen were standing on a small patch of pavement sandwiched between a public restroom and a food stall pushing dumplings and buns. Liz looked over at them expectantly, but the skin on the buns was dimpled and waxy, the dumplings glossy as a magazine cover, as if they'd been sitting out since the morning rush.

"Be thankful," Stephen said, pinching his nose playfully with two fingers, "there are some things you're better off missing."

Liz pulled out her phone and flashed the green QR code to the station attendant for him to scan. Stephen did the same, placing his phone on the scanner, and stepping through the metal turnstile. Scanning her jiankangma had quickly become a requirement to enter any public space. The colors of the health codes corresponded with who had been exposed to the virus and were directly linked with mobility. A green code allowed for travel as usual. Yellow meant there had been exposure to someone in a vicinity close enough for infection, resulting in a weeklong quarantine. Red was the most severe of all: fourteen days confined to an area no larger than an RV.

Once a new case was confirmed, the app could quickly identify where the patient had been and the people they'd been in contact with. It could even tell if they'd strayed too far from a designated radius during a quarantine order and force them to start over. Liz tried to rationalize each code's necessity by seeing it as something more physical than digital, as unique as a fingerprint. She learned to keep her phone close to her body like an appendage, an essential part of her being.

Liz had fought hard for her green status: her two-week stint at the fangcang, the mandatory self-monitoring period at Stephen's apartment after that. The code contained a travel history of everywhere she'd been for the last fourteen days, uploaded to a central server. She'd long made peace with the question of autonomy in China: Her ability to go almost anywhere was undercut by the meddling gaze of some government functionary. But to have those eyes on her constantly as an American already—was it really all that different?

Liz and Stephen walked from the bus station to the taxi stand and ordered a cab to the hotel. The driver reached over the back seat to scan both of their phones before they even had a chance to sit down. The seats were covered with a thin plastic, like the water-repellant covers slipped over mattresses in college dorm rooms. In Meihua, the seatbelts were just as inaccessible as they were in Qixian. It was a grave affront to use one, an implication you thought the shifu's driving so poor it warranted protection. But some part of Liz still wondered if, in her hometown, anything at all would feel different.

"Qu nali?" the driver asked, wiping a bead of sweat from his forehead.

Liz told him the address, then repeated it again to be understood through the layer of her face mask. Through the window, Liz could see open storefronts and people filling the sidewalks. It felt unsettling, like the very act of congregating was illicit.

"Does it feel strange?" Stephen asked, seeing her eyes widen.

"I forgot what it's like to be around people," she said. Even through the fog of her recovery, she was surprised at how quickly city life had bounced back. She never thought she'd be grateful for the jostling and the crowds, not appreciating what they would mean to her now.

"I mean being here," he said, "in Meihua."

For a moment, Liz marveled at the exhaustive series of events that had brought her to this place. It was a trip she'd considered in her head countless times, but the fact that it was happening was still hard to believe.

"I'm trying to keep my expectations low," Liz said. She still wasn't sure if she was ready to find her great-aunt Qiuting, let alone what she would say to her if she did.

"But isn't this why you came to China?"

It was the question Travis had asked her when she landed in Qixian, the same one Lin posed after they became friends. It was innocuous enough, but Liz felt that each time she had to explain herself, she found some new reason to doubt her intentions. Pearl. It was the answer she'd always given. *Yes, I will go for her*, Liz thought. *To understand something of her past she never wanted me to see.*

The car stopped and Stephen reached for his wallet, but Liz beat him to it.

"I got this," she said, peeling a red bill from the envelope Nurse Wang had given her. "I dragged you all the way down here. At least let me feel like I'm good for something."

"Fine," Stephen said, "but I'm paying for the hotel."

Liz stepped out onto the street. It was late afternoon. The sky was overcast but hot, the kind of sticky humid feeling Liz remembered from when she was five, and her dad drove her and Phil up from Akron to Edgewater Park in Cleveland. For the entirety of her childhood, Liz had never gone on an outing with just her dad. She couldn't remember what Pearl was doing, but Ron had organized the entire trip, pitching squirt guns and lawn chairs and a cooler with ice cream sandwiches into the trunk of their Honda Civic.

It was Liz's first time swimming outside of a YMCA pool and she was thrilled. She loved watching the rippling contours of the water, did laps up and down the pebbly beach, splashed and rollicked in the lake until her fingers pruned. Only, her father had forgotten to bring towels. Rummaging through the back of the car, he doled out a stack of old newspapers to Liz and Phil that they used to dry themselves off before getting back in.

It had all the makings of family lore, but by the time they got back to Akron, there was no time to joke. Within a week, her dad's belongings had been emptied. And within a month, her mom stopped referring to him at all, to the point that Liz and Phil learned that if they ever wanted an answer from her, it would have to be as part of a question that didn't mention his name. It was a subject she learned to avoid, the way other kids might have ceased talking about a dead pet or a school bully. But it stayed with Liz. The wet newspapers may have been the most enduring image, but it was also the last memory she had of her father.

"You can't be serious," Liz said, standing inside their hotel room on the fifth floor. The bed was a yellow foam mattress draped in pale sheets. The shower, a translucent box with exposed pipes that looked like frozen pig intestines.

"You should've let me talk to the receptionist," Stephen said. "I said I was happy to pay—"

"Not the hotel room," Liz interrupted. "Your plan for finding my family."

Until that moment, Liz hadn't known very much about Stephen's job. The little she had gleaned was that his company researched consumer behavior. They did it by collecting small bits of anonymized personal data from app users: how long they looked at certain ads, what articles they were more likely to read, how their surroundings influenced buying patterns. It sounded pretty boring to Liz, who'd mostly scoffed at the privacy concerns latent in everything Stephen had described.

"That could never happen in America," Liz had said, jutting out her lower lip. "Your company would be sued immediately."

"GPS and Bluetooth," Stephen had told her. "It's the exact same technologies we use here." He pointed to the phone in Liz's purse. "In fact, we learned a lot from American ingenuity."

Stephen slumped his bag down on the tile floor and shook his head. "You should have told me if you had cold feet."

"This isn't cold feet," Liz replied. "This isn't right."

Stephen had just started breaking into the field of geolocation when Shanghai went under lockdown. For weeks, everything was at a standstill as the industry tried to assess the gravity of the situation. But it wasn't long before his firm got its big break: a government contract. Stephen was staffed as Lead Engineer to a new division of research. The government paid his company to develop tracing software, to understand the patterns of where infection spread as a means of trying to control it.

"Where was I when all this happened?" Liz asked, incredulous.

"You were sick," Stephen explained. Just then, Liz remembered the week she spent in Stephen's bed, bleary-eyed and feverish. The whole time, Stephen was behind the closed door of his office, working through a cache of herbal tea and ramen. By the time the hospital workers carted Liz out from the apartment, Stephen had already finished a prototype of the app.

"I knew it!" Liz said. "You totally sold me out for your job."

"I *was* worried about you," Stephen insisted. "But I already felt guilty that I couldn't spend any time with you. I thought this was best for everyone."

"Easy for you to say," Liz said. "You didn't have to spend two weeks at a quarantine hospital."

"I couldn't risk getting sick! Everything we heard from our supervisors was that the work was too important. Forget 996, I was at my desk so long I couldn't remember what day it was. They started hailing us as national heroes."

"National heroes? Is that what they're calling informants now?"

"What are you talking about?"

"The technology you developed could be used to monitor Uyghurs and jail dissidents." It stirred up in Liz all the things she had willfully allowed herself to forget about China as recompense for living there. "Don't you ever feel bad about that?"

"It's more normal than you think," Stephen countered. "We get monitored at work, too. What we say on social media, the amount of time we spend away from our desks. Inspectors can even check our private messages if they have cause for suspicion."

"And who's the arbiter of suspicion?" Liz asked.

"You're missing the point," Stephen said. "Just think of all the good it's doing." He thumbed the green QR code on his phone. "China is freer than almost anywhere right now."

He had a point. There had been no new infections in China for seven days, a record. Shanghai had started to open up in a way that the rest of the world could only envy. Liz considered how she and Stephen had been able to leave the city, how they could have made it to Hainan or Chengdu or Kashgar—all the way to the border—if they'd wanted.

"So what? You gave people their freedom," Liz said, "you can't just go and take it away."

The truth was, Liz didn't have to imagine the nefarious ways in which Stephen's tracing technology could be exploited if it fell into the wrong hands. Stephen showed her how to do it himself.

He'd found a loophole in the system. Health data from every person in the country was uploaded from provincial and regional authorities to a national database. The data was anonymous, and local governments could access and share that data to establish if visitors arriving from another province had been exposed to the virus. Stephen swore up and down to Liz that his firm hadn't been asked to design it and that he hadn't engineered it this way himself, but the loophole allowed Stephen to see the unanonymized data that was collected and pinpoint specific users.

In addition to providing their name and national identification number, users who signed up for the app also had to register with facial recognition. It made it so that anyone scanning a QR code at a checkout line or at a train station could link the intended user with the person standing in front of them. So once Stephen could search for a specific user, it was also possible for him to access their headshot and address and manipulate the color of their QR code.

"The codes have natural glitches already," Stephen said. "False negatives are pretty common." Someone who'd been self-quarantining for fourteen days, for example, might still wake up to a red code on their phone on the fifteenth day and have to call a government hotline to get it straightened out. The users would have no idea why the code was quarantining them but would still need to comply.

"I don't care. I've already made up my mind," Liz said. "I can't go through with this."

"I have all the information right here," Stephen said, pointing at the laptop in his bag. "Don't you at least want to see it? What do you want to do, turn around and go back to Shanghai?" It was the angriest Liz had ever heard him. She was scared to look at him, awed by the kind of power he wielded but terrified of it at the same time.

"What happens if this data leaks?" Liz asked. "How is it possible to keep individual people safe?"

Stephen shook his head. "The data collected should be proportionate with the purpose to be achieved."

"What's that supposed to mean?"

"Be rational," Stephen said. "It's not like you're condemning all eight hundred Qiuting Chens in Meihua to their homes for two weeks." He wiped his mouth with his shirt sleeve. "If we do this right, we only need one."

Liz tried to imagine Qiuting in her mind. She would probably be in her sixties by now. Wavy salt-and-pepper hair, like a Chinese Farrah Fawcett. A job at the local tourism agency, shuttling flush mainlanders on shopping trips to Jinmen. Married, though God knows that didn't always end well. An adult son, perhaps, or a daughter.

Who was she kidding? Liz didn't know the first thing about her. It was presumptuous to think her yipo would welcome her with open arms. Stephen assured Liz that Qiuting would forgive her, that she would put up with being shuttered at home if it meant getting to see her long-lost niece. But it didn't seem fair to Liz that someone could unknowingly have their world turned upside-down like that. People trusted the system, lauded it as nothing short of miraculous. The codes were the key to real-life livelihoods. The last thing she wanted was to cement her legacy as some meddling delinquent, a child whose mother was too embarrassed to take back to China to meet.

"What about after?" Liz asked. "Who's going to be the person who says, 'This is over, so let's delete the data, let's not store personal data anymore.'" She wanted to know the ending, how it all got resolved. How badly did she want to meet her family, and would they even accept her if she did?

"We don't think about things that way," Stephen said. It was a tic she'd first noticed in Lin, invoking the collective voice of a billion individual people at once. She found the way Stephen slipped into that voice alarming. She'd noticed them before, but the ways in which Stephen's culture cleaved from hers were starting to add up. He was slower to criticize, less likely to express his opinions. The ways in which he bristled, or not, at Liz's takedown of the dominant culture probably sounded quaint to his ears. But the consequences of speaking out against something as a Chinese citizen were much more severe for him, too.

"You were the one who said it was yuanfen to do this, that you owed it to your mom to find your relatives," Stephen said. "How do you think she would feel knowing you got this far only to give up?"

Liz thought back to why she'd come to China to begin with. Was it really because of her mom? Or the absence that was left in her place?

She didn't know why she hadn't thought of it before. But, of course, her dad would have returned to China. He didn't have any other connections in the states and struggled the whole time he was there. He was disciplined by the university in Akron because of how long it took him to complete his research and his reluctance to publish. Pearl never said anything to her and Phil about where he disappeared to even after he seemed to have no intention of getting in touch. He'd walked out on his family without sparing a second thought.

A sharp pain rose in Liz's chest, and with it, a sensation both diabolical and charmed.

"I'm not giving up," Liz said to Stephen. "There's one last search I need you to run."

It rained all through the evening, muting the town in dull grays and foggy whites. Liz hardly slept. The bed was too small, the walls too thin. The air the next morning was cool when she left early for a walk. It was a half mile from the hotel to Meihua's commercial district: gaudy six-story mall, jewelry plastered in window displays, McDonald's cattycorner to a KFC.

But as Liz kept walking, she found areas that looked rougher than she expected. Gray brick buildings specked with black mold. A volleyball court littered with brushwood. Courtyard houses with their roofs caved in, ferns bending toward the light. In Shanghai, every building looked as if it had been built within the last decade. Here, there were places that could have been unchanged in half a century, well before her parents left.

Liz tried to imagine her mom there among the cobblestone streets, in the time before chain stores and Starbucks lattes, before the young people left to find jobs in big cities. Pearl studying at the one-room schoolhouse, scrimping to sell rice in the market, obtaining immigration papers that probably cost her everything she had. As beguiling as it once was to imagine why her mom had decided to leave Meihua, Liz couldn't comprehend why her dad had decided to come back. Was his life with her in America so bad that leaving it was inevitable?

In a park, a group of middle-aged women performed a synchronized dance. Elderly couples emerged from their homes with single-burner stoves for boiling water. Liz smelled laundry hanging from bamboo clotheslines, whole families outlined in their billowy folds.

She ducked into an indoor market, a windowless room buzzing with the sounds of hand-drawn carts and sewing machines. Thatched trays brimmed with mounds of bean sprouts and dried shrimp. Knotted bags of shiitake idled on wooden tables. An assortment of eggs—duck, goose, quail—were displayed alongside their purveyors. Liz's eyes eventually settled on a row of cats in square cages ringed with rust.

She found herself possessed by a gray cat with murky olive eyes. The more she stood watching, the more she felt a rising tide of injustice for this creature, held against its will. It had been a long time since Liz thought about Boom. But just then she remembered something Lin had said on the day they released him in Jiaocheng: Cats miss home just as much as humans do. Whether taken away or lost, their homing instinct kicks in, allowing them to do whatever it takes to return. "We're going against nature," Lin said, stepping back onto the motorbike. "It's only a matter of time."

Maybe Pearl had always wished she could return to China. It was an option Liz had never considered. Could her mom have wanted to go back and her dad insisted they stay in Ohio? It went against everything she thought she knew. She tried to recall a fight her parents might have had, but the memories played back like a silent movie, all emotion: faces twisted in grimaces, arms raised, but never any sound.

Liz came to the uneasy discovery that she could no longer place her father's voice at all. In every memory, he was mute: slumped over the dining room table, morning paper stitched between his fingers, empty ashtray at his side. It was probably a self-preservation tactic, she realized, to remember him, not as some object of menace, but as an actor in a scene completely outside his control. The sofa from Ikea and dining set from JCPenney were all just elaborate set pieces, and her dad, just a willful stage prop himself.

It was particularly jarring, then, when her father's image came to be imbued with another voice: Stephen's. Imprinted on Liz's expectations about their relationship was unresolved aggression at her father. Liz feared she would have to lose a part of herself to be with Stephen, that no matter what she did, he was destined to leave her. Liz had long assumed it was her fault that her dad left. She'd failed to live up to his exacting standards. Perhaps now, he had another Chinese daughter who would measure up in all the ways she couldn't. Why did her love mean so little to him?

Pretty soon, Liz began to see him everywhere. The man in the yellow jacket playing xiangqi on a wooden bench. The silver-haired cyclist fixing his bicycle in the town square. A hooded figure squatting along the banks of the Jinxi River, a wire fishing line at his feet. She whispered his name under her breath, Chen Rongxing, like blowing the dust off a book jacket.

Liz reached a series of squat structures spread out over a flat pitch. The path was sloping and uneven from packed dirt. It smelled like manure and grain alcohol. There were two chickens pecking in a corner, one mottled and brown and the other white with a bright red beak, like a clown wearing lipstick. A dog barked. The trees were overgrown, tall stalks of palm and wispy juniper plants propagating along the trail.

Far out in the distance was a shadowy pale of mountain ranges obscured in haze. It hadn't been that long since Liz was running past the mountains in Qixian with Travis, ducking under boughs of heavy fabric for the dust storms to pass. Or in the chilly damp of winter, before the snow got too thick to venture further.

Liz didn't expect to walk all the way there, but it seemed like her legs had other ideas. Stephen had pulled up the address and sent it to her phone, the destination shining like a beacon. She charted the path as if she'd known those streets—bleached white by the sun—by heart, until finally she reached the vast courtyard full of weeds and broken tiles. She rang the button in the aluminum box. The soaring metal door alternated straight lines and stencils in the shape of suns, treble clefs, moons. High up along the roof ridge, her ancestral name—Chen—was emblazoned in fading calligraphy.

When there was no answer, she knocked, and a bolt slid in the lock. The door cracked ajar. A man whispered something in a heavy tongue, the voice sounding like a pail dropped on a tile floor.

"Come in," the voice said, "I've been expecting you."

15

They started driving at dawn. The sun was peeking out from beyond the horizon but the roads no longer came through in colors. There was only the black tar of the asphalt and the faded white lines that seemed to bow and buckle with each turn. Lin drove barefoot while Gua slept in the passenger seat. She'd pitched her sneakers in the hatchback, wanting to be rid of them. Callouses lined her heels, a spidery red that spread along the tendrils of her feet. *Battle scars*, she thought, with a sneer.

She pulsed through radio stations full of static before a DJ's voice emerged: *His music. His word. The-the-the-The Rev.* Instead of gospel, it was as if each genre had been reproduced with a slight twist. Lin had seen this done with handbags, art pieces, computer chips—why should music be any different? Song after song were faithful renditions of what could have been Bob Marley or Tony Bennett or The Eagles. Only, there was always He. It was fascinating to Lin, like the old Communist songs of her mother's childhood, each one a rapt overture to a single man.

This He in question was like a man but unlike other men, too. He seemed to dwarf them with his greatness: more knowing, more generous, and yet more bitterly misunderstood. There were people who were afraid of him, who wanted him dead, and others who gave their life in his name. Each song seemed to reinforce the message that revering him would make you deserving of reverence, too. The pronoun rose before her like a specter. He. Lin changed the station. She didn't need saving, certainly not from any man.

"So who is this cousin of yours?" Lin asked, when Gua had woken up. They were most of the way through Montana, and Lin was staring out at the giant irrigation machines she'd once mistaken for prehistoric creatures.

"She's not a cousin, exactly," Gua said, without elaborating.

They'd gotten used to speaking less to each other, preserving their energy, expending it only when absolutely necessary. It was a way to avoid the questions they, grimly, already knew the answers to by heart. There didn't seem to be anything Gua could tell her that Lin hadn't already considered herself.

"Suan le, this relative. You said she works at Microsoft, right? Maybe she could help us get a job."

"I said she used to work at Microsoft," Gua said. "And you wouldn't have wanted her job anyway."

The wheels of the irrigation machine retreated so far back that Lin couldn't make out the end. Its sprinklers were fastened at even distances, seeds centered in long furrows, crops perfectly plotted. As if anything reaped from the earth could be that predictable.

"What do you mean wouldn't want?" Lin asked.

"Not unless you like scrubbing toilets," Gua said. "Besides, she's retired now. Imagine that? Forty years of cleaning other people's shit."

Lin shrieked. "I thought we were going to Seattle because she could help. What good is an old woman going to do for us?"

It was only then that Lin realized she knew nothing about the plan. For all their talk about needing to make it to Seattle, Lin had no idea what she would do if, somehow, they eventually got there. Had Gua been keeping the truth from her, too, or had Lin been too afraid of the answer to ask? It astonished Lin that Gua's thoughts remained impenetrable to her, the only boundary they had left.

"Us?" Gua snorted, turning to face Lin. "Now suddenly we're working together again?" Outside the window, a crumbling grain silo came into view—a shamble of wooden slats protruding from its roof—the lone structure in any direction.

"At least in Yellowstone, I knew how to take care of myself," Lin said. "Why did you make us leave in the first place?"

"For you," Gua said. "It wasn't good what you were doing." Lin heard the shadow of her mother's judgment, her conviction that Lin would never live up to her potential.

"You didn't mind so much when you were living off the food I brought you."

"I couldn't leave you there," Gua said, her voice trailing off.

"I would've been fine."

"You would've been dead." Gua straightened up in her chair. "Do you know how many women like us go missing every year?" She glared at Lin. "No one would have even noticed if we were gone."

Lin blinked back at Gua, unable to respond. For all Lin knew, she was right. It was too late to change anything now. Seattle was just another disappointment, a small bit of bad news in a sea overflowing with it, which seemed almost inconsequential by comparison.

It was dusk by the time they reached the city limits. Their first stop was a used car dealership east of downtown. There were streamers out front and a flailing, inflatable tube, but no other customers. Lin shouldn't have been surprised then when the portly manager, donning a rain-slicked windbreaker over a yellow face mask, offered money on the spot for Gua's hatchback before even looking inside.

Lin thought about asking if Gua was sure she wanted to do this. Having a car might mean being able to get a job making deliveries or having a place to sleep. At the very least, they'd have a way out if they didn't feel safe. But Lin didn't say a word, preferring not to botch the deal for Gua, who she knew had the gift of being able to tanpan from the day she could say her first word. Gua didn't disappoint. She got twice what the man had initially offered, paid out all in cash.

"Now we're even," Gua said, handing over half the money to Lin. "Don't say I never did anything for you."

It made sense why she wanted to sell it. And yet, Lin was still sad to see it go. It was as close to home as she'd been able to find in America, even if there were times when, crawling inside to go to sleep, she had to cry to stop herself from screaming. But Gua didn't have any use for it anymore. There was no chance of driving a car back to China, after all.

"That should be enough for both of us to get a ticket," she said. Lin nodded. It wasn't the outcome Lin would've wanted, but Gua had done it her way. The question of being there suddenly made sense. Seattle was the closest major city with a direct flight to Beijing, and Gua made no misgivings about her intention to buy a flight back as soon as the ticket price came down enough.

Lin accepted Gua's money, slipping it between the pages of her passport. She would wait and buy a flight home, too. It felt like giving up to leave without having earned her degree, to return to China no better off than when she'd left. But she'd given this country her best shot. Lin couldn't understand why anyone would come all this way to study in a place without the barest regard for safeguarding even its own people. It had only been four months, and yet long enough to contain several lifetimes.

"She's going to let me stay with her until I can leave," Gua said. "My yinainai."

"And what am I supposed to do?" Lin asked.

"There's an opening in the building where she lives."

Jackie, the building manager at Hirabayashi Place, swung open a makeshift door made of thick plywood.

"Homeless," she said, before battening it with a chain behind her, and Lin was careful not to mention where she and Gua had been living for the last several weeks.

"The same people who smashed all the windows in the neighborhood, too," she continued, doing nothing to help her sales pitch. "Some days I don't know which is worse: the virus or this."

The apartment building was a creaking six-story walk-up. The only light came from a naked bulb dangling from a pull string. Lin counted the missing tiles in the vestibule, the sag of each wooden step fastened with metal struts, the peeling chips of green paint that gathered in the corners of the landings.

"Be careful with the railing," Jackie warned as they made their way upstairs, a slippery Mandarin infused with her native Cantonese.

It didn't feel altogether foreign to Lin. She recalled the preserved tenement homes near Yuci that she'd toured as a kid. But even rural Shanxi had cleaned up its act, fortifying damaged walls with sheetrock, spraying the ground with concrete. It was nearly impossible to view history objectively, the way you might count rings on a tree trunk. That it needed to be distorted—enhanced or obscured—was in effect the story of her own country. Survival was as much a testament to persistence as it was any true act of self-determination.

"This is your room," Jackie said when they reached the top floor, pointing to a door with the number 64 on the front. She opened it for Lin and Gua to look inside. "You're very lucky. The previous tenant died unexpectedly." For a rent-controlled apartment, Jackie explained that there would normally have been waitlists and forms to fill out. But Lin knew that no one was all that eager to move closer to the city, into housing with a bunch of at-risk seniors.

Jackie fished in her pocket for the key. "In addition to the first month's rent, you'll need to pay a security deposit and insurance."

Lin gaped helplessly at Gua. She hadn't budgeted for the extra costs. Lin counted out the money from her passport case and handed it to the building manager.

"You're two hundred dollars short," Jackie said, flinching. "I gave you a discount, and now you try to pian me like this?"

Lin was already wary of spending any more than she needed. The room itself was austere: single cot with a thin metal bedframe, closet with hangers that looked like they'd been scavenged from department store dressing rooms. The contract she'd had to sign made it clear that even walking too noisily after the 8 p.m. quiet hours was grounds for eviction. It felt more like penance than any place she'd choose to live, but Lin conceded that if she had to bide her time in America any longer, some part of her yearned to stay put, no matter what.

"I don't—" Lin started, her voice catching in her throat, when Gua piped in.

"There are lots of residents in this building and only one of you," she said, giving a pointed nod up and down the hall. "You make up the difference in rent, and Lin can help you with the rest."

Earlier that spring, when it had become unsafe for seniors in the International District to leave the house or get food for themselves, community organizations began rounding up surplus groceries and donating them to neighborhood residences. Lin soon became responsible for distributing those groceries to the elderly residents of Hirabayashi Place. The job wasn't complicated, but Jackie was specific with her instructions: Wait to meet the delivery driver, never prop open the front door, don't overstay your welcome.

Lin received a list with names like Hsieh and Tolentino and Okada, sixteen residents to each floor, eight on each wing. Every Monday and Friday, she knocked on the door of each unit and left a sack of food outside. She learned not to go after lunch, when some of the residents slept, and got to know which ones had hearing problems—like Gua's great-aunt—so that she could key into their apartments with the bags instead.

Outside, Lin quickly understood Jackie's glibness about the smashed windows. Seattle already looked like a construction zone, with cranes that peered up from the bottom of ditches like startled animals. But it was as if the builders—in a zealous rush to finish—had covered up the openings meant for windows and doors, too. Each restaurant had wooden boards erected in place of glass, their hours scrawled in paint. And then there were other buildings whose wooden panels were permanently closed, affixed with chains and padlocks, a response to the break-ins or out of an abundance of caution that the owners might be targeted next.

Hirabayashi Place, along with the rest of the International District, was bisected by the overpass to I-5. Underneath, concrete columns buttressed a parking lot teeming with tents. Lin got used to maintaining six feet and holding her breath every time she passed. It wasn't uncommon for police to periodically sweep the area or for the fire department to turn their hoses on a smoldering trash fire. Lin couldn't decide if Jackie's warnings had been well-founded or whether she should feel sorry for those getting by with even less. The depth of her empathy was wearing thin.

As a building resident, Lin got her own allotment of whole wheat pasta, garbanzo beans, canned vegetables, and stewed meat. Occasionally, there were additions that surprised her: haw fruit, blocks of dried chrysanthemum, preserved beans with ginger, cured cod, salted duck eggs. She imagined the people who packed the bags: students who'd lost a summer internship, perhaps, or workers who'd been furloughed from other jobs. Lin still needed a way to support herself and thought maybe she should look for openings at Golden Hong, too.

She thought of Gua's great-aunt, who labored in a light-blue uniform for forty years. How she'd come so far just to do something she could've accomplished without ever leaving home. She'd never married in the states and never had children. A wasted opportunity as far as her family in Shandong was concerned, who weren't even able to sponsor a single relative through her. Maybe Gua leaving to go back to China was just as well. Neither of them had any claim to the America of Lin's imagination, a vision Lin herself was finding increasingly hard to invoke.

Lin was on the second floor making her round of deliveries when a resident stopped her.

"I haven't seen you around before," the voice said, poking out from behind the door where Lin had just knocked. "Are you new?"

Ruth Osada, room 203, according to Lin's roster. She looked to be in her eighties, with a hunched gait, wirerimmed glasses, black knee braces on each of her legs. She flashed a tight smile, deepening the lines that creased along her eyes and cheeks.

"I'm helping out the building manager," Lin said, ungainly in her full disease-prevention regalia. She turned and got ready to keep walking, but Ruth beckoned her back toward the door.

"Have a little tea, will you?"

Jackie, despite her litany of instructions, had said nothing about whether or not she could accept a resident's invitation. Ruth wasn't wearing a mask—it was her apartment, after all—but with a suit covering practically her entire body, Lin felt she wasn't being entirely irresponsible.

She stepped inside. Against the back wall of the apartment were canvas bags that had been stuffed onto makeshift wooden rafters. Shirts and other garments hung as if in a vintage window display. Piles of VHS tapes formed a mound near the slippers by the front door. Magazines and newspapers dating back several decades were stacked atop nearly every surface. Lin wasn't sure which was more remarkable: that Ruth or the apartment had survived longer.

"Make yourself at home," Ruth said, shuffling around in rubber slippers. In the kitchen, Lin reached for the kettle, passing the plastic musubi maker—a rice paddle in the shape of a cat—and black enamel bowls with red engraving. She eased into a chair with little stockings on the legs to prevent scratching.

"I'm saving this for you, you know," Ruth said.

"For me?"

"For the future. Everything you see—the photos, the newspaper clippings—down to the smallest details." She unscrewed the cap of her thermos and took a sip. "How else will people remember?"

Lin paused to look at one of the black-and-white photos on the wall, of a young girl staring into the camera.

"Is that you?" The girl in the photo was not quite smiling, her mouth slightly agape. Her hair was tied in pigtails with tiny ribbons. The photo was faded and dogeared, but unmistakably Ruth.

"We used to have to make our own fun," Ruth said. "We made fishing lines to go out to the lake, picked flowers to wear in our drill team headdresses. Hell, we even used to cover rocks in newspaper and wrap them in twine because we didn't even have balls to play with."

"Where was this?" Lin asked.

"Topaz, Utah," Ruth replied. "I was born in the camps."

Lin had read about them in high school. She remembered her teacher talking about the wartime history of Japan with perverse glee. Even though the Japanese in America weren't the same ones who had come to occupy cities across China—whose armies had raped and killed girls not much older than her—it was small penance that they were getting what they deserved. Lin had been taught never to forget that Japan was still the enemy. She never expected to have a conversation with a Japanese person, much less someone who'd experienced the internment firsthand.

"What were they like?"

"The exact opposite of here, if you can believe it," Ruth said. "Dry. No trees or flowers. Not a speck of grass in sight. My parents lived in Seattle before the war. When they were forced to move, they gave up everything they owned. When we got out, they wanted to come back, but we basically had to start our lives over from scratch."

Lin looked around the apartment again, and it began to make sense. Ruth's belongings were a form of resistance, a way to reclaim a history that had been denied to her family. She suddenly thought of her mother and the artifacts of her life in Yuci. A shrine to her missing daughter.

"Do you miss them?" Lin asked.

"All the time," Ruth said. "I think about what my parents would say about the world if they were still alive. My children and grandkids are halfway across the country." She paused. "Of course, there aren't many of *us* left anymore."

Lin nodded. It had been weeks since she last texted her mother, ever since Qi Fei cut her off. She realized she had no idea how she was doing. No matter what had come between them, Lin knew she would never be able to forgive herself if her mother had suddenly fallen ill.

"Right now, I've been fixated on the block below me," Ruth said. "Lights change. The occasional car goes by. I observe the empty cityscape in the distance." She flashed a smile to Lin. "The tranquility is almost deceiving. I like to joke that quarantine is good practice for internment."

Lin froze. The truth was that nearly the entire time she'd lived in America, Lin feared there might be a different kind of internment. That if the aggression with China escalated into a war, she would be slated for detainment. She'd told no one about this fear, not even Gua, outlandish as it seemed. It wasn't shocking to Lin that America was using a competitor as a way to divert attention from its own problems. Her own country had done the same. What was surprising was that it took until this moment to finally come to light.

"Aren't you afraid?" Lin asked. "That people will come after you again?" But Ruth shook her head.

"You can't let them see your fear. We lived through much worse and never expected anyone to protect us." She drew a circle around herself. "Around here, we look out for each other. What you're doing with the groceries is no different." She pointed down at the street below. "See for yourself."

The gray broke on the day of Lin's next set of deliveries. It was still chillier than Lin expected for May, but even in her coat and gloves, she was grateful for the sun peeking out from behind the sheet of clouds. People on the street looked almost delirious, like awakening from a long sleep, the light doing as much to change their moods as it did the appearance of the neighborhood.

Lin began to see the storefronts differently. While some of the wooden boards were bare, others were painted in bright colors. She studied the stencils and patterns: koi fish, snaking dragons, dim sum nestled in a bamboo steamer. There was the flourish of a soaring egret, Bruce Lee with his muscles bared, two children holding flowers: peonies for bravery and plums representing strength. Lin was struck by how unafraid the community was to show its true spirit. A small display of beauty in something so ugly.

Back at Hirabayashi Place, Lin padded over the carpeted hallways, going door-to-door. Many of the residents stepped out of their rooms to thank her. She came to know their names, asked questions of them, always made sure to smile back through the crinkle of her eyes. Lin had always struggled to read social cues in China, but in America, she could get away with not always knowing what was going on. The residents didn't have the same expectations of Lin as her old classmates did. Their hearts and minds were different. And yet, they were still bound together by a collective strength.

At the end of each set of deliveries, Lin returned to her room, exhausted but fulfilled. She felt like her body could accomplish great things, the life poured back into it, as she did when she was hiking in Yellowstone. She'd never lived alone before. It was comforting to return to a room she could fashion in her own way: arranging the clothes in her dresser, replacing the dull curtains, buying a new wok for the stove. Even if it was a temporary place, it was more than she'd come to expect, and that was enough.

"Everyone's going home," Gua said, when Lin reached the apartment of her great-aunt. "What are you waiting for?"

Lin had heard about the wave of Chinese citizens who were flowing back into China, nearly as quickly as they'd fled in January. There was an expression for people like them: those who run when it's convenient to go away and come back when it's already too late to help. Lin was a traitor for leaving when her country needed her most and would be a coward for only now going back.

"I don't think I'm ready yet," Lin said.

"What are you talking about?"

"I'm just not sure I'd recognize myself there anymore."

"And you can see yourself clearly here?"

Gua had a point. It wasn't as if Lin felt any more accepted in America. But there would be too many compromises to make in China, realities she would have to either swallow or ignore if she had any chance of being content. There was something fastening about being here, like a braised duck in a shop window, that held her and wouldn't let go. She knew that if she left, it could be years—decades—before she'd have a chance to come back.

Lin left the bag inside for Gua's great-aunt and turned back toward the door.

"You're insane," Gua said, calling after her. She shook her head at Lin in the doorway. "Just remember, as long as you're here, you'll only have yourself."

Lin began visiting Ruth a few times a week, then nearly every day, the delivery runs just another excuse to spend time with her. Ruth was warm and doting in a way that Lin's mother had never been. Lin's face softened when they talked. She could momentarily neglect the anxious sensation of always having something she needed to explain.

They were having dinner together in her room, a stir-fry Lin had prepared just as she had for Phil back in Cleveland, this time using ingredients from the weekly groceries she sometimes pooled with Ruth's. Ruth had a few photo albums spread on the table, pointing at pictures of her and her parents against the backdrop of barbed wire and tar-paper barracks.

"There's something I wanted to ask you," Lin said. "When you had the chance to go back to Japan after the war, why didn't you?"

"It wasn't that simple," Ruth said. "It cost a lot in those days to travel and start up somewhere new. Besides," she said, "we didn't have any home to go back to."

"What do you mean?"

"Many of us were born here. My siblings and parents, too. We never knew a life outside the United States."

"So you were American?"

"Not exactly," Ruth said. "Even if you were from here, your allegiance was questioned. It didn't matter how long our family had been in this country; it would've been the same. To many people, we were still foreigners and therefore couldn't be trusted." She flipped the matte pages to a photo of her and her classmates holding their hands over their hearts.

"America made us swear loyalty and then still put us into camps."

Lin shook her head. To be severed from one's homeland seemed like loss enough. It shouldn't have to be bartered as currency to purchase another government's trust.

"My father tried to wear the pin, you know," Ruth said. "*I am Chinese.* Not that it helped him any."

"I don't understand," Lin said. "Why would he pretend to be Chinese?" The very notion to her seemed unthinkable.

"You were OK if you were Chinese," Ruth said. "People would've given a lot in those days to be your shade of yellow and not ours."

Lin considered her arms for a moment, tugging at her skin. "I guess it doesn't matter so much now."

Ruth nodded. "We all get lumped together. These days, people are less willing to accept outsiders as anything less than a threat."

Lin let her eyes linger on the room, at this life Ruth had built for herself. She was simultaneously fascinated and bewildered by her, to have lived this long in a place where she'd had to fight for every rung she managed to climb.

"What made you want to stay?" she asked, finally. Ruth blinked back, seemingly puzzled by the question.

"I didn't want to leave," Ruth said, the silver in her hair glinting in the light. "I have as much right to this country as anyone."

It suddenly made sense to Lin. Whether or not she would ever decide to stay was irrelevant. Didn't being American, fundamentally, mean being from somewhere else?

"We may never fully be accepted," Ruth said, "but we're something, aren't we?" She smiled at Lin. "This is our home, too."

The sun hadn't yet risen, but the trains were running a limited schedule, and all the flights leaving the West Coast seemed to depart before dawn.

The terminal at SeaTac was nearly empty, the rattling of Gua's suitcase the only sound puncturing the silence. Lin and Gua strode past the single agent at the check-in counter, each with their faces and eyes covered.

"You can still change your mind," Gua said, when they reached the security gates. "Ticket prices are starting to go down."

Lin nodded. She'd already imagined what it would be like to go back. Trading in agency for restriction, safety over freedom. All her life, she'd accepted the ideas others put on her—her mother, Liz, Gua—never having enough faith to follow her own.

"Is there anything you'll miss?" Lin asked. Gua thought for a moment.

"Corn," she said. "It's so bland in China. Here's, it's sweet and cheap," she paused, "like everything else."

Lin laughed. She remembered driving past endless rows of cornfields, Gua in the passenger seat with her head lolling out the window, shouting obscenities at the empty roads, her words evaporating in the wind. Lin had never hugged in China. There was never any reason to. And already the concept was becoming foreign in the states, too. Without being able to explain it, Lin took off her mask. She reached out for Gua's arms and slid them around her waist.

"This is it," she said. They embraced. Lin counted the seconds. The last hug they would ever share.

"Goodbye, Lin," Gua said, as she started down the moving walkway. A puff of breath passed between them, at once both menacing and dear.

16

The room was dark when Liz stepped inside. Shades heavy as tapestries hung in the windows. In the corner was a wood-burning stove and, above it, a watercolor painting of horses stampeding through a field. The cavernous living room was otherwise nearly empty, with cracked plaster forming the sole patterns in the sheetrock.

"Can I get you something to drink?" the man asked in English, his words curling up at the ends like an old rug. It might have been years—decades even—since he'd had to use them. Liz was tempted to switch into Mandarin for his benefit, but she wanted, after all this time, to hold something over him. To remind him of the life he left behind.

"Nothing," Liz said. The floor was covered with tiles that looked and felt like stone. Liz slipped off her shoes and rubbed her soles against the bottom, trying to reconcile the memory she had of her father with the man standing before her, offering her a drink like they were prospective business partners, one step above strangers.

"Have a seat," the man said as he returned from the kitchen, placing a box of tea leaves and a glass pot on the coffee table. Liz sat down on a stool opposite him, their bodies facing like chess pieces.

There he was. The man whose face she could barely conjure. The person she spent years pretending was dead to avoid having to remember. Liz still wasn't sure what to call him. Sure, he was her father; biologically, he'd been coconspirator to her birth. But Liz felt like she was looking at a hologram. The edges around him were fuzzy, making the rest of his body hard to trace. She wanted to memorize the wrinkles in his brow, the grooves cast like a drought-stricken lake across his cheeks, if only so that if he ever ran out on her again, she'd know exactly how to describe the kind of man he was.

His hair was parted down the middle like a book with a warped spine, the gray leaves pleated on each side. His face was rounder than she remembered, a slight paunch beneath the eyes. But his limbs were long and thin. The slacks he wore hung off him like a rag doll. He had on a faded gray T-shirt, the name of the academic conference where he'd received it barely legible, but Liz could still make out the date. 2002. Liz had been five. It was the last time she ever saw him.

"How did you find me?" Rongxing asked.

"My boyfriend's good with computers," Liz said. It was the first time she'd ever described Stephen that way, and she didn't have the slightest concern over how her father might respond.

"I thought you might've been sent from Beijing."

"Beijing?"

"You know, the government," he said, drawing out the last syllable with a thump. Liz blinked at him, cocking her head to one side.

"Oh, come on," Rongxing said, and then, switching to Mandarin, added: "you're sure no one put you up to this?"

Liz was incredulous. "Do I need an excuse to go looking for the father I never had?"

Rongxing didn't say a word. He picked up the pot of hot water and swirled it into two porcelain cups sitting atop the wooden table.

"Forgive me," he said, pouring the water from each cup into an empty beaker. "It's just hard to know who to trust these days."

Liz knew about Party-owned news, persistent surveillance, even the secret police. But for them to use her to get close to her father just didn't make sense. She began to doubt what she was even seeking in tracking him down.

"Why would the government be looking for you?" Liz asked, swallowing the lump in her throat.

Her father sighed, stuffing a clear glass with leaves from the tea box. They were full blooms, like dried flowers, all the leaves and stems intact.

"Juhua all right?" Rongxing asked, holding up the glass in front of him. For a moment, Liz thought he was going to have her smell it, stick her nose in the stamen and breathe, like he might have done when she was a child.

"When I came back to China," he said, pouring boiling water over the flowers to steep, "I started to notice someone following me." He placed the lid over the top of the glass.

"Little things at first," he said. "I used to see a white car in the parking lot of my danwei. Then, on my way home, I would see the same one idling outside my house. He followed me on the road, stopping where I stopped, never letting me stray too far." Rongxing laughed to himself. "In a rural area like this, you can imagine how conspicuous it was."

He dug the lip of the lid into the glass and poured the clear, unblemished liquid into the porcelain cups.

"Try it," her father said. "Not too bitter." The whole setup, from the slatted holster inscribed with running script to the metal strainer and matching tongs, struck Liz as overkill. She wondered if her father had always been into jingcha or whether it was part of this whole other life he'd kept from her.

"I don't understand," Liz said, shaking her head. "Were you really important enough that someone would need to follow you?"

Despite the few memories she had of her father, Liz remembered clearly what happened after he left. One day, the four of them had been living in faculty housing on campus, and the next, she was pulling up in a U-Haul with Phil and her mom to an apartment complex piped in tinsel-colored fencing with a vestibule that smelled like stale piss. What about her father could possibly make anyone curious, much less suspicious?

"It wasn't like it is now," her father insisted, "thousands of students coming and going between China and the US. Back then, anyone who returned from being abroad was thought to be suspect. Exposed to dangerous thoughts."

He held one of the porcelain cups in his outstretched hands. Liz took it, her fingers grazing the skin of his palm. It was soft, despite the rough exterior, like the peel of a persimmon. How she would have loved to reach for his hand when she'd first fallen off her bike, after she'd had her first breakup, the morning she'd emerged from the hospital—bleary-eyed and inconsolable—after Pearl passed away.

"And besides, anyone married to your mom was going to be scrutinized."

"Mom?" Liz asked, her face twisting up in a scowl. "What does she have anything to do with it?" Steam rose from the top of her cup. Her father turned toward the window, his visage partly obscured by the haze.

"Liz, your mother was an exile."

Shortly after Rongxing left and the weather changed from summer to fall in Northeast Ohio—that most illusory and magical of seasons—it was Liz's job to sweep up the fallen leaves that had gathered in front of the apartment complex. Liz and her mom descended on the gum-stained front stoop, Liz crouched with a rake, and Pearl using a garbage bag to catch the brush and dust.

"Stop," she said suddenly, motioning to the ground. "Yezi." Pearl pointed a long finger at the oak leaves, the tips fanned out like mini tridents. Liz marveled at the colors, the green leaves specked with spots of orange and brown.

"What's that one?" she asked, of a yellow leaf curved like a paper fan, or a red one rounded at the bottom like the hull of a ship.

Her mom taught her the words for different species of trees: yang and tao and song and liu. She explained that dangling willow branches had long been likened to a woman's slender hips. How pine trees could withstand even the most severe winters. Peach trees were associated with the fleeting nature of youth, the misfortune of girls born pretty but whose beauty faded with age like blossoms slumped from the branch.

"Not like you, my little taohua," she said, "you'll be beautiful forever."

"What trees did you see when you were little?" Liz asked.

"I—" Pearl started, and then stopped, the color draining from her face.

Years later, Liz would learn from Phil that Pearl grew up picking ginkgo nuts in Meihua. She and her mother went out in the morning with a pair of shears and a woven basket, cutting the fruit from the tops of trees. Pearl would hug her limbs around the branches, fitting into the crevices where the clippers wouldn't reach. The ginkgo nuts reeked, a smell like sewage dredged from the bottom of a ditch. And yet, when boiled in a stew, the sweetness of the fruit emerged from the withered husks.

Liz still remembered the sound of the wind whistling through the trees that morning, the ache of the leaves as they released their grip and tumbled to the ground. After that day, Liz stopped asking stories about Pearl's childhood. She came to understand that when a person leaves behind a country, she does so knowing it is an entire life, full of its own landscapes and rituals and memories. It was one thing to decide to move to a place without having anything to lose. It was an entirely different one to know you could never return to the country you were leaving behind.

Rongxing reached for a pack of cigarettes from his pocket and began smoking, wispy trails that curled across the room.

"Why didn't she ever say something?" Liz asked. "All this time, she could've just told us she couldn't go back."

Her father shook his head. "Your mother was very stubborn. For her to say anything would be to admit it was true." He refilled his cup with hot water from the glass pot. "If she exposed you and Phil to the reality, then she could never let go of the past. She would have to live with it every day."

Liz considered whether learning to live with America's flaws was its own kind of reclamation. She never saw her mom as someone who would make waves. But there always seemed to be parts of Pearl suppressed beneath the surface.

"What does a person even have to do to get banned from entering a country?"

"When we left China, we didn't know the next time we'd be back," Rongxing said. "The university paid us a large enough stipend to live on. I felt for the first time like I could say whatever I want, publish whatever I want." His PhD was in political theory, his thesis on the possibilities and limitations of state-run capitalism.

"But things began to get worse for your mom's parents. We sent money home, but their health was failing. That's when we started having second thoughts. We still had no community in America. It was a few years after you were born, and I saw the planes hit the Twin Towers on TV. I knew that no one would have our backs if we needed help. Or that people who looked different would ever truly be accepted." He ashed his cigarette in one of the slats in the wooden tray.

"By that point, things were deteriorating between your mother and me. We couldn't agree on how to raise you. We fought constantly. She wanted to do things the American way, have you and Phil be just like all the other kids you went to school with." He shook his head. "She told me I was too traditional. But I said her thinking was senseless. You'd never be at the same level if you didn't work twice as hard."

Liz remembered the way her mom never asked about her homework or what she was doing in class. She was always so focused on Phil that Liz learned to trust in her own abilities regardless of the expectations other people set for her.

"And that was reason enough to leave the country?" Liz asked. She felt like she and Stephen had already had worse arguments than that, and neither of them had threatened to leave.

"I remember coming home from the university one night and she had all these books in her hands, the books I needed for my research. She started shredding pages out and then tossing the books at me. I couldn't stop myself. I threw the books back. The neighbors eventually called the police because it sounded like gunshots." Rongxing sighed, bringing the cigarette back to his lips.

"I was miserable. My research wasn't fulfilling, I couldn't stand my colleagues, I didn't feel safe at home. So many years in that country and so little to show for it. Hard as it was, I knew my time was over. I told your mom I was leaving and wanted to take you and Phil back to China with me. I don't know if she believed I would go through with it or not, but I drove to the Chinese consulate that afternoon. Only, when I did, they told me there was something wrong with my passport."

"But you had a Chinese passport."

"Exactly. But they said I'd been placed on a list. They wouldn't tell me outright, but I knew what it was."

"A list of dissidents," Liz whispered. For years, she'd seen his dissertation bound in a bookshelf high up in the living room, but never even considered what her father had written.

"They had me trapped." He gripped the cigarette with his fingers, his hand shaking. "I'm not proud of my decision, but I did the only thing I could think of. I told them your mother had made me write it."

Liz froze. She felt a screeching pain in her chest, an ache so large and heavy she thought she would be crushed under its weight. She'd spent her whole life protecting her mother, interpreting for her, putting herself between her and rude strangers. But she couldn't shield her from this. Liz grabbed her things and bolted for the door.

The towering building, with its granite slabs, had reflected the heat, but outside, the sun was scorching. The humidity in the air made her limbs heavy, but Liz strained against them, pumping her body as fast as her feet could take her. Each step away from him brought a new layer of clarity. It confirmed for Liz what she'd learned when she first arrived at the red-brick flat in Qixian but hadn't wanted to admit: that to be a Chinese woman was to suffer for a man's greed. She saw how easy it would be to condemn a woman to a fate she didn't choose for herself, how her own choices in life could be seized from her grasp.

"Liz, wait," she heard a voice call out. When she turned around, she saw her father running toward her. In the light, he was smaller than he looked inside. She could see the sharp curve of his widow's peak, the strands of silvery stubble clinging to his face.

"It should've been you who was exiled, not Mom," Liz shouted.

"It was a mistake," her father said, catching up to her. "But I did what I thought was right. For the sake of our family."

"Our family?" Liz yelled. "So you could live alone in a mansion halfway around the world?"

"This house is owned by the entire village," he said. "The whole town is full of them. Monuments to people like us, who left."

Meihua's landscape was inscribed with traces of overseas Chinese wealth: water towers, electric generators, concrete driveways. But most of the structures were empty, paid for by the guilt of those who hoped to leave their mark, but who rarely came back.

"I don't even live here," he said. "Look at what I'm wearing. These are the only clothes I keep in the house." Rongxing explained that he registered himself there to guard against the minder he'd been assigned. Even though the embassy eventually accepted the reason for his publication history, the government still wanted to keep tabs on him.

"Remember the white car I told you about? I never talked to the guy who drove it, but for a while we just nodded at each other," Rongxing said, his breath slowing. "He never really intimidated me or did anything, but that wasn't the point. The government wanted to send a message that they were always watching. After a few months, he was gone, off to stalk other malcontents, I suppose. But they succeeded in making me understand that I would never be free."

Liz remembered the security cameras in Qixian, the lockdown in Shanghai, the app that had traced her father's movements—and her own. In coming back to China, he'd had made a conscious choice to give up some of his freedoms, but perhaps, for him, it had been worth it.

"We're all dancing with shackles," he said.

"What?" Liz asked.

"It's what people here like to joke. We can be as free as we want, until we feel the tug of invisible cuffs around our wrists. We dance as we breathe surveillance in. You must reconcile that with yourself—give in completely—or risk never being able to be survive."

Liz didn't know what to believe. She wondered who the real man standing before her was and whether she would've felt as disillusioned if he'd not been her father but merely someone she'd met here, in this manor that bore her name.

"My real home is across the river, on the opposite side of town. I have my ID registered here but that's about it." He pulled the T-shirt over his slender arms, as if embarrassed by them.

"I rarely stay here, you know," he said. "When the border closed with America, I thought they were doing it again. Like maybe they thought I was agitating resistance. I felt a strange sensation every time I left the house, a feeling I hadn't had in years. When I got the alert to quarantine, I knew something had changed."

He looked scared suddenly, the veneer of toughness stripped away. Liz had a flickering image of her dad, back from when he still lived with them in Akron, reading her a book in the bathtub, the water coming up past both their chests. Liz could see that her father was trying to tie their fates together, like they both wanted to reclaim a part of their past that had vanished.

"Don't try to drag me into this," Liz demanded. "I'm nothing like you."

"We're more alike than you might think," Rongxing said. "Think about it. Each of us has been uprooted from one place and, through a great series of chance and circumstance not entirely our own, been made to reinvent ourselves somewhere else." He paused. "Only, it's never quite that simple, is it? We're both caught in between, Liz."

"Maybe," Liz conceded. "But I didn't leave my family behind to do it."

"Believe me, I didn't want to. This house was meant for all of us," he said, "when eventually we came back here to live."

Liz looked back at the building draped in wisteria, its covered balcony and arched columns. There were buttressed staircases that ran to small portages on the outside, roof tiles that had been curved and embroidered to resemble Grecian temples. It looked gaudy and out of place with the surrounding countryside, dappled in moss-green grass. A rooster crowed. Lines of laundry hung limply in the heat. Liz could hear the yaw of plows somewhere in the distance.

"Did Mom ever tell you she wanted to go back?" she asked.

"Of course," he admitted. "She knew her parents would die without ever seeing her again, without ever meeting you. But she believed that America was the best place for you and Phil." He combed his hand through his hair. "She was wary of putting you in any danger. After seeing what this country could do to me, she didn't want to take any chances."

It suddenly made sense to Liz, what her mom her whole life had been trying to warn her. She didn't want her daughter to go back to China because she was afraid that, even as an American, she wouldn't be allowed to return.

"And what about you?" Liz asked. "If you knew she couldn't go back, why didn't you ever come to Ohio? Were you happy with never seeing us again?"

"Leaving you and Phil was the hardest thing I ever did." He turned his face away from her. "I tried to rationalize it. Moving here, to support your mother's parents until they died. Not that it matters very much now."

"What do you mean?"

"When I arrived back in China, they took away my passport. Your mom may not have been able to come back to China, but I couldn't leave either."

She understood then that her father, in his own twisted way, had made his own sacrifice. The relatives he had relegated himself to caring for were gone, the village a shadow of when Pearl had lived there as a girl. They were dead now—all of them—and yet here he was, still tending to the broken pieces.

"To this day, I haven't forgiven myself," Rongxing said. And when Liz looked at him, she actually believed him. It was too pathetic to have been a lie.

"I wanted to tell you all of this. I knew one day you'd come looking for me. When you were ready."

Liz knew it too. From the moment she first bought a one-way ticket to China, she would seek out this last vestige of herself. She arrived in Qixian thinking she could finally pull back the curtain of who she was. But she didn't know then about all the things others could place on her, too, the way her identity was formed as much in her own mind as by people like Lin and Travis and Pearl.

She was still wearing her mourning plainly on her face when her father started in again.

"I'm sorry for your loss," he said, finally.

And Liz knew then that he didn't only mean her mother. It was that she'd tried to find some connection to a future in Meihua and had failed too. No matter how good her imagination, it was an experience, at its core, that she would never truly understand. She would always be an outsider here. Meihua had never been hers to claim.

And so, despite her vow to the contrary, Liz realized she needed to go back. Her version of China would have to be predicated not on what had come before, but on what would remain after she left. She would have to return, as her father had, if only to resolve something left unfinished.

That night, in the hotel room with Stephen, Liz explained the whole situation as best she could. She started with her father's confession, his betrayal, the sequence of events that would forever estrange him from Liz. She was lying down next to him, quietly sobbing, her face burrowed into his chest. When she was finished, he only had one question.

"You're sure you don't want me to come with you?" Liz paused for a minute, appreciating the touch of his body against hers, but shook her head.

"I have to do this by myself." And this time, she knew he would relent.

The sun rose with Liz as she climbed the hill the next morning. At the top of a peak, in front of a wide clearing, she saw the gravestones that her father had pointed out in the map he'd scribbled down before she left the village. The markers were of the town's forebears, small headstones that had been squeezed and stretched up to the limits of the property, where high-rise development licked at the outer edges. Qingming had just passed and Zhongyuan wouldn't be for a few months, so the cemetery was empty and quiet.

Pearl had believed in reincarnation. It was funny to Liz that this relic of her mom's Buddhist upbringing had survived the journey to America. It didn't matter how often they passed a patch of wildflowers off the side of a highway median or the tangle of honeysuckle that used to grow wild by their apartment complex. If ever a white butterfly appeared, her mom insisted it was the spirit of their ancestors.

"Flew all the way from China," her mom would say, as if further endorsement of the American dream.

For a long time, it was a comfort to Liz. This physical embodiment seemed to almost make up for the lack of family photos or her mom's own stories of China. The fact that the butterfly was here, in Akron, allowed Liz to feel some sense of grounding, that she had had a reason for being there too.

But as she got older, Liz began to question why the spirits would have chosen a butterfly to begin with. Of all the living things in the world, it seemed silly to Liz to return as something so pointless: an object of beauty but no substance. And yet, there was a part of her that never stopped believing it. Ever since Pearl's death, every time Liz saw a butterfly, she maintained the stubborn position that her mom was living inside of it, too, watching over her.

There were small paths between the rows of gravestones, and Liz stopped to pull out the squat metal tin she'd carried on her back. The gravestones she paused at were of the grandparents she'd never met. There were no adornments, just the script of their names carved into stone. Pearl might have been buried in America, but the spirits had a way of returning. Liz remembered an old saying: The motherland is eternal. No matter where you die, you will always be Chinese.

Liz opened the two packages of brightly colored paper sold in thin squares. Beneath that was another ream, this one thick, the front soft and tender as sheepskin, with a streak of gold embossed over it. Some of the paper had been folded into designs: red qipao, gold bars for prosperity, a watch to tell time. The gifts she wished her mom could have, now sent to her in the afterlife.

Liz took a match to the bundle and placed it in the tin, then slowly added the paper, low and flat to guard against the wind. All of it burned easily. The smoke clung to her hair and clothes, making her eyes burn. She opened a container in her bag containing four teacups and a bottle of rice wine. She lined them up in front of the metal tin, pouring a small amount into each. On a white sheet, she arranged bao and danta she'd bought from the bakery that morning.

There was beauty in this simplicity. Perhaps, Liz thought, in her next life, Pearl would finally be surrounded by the relatives she'd never had the chance to see again. A recognition, not of the time that was lost, but of having finally made it home. In Chinese, there was a difference between hui qu and hui guo—of returning home versus merely traveling to it—though Liz wasn't sure, in her case, which one was true.

Liz poured out the wine and put away the cups. She cracked an egg and left the shells to feed the soil. The bits of paper burned away, billowing up toward the sky. She saw the scraps of them, the ash flickering like moths, bobbing gently in the air, before disappearing into nothing.

17

The chill from the morning dew languished on Lin's windowpane like a spilled drink. Her room smelled like cooking oil, old paper, and the must of a mildewed radiator. Lin counted the bubbles of condensation outside as they gradually multiplied into rain. At night, it was still cold enough that Lin slept with the blankets pulled up to her ears. But despite complaints from the other residents, the building manager had already switched off the heat.

"Is Jackie trying to kill us?" Ruth asked during one of Lin's nightly visits. "If we don't die from what's going on outside, we'll wake up with our hearts stopped from the cold." She shuffled two places in her fuzzy slippers. "Is there any justice?"

Lin shook her head. It wasn't the first time she'd heard this particular Ruth rant and knew it wouldn't be the last. It didn't seem to matter that Ruth had stockpiled duvets like sacks of rice or slept with wool socks rolled up past her calves. Before she started training to become a nurse, Lin had no idea just how sensitive older people were to even small fluctuations in temperature.

"It's too bad we can't control the heat ourselves," Lin said. For all America boasted of individualism, Lin found it ironic that the residents of Hirabayashi Place were subject to the same collectivist rules that governed when northern provinces in China could access the heat grid.

"Save your energy for the things you can change," Ruth said, shrugging it off. "Would you help me with the sheets?"

Lin walked over to the dresser and pulled open the bottom drawer. By then, Lin was as familiar with Ruth's apartment as her own. Ruth had even told her to take off her mask.

"Is it so much for an old woman to want to see your face?" she'd asked.

Lin, at first hesitant, eventually obliged. Some days, they talked for only a few minutes, Ruth remarking on how heavy the clouds looked or whether she'd go out for a walk in Donnie Chin Park. Other days, Lin would settle in for an entire evening, making them both steaming mugs of hot water and getting Ruth ready for bed.

Lin balled up the dirty sheets and stretched the new ones in their place. Ruth's bed was the same double mattress Lin had in her own apartment, outfitted in bright red sheets adorned with the characters for fortune, prosperity, and love. Lin was reminded not of the dorm rooms in Qixian, where she and her unfortunate roommates—names she'd already begun to shake loose from her memory—slept stacked on top of each other like tins of preserved vegetables, but the beds in the red-brick flats where the foreign teachers lived.

Lin guessed that the furniture and decorations never changed much from year to year. Every summer, old teachers would leave, and, every fall, new ones would be hired by the waishiban to take their place. The teachers might be different in any number of ways, but the rooms and the lives they occupied would bear the invisible traces of the occupants who'd come before. Lin began to wonder about Ruth the same way she used to about Travis and Liz. She understood that her own story was a tapestry composed of all the people in her past. It was important to honor that lineage because, in some way, it would come to define her, too.

Ruth moved from a seated position to lying down, drawing the fresh sheets over her.

"Oh and could you refill Tomo's bowl?" she asked.

Lin had helped Ruth get Tomo—a shaggy-haired mutt with a slightly smushed nose—from the shelter, nearly the last dog available anywhere with the sudden uptick in adoptions. Dogs were needier than cats, but Ruth was all too happy to oblige. Lin liked to give Ruth a hard time, insisting she treated him better than she did most people.

"What did you learn in school today?" Ruth asked.

"Dressing wounds," Lin said. She scooted up in the red plastic stool next to Ruth's bedside. She placed a plastic cup of water by the nightstand and wrung her hands over her knees. It felt like being a child again, sitting inches from the floor, looking up at her grandmother as she spoke.

"Wonderful," Ruth said, "maybe you can help me with my ankle?" Ruth had undergone surgery the previous year for a fall, but the wound hadn't yet fully healed.

"My professor still hasn't said anything yet about practicing," Lin started, but Ruth just waved her hand.

"You're going places, I can tell," she said. "Didn't you say you were already at the top of your class? If I wanted someone else's help, I would've asked for it a long time ago."

For years, Ruth resisted the idea of having a home health aide. But she made an exception for Lin. She was better off than the patients Lin had been taught about at Seattle Central—where she'd recently had her transfer request approved—who couldn't take care of themselves. Ruth didn't have diabetes or congestive heart failure or psoriasis, illnesses whose names Lin had to sound out and repeat before being able to commit to memory. She'd long felt that the only thing Ruth was sick with was loneliness.

"Have you ever considered a nursing home?" Lin asked. In China, nursing homes were still a foreign concept. Most of the elders in Yuci lived in small communities with extended networks of relatives or neighbors and relied on each other for help. Increasingly, that was beginning to change—as younger generations felt less guilt about institutionalizing relatives—but their lives still didn't feel as isolated as they did in the states. Lin thought she'd be the last person to espouse the value of company. But if the preceding six months had taught her anything, it was that there was something useful—if not vital—about human connection.

Ruth shook her head. "Independence," she declared. "I didn't leave the camps only to be trapped in someone else's idea of home."

"So instead you're stuck here with me?"

"When you get your degree, you'll be too busy to deal with me anymore," Ruth said, turning to face the wall. "Either that, or I'll be dead."

"Don't joke about that," Lin said, "it's only two years away."

"Not for someone with a cold heart or a weak stomach," Ruth said. "Luckily, you have neither." She turned back toward Lin, her face suddenly glowing. "You know, looking back, it really feels like I've lived such an ordinary life. But whose life is truly ordinary?"

Lin smiled. To have lived through internment. Relocated far from home. Persevered into her eighties. "It sounds like a pretty extraordinary life to me."

Ruth pointed a finger toward the door. "I left a little extra on the front table," she said, "don't forget to take it on your way out."

"I'll see you tomorrow," Lin said, looping her bag over her shoulder and squeezing past the boxes in the foyer.

"The relationship between an elder and a caregiver is one of an empty and a full vessel," Professor Reynolds said in class. "The caregiver pours resources into the empty elder."

Lin was sitting in the lecture hall, three students to each row, with masks on and the windows open. She was grateful not to be stuck taking remedial English a second time, but all the requirements she needed for the nursing major were new. Her familiarity with animals didn't carry over to all the practical skills necessary for adult critical care: taking vital signs, assisting with mobility issues, administering medication.

Lin scribbled the words down in a notebook. But if a caregiver pours all their resources into the elder, then isn't the caregiver depleted?

"The elderly retreat even faster into themselves as their confusion and uncertainty grows, thereby speeding up their own decline," Professor Reynolds went on.

Lin had already begun to feel that deep, sad exhaustion during some of her visits with Ruth. When Ruth had asked Lin to visit more frequently, she didn't fully grasp how physically demanding it would be. She wasn't even sure why Ruth had taken a liking to her. There was no such thing as an Asian consciousness in China. Everyone had a national ethos or a regional pride or a fondness for a local cuisine. You weren't even Chinese so much as you were Fuzhouren or drank Shanxi fenjiu or rooted for the Beijing Shougang. Years of habituated animosity were hard to remedy.

And yet, in America, things were different. Asians were lumped into a single category, forced to sink or swim as one. The very idea of the International District seemed antithetical to all the animosity and bloodshed that stained the Asian continent. To believe that something as tenuous as a pan-Asian identity could even exist seemed delusional. Lin ran down the roster of residents in her head: Yu and Chin right alongside Ng and Patel. One floor down, Shin and Po around the corner from Ramirez. If it could work at Hirabayashi Place—and with her and Ruth—Lin conceded, at least that was a start.

"Each of your patients will be unique, and there is nothing quite like getting to see firsthand the positive impact you will have on someone's life," the professor continued. "We can be a kinder, gentler nation when we allow individuals to recover. And nursing is the perfect vehicle to do that."

Lin found pleasure in helping Ruth age gracefully. Of knowing that death was imminent but doing everything she could to make the best of the time that was left. She'd learned to master the delicate art of mourning, the grief of losing those closest to her—her pets. And yet, she'd already begun to blur the line between personal and professional, the first cardinal sin of nursing. There was a camaraderie she felt with Ruth that surpassed the warmth she had for her gerbils or her snakes or even Boom.

If she'd learned anything from Ruth, it was that it was impossible to ever judge a person fully. Lin found it hard to imagine other clients, the kinds of people who, perhaps, had made life in this country for her so volatile. But for every person who let her down, there would be someone to reaffirm her faith in humanity. Each time Lin had been pushed to the brink, she learned to trust in those around her. Since having left China, she'd never anticipated missing the joys of being part of a collective. This vocation, more than the need brought on by the virus, was also, for Lin, the desire to make sure her community would be protected.

Chi le mei you? a text flashed across Lin's phone. Lin rolled over in bed to answer, but before she could respond, a flurry of other messages followed:

> *Is it still raining there?*
> *Do you have enough clothing?*
> *How were classes yesterday?*
> *Are you feeling sick?*

What began as a tepid attempt by Lin to get back in touch with her mother had quickly developed into a daily torrent over WeChat.

Everything's fine, Lin wrote back. She knew her mother would never come to the states, and that this was the closest she would get to being part of Lin's life.

I need you to text me when you go to sleep, Qi Fei insisted. *I want to make sure you're safe.*

I will, Lin wrote, knowing that her concern wasn't without merit. She had considered regular calling or even video but, for the moment, didn't want to push her luck.

Don't go out past dark, and always make sure you walk in groups.

Hao le, hao le, Lin thumbed back, before adding: *Make sure you take care of yourself, too, Ma.* Lin still wasn't used to the feeling of holding her mother in her hands, the way she'd had to keep even the people she cared about most at arm's length through these many months.

Sometimes I just wish you were closer, Qi Fei texted.

Lin and her mother both seemed to agree on the subjects that were to be avoided: career, marriage, the future. The path that had once appeared so straightforward to Lin was now entirely up in the air. She knew she couldn't stay in the US forever but didn't know how long it would be until she went back.

I have to finish what I started here, Ma, Lin wrote. For a long time, Lin withheld her degree program from her mother. She thought Qi Fei would be disappointed that Lin was only studying to be a nurse and not a doctor. But Qi Fei surprised her.

In every river, there are small fish and big fish. But they swim just the same.

In the mornings, Lin left for classes at Seattle Central. By the afternoon, she was at Hirabayashi Place doing deliveries. Then it was back for more classes in phlebotomy, learning how to drain a catheter, or changing a pressure dressing with compression wraps. In the evenings, she bought whatever groceries she still needed at Lam's Seafood or Hau Hau or Golden Palace before visiting Ruth, sometimes cooking for her too, or just talking until it was time for bed.

On the weekends, without school or work, Lin tried to get away. She boarded the bus at Mt. Baker that went all the way to the Issaquah Alps. There were two hiking routes she got to know by heart, learning the curves in the bend that led to a small creek, the scenic overlook hidden beyond a half-closed trail, the best place to pick salmonberries among the overgrown brambles. The mountains at Yellowstone may have been more majestic, but Lin had felt like she was teetering at the remotest reaches of the globe. Here, as she headed back toward the city at the end of the day, she never ceased to be amazed at just how close she could live and still touch the natural world.

Lin didn't think much of Gua in the weeks that followed. Of her round face, dimpled like a qianbao, poking out of the mesh of her green sleeping bag. Or her quick mouth that could stanch an argument—or exacerbate it—in a minute flat. How there was a time when Lin felt she might very well not have made it this far without her. Gua would have been back in Jinan by now, American degree in hand. She'd done exactly what she'd set out to do, which, considering all that had transpired, felt even more remarkable than it might have a year prior.

For all Lin knew, she'd already gotten a job and started working. Lin wondered whether Gua's new boss had been impressed by the neat rows of English letters embossed on her Tri-C cardstock. Gua wouldn't have been anything unique before. Hundreds of thousands had been educated on American shores on the way back to China. But because of the travel ban, Chinese students who had left the states in the spring couldn't return to classes—and no one knew for how long. Perhaps it was possible, in the end, to be the last of something, the only one remaining inside after the surrounding walls had been sealed shut.

Lin would have nearly stopped thinking about Liz, too, had she not received a message out of the blue. She was leaving an afternoon lecture class when a green chat bubble on her phone lit up.

You'll never guess where I am.

Lin reeled. The last time she'd communicated with Lin was back when she'd still been in the fangcang in Shanghai, the view of the convention center piercing the grainy video. Had she really forgotten to write back to see if Liz had recovered? She felt awful. How did she expect to care for patients when she couldn't be bothered to remember her friend?

But just as quickly as the thought arrived, Lin's phone pinged again, this time with a call and a video of Liz on the other line.

"Hold on," Liz said. She was wearing a blue headband and no mask, her bangs swaying. She looked healthy, almost jubilant. The camera pivoted away from Liz's face and Lin saw the front gate of the university in Qixian, the streamers strung between the thick pylons welcoming students back to campus.

"You went back?" Lin asked, almost in disbelief.

"I just arrived," Liz nodded.

"Did you need to pick up your stuff?" Lin remembered how adamant Liz sounded on the phone about leaving Qixian for good and couldn't conceive of why else she'd want to return.

"I'm staying," Liz said. Lin could feel the glow of her smile through the phone. The camera kept panning, and Lin saw the gate where she'd first squeezed through her crates of pets with Qi Fei a year ago. She remembered clutching the hongbao as she watched her mother turn back to her motorbike to leave. Part of Lin felt sad to see it, a time in her life when her biggest disappointment was having not made a single friend. She had sympathy for Liz now, and how hard it was to make a new life somewhere else. There was no way to properly convey to her—or her mother—all the travesties, big and small, that had occurred since.

"Liz," Lin said.

"Yes?"

"Can I ask you a favor?"

"Anything."

"Would you promise to check on my mom for me?"

Before Lin knew it, the days were becoming longer, the evenings warmer. Walking around at night, Lin was comforted by the neon lights on the signs in Chinatown, the soft curve of the pagoda roofs. Despite the doors and windows still boarded up with plywood, the junkies and beggars who loitered down alleyways, she felt emboldened. At Tri-C, she couldn't turn a corner without drawing stares, but in the International District, no one saw her as any different. It was easy being an outsider in America, Lin thought, so long as she was surrounded by other outsiders, too.

Above the restaurants with their glowing noodle boxes were apartments connected by a series of fire escapes. Some of the top floors had balconies with large columns and trim white railings, black characters embossed in gold. Lin had heard of the first Chinese people who, a century ago, left to go abroad to make a name for themselves. If they were successful, they would start a family association, proof that anyone who immigrated after would know their forebears had made a mark, a claim to the land.

If not quite at home, Lin felt like a weary traveler, granted access to a door after having finally proved her worth. The same door, now behind her, might allow her to come and go, but there would always be the looming threat of being barred from entering once more. Ruth had told Lin that the worst of the violence and stigma would gradually lessen, as it did with the Japanese, but would never go away entirely. There were conditions to any kind of freedom, both good and bad. Racism was an endemic fact of this country, but resistance was just as foundational.

"Remember that old line we were fed in the camps?" Ruth had said. "With liberty and justice for all?" She brought her in close. "I'll tell you a secret. I still believe it."

"Today's the Obon Festival," Ruth announced. It was Friday morning. Wildfires had been burning out east, forcing evacuations, and smoke was blanketing Seattle. Lin had arrived early to Ruth's apartment because classes were canceled and grocery deliveries postponed on account of the flagging air quality.

"What's that?"

"A day of remembrance. Every summer, people dress up in kimono and yukata and dance to the sway of the minyo band." Ruth smiled. "Of course, the obaasan have all the best moves." She jutted out her hip and did a slow twirl in front of Lin.

"I used to look forward to it all year growing up," Ruth continued. "Why don't we go somewhere to celebrate?"

"Have you looked outside?" Lin asked. Through the window, the sky was a hazy auburn, the color of rusted pipes.

"Doesn't scare me," Ruth said, pointing a thumb at her sternum. "They're going to need more than a little smoke to keep me out. Besides," she said, hooking an arm around Lin's elbow, "at my age, you can't afford to waste a minute."

It was noon by the time they made their way to the first floor and stepped onto the sidewalk. The sun was out, but it was impossible to tell through the smog. The air was humid and thick, like the autumn in Shanxi before the sandstorms arrived. Lin didn't think to check the AQI—it would only have made her worry more about Ruth—but with masks already looped around their ears, she didn't feel quite as guilty.

Lin would have preferred to go all the way to the Sculpture Garden, to the grassy knoll at the top of the winding path with a view of the Sound. But she conceded, for the sake of time and the air sticking like hot haw fruit to her lungs, on heading due east on Jackson, to where the street dead ended at the piers, and where they could still see the water.

"Lin," Ruth said. "Hold my hand."

And Lin did. From the outside, it didn't look the least bit strange. The area was a tapestry of intersecting streets with a rumpled, unfinished quality. They strode past empty bus stops, trash that languished in corner bins, streets crossed by rail tracks and others lined with construction.

Lin never tired of seeing it. At the water's edge, Lin gaped at the shimmering lights of West Seattle, the armada of cranes like steel giraffes floating on the surface. She could still make out the islands of Bainbridge and Vashon beyond, obscured by fog. Her home province was landlocked, and it was a thousand kilometers to the coast. Lin loved watching the ebb and flow of the waves, how some of the seaweed lapped up against the rocks and remained rooted to the shore.

Ruth still hadn't let go of Lin's hand, and Lin didn't make any motion to take it back. Without warning, Ruth stopped short, and Lin turned, fearing that something was wrong. But Ruth simply opened her arms to the breeze.

"This reminds me of when we used to dance odori and kabuki after the war."

Ruth told Lin that cultural activities were forbidden in the camps, both on account of the guards, but also to avoid accusations of demonstrating loyalty to Japan. The games they did play were devoid of any cultural baggage. They sang English songs, watched American baseball, practiced English penmanship.

"But we kept the dances alive in our minds," Ruth said. "We had to be resilient. But resilience wasn't all teeth gritting and muscle flexing. We had to make our own joy." It was easy to lose sight of joy when every day away from home was a battle of endurance. But as long as she stayed in this country, Lin vowed to never lose that sense of wonder.

"When we were allowed back to Seattle, the cultural groups gradually got together again," Ruth continued. "Matsuba Kai, Mimasu Kai, Hatsune Kai. Not all of them survived, but there was something special about being able to express this thing we'd all kept buried for so long."

Elders had become known to Lin as a critical connection to history, the only way to learn from the wrongs of the past and correct them. Lin looked out at the Olympic range in the distance, hazy inkblots rendered by a calligrapher's thick brush. For Ruth, the past was as stark as the present, as if the two were painted on adjacent canvases, hanging side by side.

"Can you show me?" Lin asked.

Ruth, nodding, placed her other hand in Lin's. They moved slowly, Lin supporting Ruth's wrists with her fingers. Ruth stretched out one leg and then turned her body in a circle.

"You try now," she told Lin. Lin turned and, as she did, she took in the docks, the ferry terminal, the wide stretch of water that separated her from her birthplace. Lin smelled salt water in the air but something else too. The smoke called to mind the coal furnaces in Qixian during the winter, grainy filaments of charcoal and soot that blotted the sky. The scent was both familiar and coarse, and though it wasn't pleasant, Lin breathed it in, smelling as she did the taste of freedom wrapped up in obligation, of responsibility to family entwined with responsibility to oneself, wondering all the while what it meant to belong somewhere and nowhere at the same time.

As long as you're here, you'll only have yourself. Gua's warning echoed in Lin's head, as she and Ruth stood dancing on the shore. She wasn't wrong, Lin thought. But for now, at least, we have each other.

18

Liz had never seen Qixian half as beautiful. Hot, but not nearly as humid as Shanghai, with the kind of blue skies she thought were only reserved for special delegations. It was still warm enough for a long skirt in the daytime, clear with a crisp chill at night. The sky was the same gash of purple and aquamarine she remembered from her first year, the smell of vinegar permeating the still air.

Having arrived on campus the previous November, Liz had missed the fall. She never knew that Qixian could have the kind of autumn she relished from her childhood: leaves in shades of reds and yellows, sidewalks crisscrossed in acorns and brown stems. It was like the months she'd been away had ceased to exist. Students crowded shoulder to shoulder in the cafeteria. The underground supermarket was fully stocked. Food vendors had returned to South Yard, replete with shoddy cooking oil. Liz found herself reveling in a kind of normal she didn't expect.

"Why are we doing this again?" Stephen asked, his arms looped around a bright red toaster oven. He'd just arrived from Shanghai that morning and didn't even have enough time to put down his bag.

"Doing what?" Liz asked. She dashed up the narrow path that led to the teaching building, a tray of cooking utensils and ingredients in her own outstretched hands: flour, eggs, bananas, baking powder.

"I thought you were an English teacher, not a contestant on *Dingji Chushi*," he said. Liz laughed. Stephen had made them watch reruns of *Master Chef* back when they were still in quarantine and Stephen was convinced his omelet-making prowess would've landed him a spot on the show. Liz, on the other hand, had fantasized about being a judge. She'd seen so many episodes that she could repeat their overblown adages word for word.

"*There is no innovation without risk,*" she quipped. "Besides, who says teachers can't have any fun?"

They hurried up the paved steps and through the long corridor. The walls had been repainted over the summer, but the color was already fading, chipped paint gathering in a patchwork of blue pastel at their feet. They passed the school nurse's office, the chemistry lab lined with beakers and vials, the still-partitionless bathroom that Liz had learned to avoid during class.

"On the right," Liz said, motioning Stephen with her elbow. He opened the door to her classroom, room 215, and set the oven down on the window ledge.

The roomful of students inhaled a collective breath. Elvis, the class monitor, a tall boy with foppish hair and appropriately long sideburns, stood up to help Liz arrange the items across the two front desks. The others were murmuring in Mandarin: *What was the oven for? Did Teacher Liz look different today? Is that man really her boyfriend?* Liz tried to ignore them and focus on her lesson plan. She still got nervous each time she went up to the podium. It wasn't until she broke the silence, heard her own voice echoing across the narrow room, that she could really believe she was a teacher.

"How are you?" Liz announced, scanning their still-new faces. Her students looked a lot like her previous ones, save for the addition of blue surgical masks.

"Fine," the class replied in unison, a holdover from primary school English that Liz was intent on rooting out.

"We have a special guest today," she said, pointing at her assistant-slash-sous chef perched in the front row. "Everyone, say hi to Stephen."

The class broke into spontaneous applause. Stephen turned and waved to the back of the room with the regality of a British nobleman. Despite having just spent twelve hours on an overnight train, Stephen was dressed to the nines: slacks, brown loafers, plaid shirt. Liz had tried to convince him that it wasn't necessary—most of what she used to wear to class was rarely more than a cardigan hastily thrown over a T-shirt—but he was insistent.

"When's the last time I got to dress up?" he'd asked. And even Liz decided, then, to wear a necklace and earrings, apply lipstick. In the mirror, it was almost easier that way to convince herself she was an entirely different person.

Stephen was facing the front of the classroom again, but Liz could still see the stares from her students boring into the back of his head. Evie, one of the more precocious girls, raised a thumb at Liz, before giggling and burying her face in a neighbor's shoulder. Liz was surprised to feel a new sensation at the podium: wonder. Her students preened at her and Stephen, not for the exceptionality of her foreignness, but for her novel approach to teaching.

"I hope you're hungry," she said, "because you're going to have to work for breakfast." Liz passed around the ingredients, already surprised at how comfortable she felt seeing a bunch of bananas or a tub of baking powder not being first wiped down with disinfectant.

"Can I have two volunteers, please?"

Elvis and Evie filed up to the front of the room. They each demonstrated measuring, pouring, and mixing the dry ingredients as Liz went over pronunciation on the board. She instructed them to crack an egg into each bowl and whisk it, eliciting a whoop from her other students like they were a live studio audience. The competition was a new addition to the baking lesson she'd piloted in her first year. It was part of a group of lessons so successful with her former students that Liz had made a note to do them again, tweaking them over time like a good stand-up routine. Teaching sometimes felt that way to her, this long, meandering search for the punchline.

"Time's up," she declared, like Cao Kefan in his blazer and sunglasses, sporting a mean grin. The judges on *Master Chef* always seemed so unapologetic when it came to making their outlandish demands. There was always some twist half-way through the episode, a secret ingredient the contestants hadn't prepared for.

"Who wants to share their recipe?" Liz asked, as she placed both loaf pans in the oven and set the timer.

At first, no one said a word. Liz was tempted to call on Stephen, just to tease him, until a girl in the back row raised a cautious hand. Liz didn't recognize her. She'd had each student, on the first day of class, pose for a photo with their name—like convicts getting booked into a county jail—and, at night, she flipped through them to see how many she could remember. But by the third class, Liz was still struggling with her roster of 120 students across four sections and drew a blank.

"Alma," the girl offered, and Liz nodded, impressed she'd chosen such a unique identity in English.

Alma read out her recipe for banana bread, and, when the timer buzzed, Stephen helped Liz pass out the muffins that had blossomed in the baking tins. Liz indulged her students in the fruits of their labor—warm, fragrant, and altogether foreign—before eventually crowning both contestants as winners. When "Fang Xue Ge" blared over the loudspeaker, the students wiped down their tables and filed out. All of them, except for Alma, who waited by the door of the classroom.

"Your recipe was perfect," Liz said, motioning to leave.

"Teacher Liz," Alma asked. "Would you like to get lunch sometime?"

Whenever Liz ran into any of her former students, she flushed with shame at having abandoned them halfway through the school year. Liz felt the same creeping guilt in the pit of her stomach, this time the fear of getting too close with another student.

"I don't think—" Liz started. Alma was petite with dark green eyes and sideswept bangs. She was a freshman this year, just like Lin had been. Liz remembered all the trips to the market with Lin, the meals in South Yard, the hours they spent talking by the track after dinner. None of it felt the same without her there.

Liz smiled, extending her hand. "It would be my pleasure."

"Not bad," Stephen said, as they walked back from the classroom. "I wish my English classes in college were that much fun."

"Maybe you would've learned something, too," Liz joked. She turned to face him. "I was actually worried for a minute. I never asked permission to bring a toaster oven to class."

"What do you mean?"

"My first year, the Foreign Affairs Office couldn't care less what I did in class. But this term, I had to hand over my entire teaching syllabus to Headmistress Zong to check for 'sensitive material.'"

"Par for the course," Stephen said with a shrug.

"It just goes against everything I learned in school," Liz said. "What's the point of teaching without freedom of expression?"

"You should ask your government the same question," Stephen said. He reminded Liz of her country's own Patriotic Education Campaign—banned books, revisionist history, attacks on public education—and she wondered if it may not be all that different.

Liz hadn't forgiven the administration in Qixian for what they did to Lin, but she didn't think it was right to punish her students for her refusal to see eye to eye with them. Not having a foreign English teacher didn't benefit anyone. It may have been naïve, but Liz had faith in the next generation and her obligation to teach them. She wanted to believe she could have misgivings about the government while, at the same time, contribute to a better future. How else, by the same logic, could she ever rationalize going back to the states?

"I'm sorry in advance about the accommodations," Liz said. "Let's just say it's going to be different from what you're used to."

"I don't know, I kind of like it here," Stephen said. "It's peaceful. I bet you can even see the stars at night."

It was Stephen's first time in Qixian—his first time in the province, period—and Liz delighted in being the one who knew the best restaurants for mengmian or juanjuan, who got to show him the fields studded with sorghum and dates, for a change.

"Isn't it Mid-Autumn Festival this weekend?" Liz asked. "We should look for the moon tonight."

"I'd like that," Stephen said.

It seemed so novel, after living in a big city, that Liz should celebrate something as ordinary as the night sky. But even in Qixian, where plumes of factory smoke clouded the air at night, she knew it wasn't something to take for granted. It had taken a lot for her to convince Stephen why she wanted to move back to Qixian after their trip to Meihua, though an equal part of that exercise had been in rationalizing the decision for herself.

They arrived at the front door of the red-brick flat, the very same one Liz had lived in before leaving for Dandong. The only difference was that she now lived alone. Travis was gone, as were Collin and Jim. The school was locked down over Chinese New Year, and anyone outside was told to stay away until the situation improved. Classes only resumed online that spring, and, Liz assumed, when the other foreign teachers were offered the chance to take one of the last flights out of the country by the American embassy in Beijing, they all did.

All she knew was that when she bit her tongue and told Headmistress Zong she was interested in coming back, the headmistress agreed right away. Visas were frozen, and the restrictions on immigration didn't appear to be lifted anytime soon. It was the other Americans now—and not Liz—who would have to wait for paperwork that might never materialize.

The school had eventually hired new foreign teachers, but they were all teaching remotely. The most coveted class by far now was with Liz. Liz couldn't imagine doing something like her cooking lesson over the internet, already kneecapped by the Great Firewall. The old precedents for what it meant to teach—along with being a foreigner in the small town—had seemingly vanished overnight. Liz was no longer bound by the code that compelled her fidelity to the other foreign men. She could be her own representative of what an American could be.

Liz propped open the screen door and Stephen strode in, setting the toaster oven down on the small stool in the living room.

"So this is it," Stephen said. "I've heard so much about this place."

The house Liz had left for months hardly felt any different when she returned. Liz felt a little like she did when she first arrived, when past students would come over and tell her about the foreign teachers who had once lived there. They spoke of them like people they might both know intimately, referencing them only by their first names. Liz had learned so much about their lives, despite never having met them.

"Is that toaster yours?" Stephen asked. Liz shook her head.

"Why do you keep it in the living room?"

"I guess I never thought it felt out of place." She motioned to the cupboard full of house shoes, the bookshelf that stayed stocked with titles like a lending library. "To be honest, I can't tell you where half this stuff is from."

Liz remembered being surprised the first time she was told that she'd stolen Ray's life. It was true she'd inherited Ray's job, her room, some of her old belongings. Even greeting her by the front door were Ray's rubber slippers. She hadn't ever thought of it that way before, but the same was true of her now. Liz knew that whenever she left, someone would arrive to take up the remnants of her previous life and try and make sense of them, too.

Stephen sat down on the couch. The green-print fabric now seemed old-fashioned to Liz—even dour—after having spent so long in Stephen's apartment. It was noon and the students were all breaking for lunch. In the distance, Liz could hear the same odious Kenny G ballad bleating from the musical fountain.

"Let's skip the living room," she said.

In her bedroom, Liz lowered the blinds. She was back to contending with people loitering outside her window, the Foreign Affairs Office knocking on the front door at any moment. Only, something was different now. Travis wasn't on the other side of her wall. She wasn't fantasizing about taking a street vendor to South Yard. She had every right to what she was doing.

"I've thought about this for a long time," she said, reaching for Stephen with both hands.

On Sunday night, Liz shared a cab with Stephen to the train station in the center of town. It was the same place where she'd taken so many weekend trips to Taiyuan with the other foreign teachers. Stephen had booked an overnight berth in the soft sleeper again, with its own door and attendant in the morning to wake him up when he arrived in Shanghai.

"That went by way too fast," Stephen said, his backpack looped over one shoulder. "I don't think I can make it all the way until October."

Liz had already booked her train to Shanghai for the National Week holiday, but on the hard sleeper instead. She didn't make nearly as much as Stephen did, but at least now she didn't have to rely on anyone else.

"I'll miss you, too," Liz said. She remembered when she'd first made the decision to go to Shanghai with Stephen. They were finishing dinner in Dandong and, the next thing she knew, she was boarding a train. She laughed a little at how naive she'd been then, how easily it was to lose herself in the idea of something larger—her lineage, her family, her mother.

"It's not too late to come join me."

"Long-distance isn't so bad," Liz said. "We may both do better with a little space. Besides, my contract only goes through next spring. What difference can a year make, right?" She smiled, but Stephen's face was stern.

"After everything you told me, I'm just worried about you."

He wasn't wrong to be concerned. Probably the most challenging part of returning for Liz was that she had no way of knowing whether the feelings she experienced in her first year would come back to haunt her again. But this time, she felt like she was ready.

"I'll be all right," Liz said.

"Have you considered getting a cat?" Stephen asked, and Liz gave him a shove.

"I'll see you in October," she said, wrapping both arms around him and squeezing tight. "It's not like you don't know where to find me."

She followed Stephen's shadow until it disappeared into the tunnel. It was both a comfort and a worry that Stephen could track her—turn the health code on her app red too—if he so wished. Still, Liz didn't have any reason to suspect that he would. She wanted things to work out with Stephen, but she knew she needed to live her own life, too. There was enough uncertainty in the world.

The following weekend, Liz was on the bus to Yuci when it stopped without warning. She peered out the window and saw the source of the delay: a funeral procession. The crowd stretched the length of the block, a swell of older men and women at the front. They were dressed in white head scarves and flowing white robes. Liz was shocked at how pure it looked, like dying was an act tantamount to being cast in light and reborn. She had never seen anything like it. Their heads were bowed and their hands adopted a praying position at their chests. Behind them, a caravan of white pickup trucks adorned with large peacock-colored wreaths bore through, obscuring the flow of traffic.

When Pearl died, people had worn black to the funeral. Liz had done so herself, not knowing any better. Her mom would likely have been the only one to correct them, but she was gone. As in all things, Liz would have to learn for herself. Stumble. Make mistakes. Accept the consequences. It had been that way with Phil. She never should have entrusted him with

Lin. But at the same time, could it have been any other way? Lin was in America, and Liz was in China, each doing what they felt they needed to survive.

"Sometimes there isn't another way," her father had said. "Eventually you learn to make do with what you have."

Maybe Nurse Wang was right. All her life, she'd carried too much of her mom's energy. Liz needed to remember that there was always light in dark places. Loss had come to everyone, and many had not survived, but those who did now had a choice about how they lived. Liz would need to write a new history, with her at the center.

"I'm sorry I'm late," Liz said, when she reached Qi Fei's door.

"Don't be," she replied, welcoming her into the narrow hallway. "I'm just happy to see you."

Qi Fei prepared dinner, and the two of them sat down, a plate of pork slices and spicy cold cucumber between them. Periodically, Qi Fei disappeared into the kitchen and returned with more dishes: albacore and bok choy, pine nuts and corn kernels, noodles with pork sauce.

"You didn't have to make so much," Liz said.

"How often do I get to see my daughter's best friend?"

Liz paused. "Do you still talk with Lin?" she asked, like dipping her toe into a hot bath.

"We send messages every day," Qi Fei said, beaming. There were photos of Lin everywhere, even more than the last time Liz was at the house.

"I brought something for dessert," Liz said. At the table, she slid across the metal tin of mooncakes that Stephen had brought up from Shanghai. A week had passed since Mid-Autumn Festival, but she'd wanted to bring them over nonetheless.

"These are sweet," Qi Fei said, biting into one.

"Aren't all mooncakes sweet?" Liz asked. In the states, Liz had only ever seen mooncakes with a thick filling of red bean or lotus seed studded with an egg yolk.

Qi Fei shook her head. "In the north, our mooncakes are made with meat and nuts," she said. "They have a flaky crust, more like a pastry than a cake. They go especially well with wine."

From the cabinet, she pulled down a bottle of guihua jiu and poured Liz a tumbler. It tasted like a cross between an apricot and a peach with a touch of cinnamon. It was a floral wine, mellow and sweet, customary for reunions.

"To the new semester," Qi Fei said, holding a glass up to Liz before sipping it down. Liz finished her drink and looked through the window at the moon. It was glowing bright in the night sky, though not quite as large. Tomorrow, it would be waxing or waning, Liz thought, never in one constant state.

"I hope she's found the right place," Qi Fei said finally. "I don't think I ever told her how proud of her I am."

"It's not too late," Liz implored her. "It would mean everything coming from you."

The light in the sky was dim now, just a haze on the horizon. Liz headed back to campus, but instead of taking the bus, she decided to walk. A couple of street stalls were set up on the curb. Single lightbulbs dangling over a charcoal spit. Glass display cases containing cold translucent noodles. A man roasting sweet potatoes in a refashioned oil drum. She passed black cabs offering rides, hawkers with wares spread out on large cotton print mats, closed retail stores and pay-by-the-hour hotels, dark and ominous, like the concrete hulls of wrecked ships.

Some days were easy: the freedom to go outside safely, to explore different pockets of the city. Other days, Liz was overwhelmed at the prospect of starting over. She felt at the mercy of some larger force, like being tossed to the wind, with no control over where it might take her. The thought of returning to America had crossed her mind more than once. Part of her yearned for the feeling of being back in a place where, even if she didn't agree with everything that was being done, at least she understood it.

But despite the shoving and shouting, the poverty and the dust, the censorship and the surveillance, being back in Qixian was cathartic. She'd begun to appreciate how things worked: how to make amends, to cope with the surprises and disappointments that occupied each day, to interact with the people who populated this tiny town at the edge of the world. It was impossible to know how long this feeling would last, but Liz vowed to savor it while she could.

It was late by the time she reached her door. On her phone was the picture of her and Qi Fei that she'd taken when she left Yuci. Later, sitting on the edge of her bed, the curtains billowing out like sails, she wanted to send it to Lin. She scrolled through her other photos. Liz posing with her class at the top of Mt. Feng. Lunch of doujiang and bing at the underground supermarket. The lifeguard at the swimming pool doing the butterfly stroke. A kitten, its nose marked by a white smudge, crossing back and forth in front of her window.

She wouldn't have been able to explain what made her do it, but it seemed better, in that moment, to put her phone away instead.

Liz wrapped her feet under the thick sheets and turned off the light. A gust of wind had blown the latch on her window open, and she breathed in the smell of date trees and salt in the vinegar tannins. She heard the crickets and the tree frogs croaking in the distance, the sound of their noises communicated across the dark sky, as they slowly lulled her to sleep.

Cover and Section Photo Credits

Cover by Elisha Zepeda. See below for photographer information on individual pieces:

Cat head: NYPL From the Public Library

Peach Blossom: Ngoc Mai Pham

Grain: Melissa Askew via Unsplash

Rice Paddy: Joel Vodell via Unsplash

Tea Ticket: Wikimedia Commons Zhengzhou Railway Administration

Fall Leaves: Freepik

Snowflakes: Freepik

Cherry Blossoms: Freepik

Cocktail glass: Freepik

Starfish: Freepik

Acknowledgments

Writing and publishing a book depends on the enormous sacrifice and generosity of so many individuals. While this list will necessarily be incomplete, I'm so grateful to everyone who has offered encouragement, support, and free therapy at various stages of this novel's journey.

Thank you first and foremost to my agent and friend, Chad Luibl, whose tireless advocacy and dedication made the publication of this novel possible. To my editor, Caitlyn Limbaugh, for believing in this book and offering invaluable improvements. To the entire team at Janklow & Nesbit and Regalo Press/Simon & Schuster for their care and attention in championing this novel and bringing it to fruition. Kate Post, for her impeccable copyedits, Aleigha Koss for managing the process, and Alisha Gorder and Jennifer Huang for all things publicity and promotion.

Thank you to my first readers for their unsparing time and feedback, as well as those who offered sage counsel on the novel in its early drafts: Roma Panganiban, Jane Chun, Lillian Huang Cummins, Robin Boord, Leah De Forest, Scott Grabel, Ian Shapira, Peter Turchi, Isabelle Bleecker, and especially Lauren Groff, without whom this book would not exist.

To the incredible community at the MFA Program for Writers at Warren Wilson College, where I first learned to call myself a writer. My faculty supervisors, whose guidance propelled this novel and the stories that inspired it: Anna Solomon, Chris Castellani, CJ Hribal, and Lauren Groff. Deb Allbery, for the call that changed my life. My incredible cohort, Phantom Cows, and the friendship and support of so many classmates, including Sarah Audsley, Lillian Huang Cummins, Joy Deng, Jodie Free, Sonya Larson, Kirsten Lind, Yiming Ma, Juli Min, Roseanne Pereira, Jeremy Scheuer, Aaron Strumwasser, and Annette Wong. The afterlife is bright.

To Hugo House, where I wrote the first words of this novel, and to my extended literary family in Seattle, for inviting me into a writing community beyond my wildest dreams: Rob Arnold, Sarah Blood, Margot Kahn Case, Joyce Chen, Courtney Emerson, Katie Lee Ellison, Josh Fomon, Cal Lee, Bonnie Lei, Susan Lieu, Pepe Montero, Abi Pollokoff, Bretty Rawson, Juan Carlos Reyes, Yitka Winn, Kate Wang, Jane Wong, Diana Xin, and Kristen Millares Young.

For patiently sitting through interviews that greatly informed the writing of this book, thank you to Katie Abbott, Kent Chen, Lynn Chen, Jason Fields, Chiayo Kuo, Liang Li, Meher Makda, Juli Min, and Qiuting Tam. For additional research assistance, thank you to Josh Chin, Bethany Ellington, Evelyn Hsieh, Taiyo Scanlon-Kimura, Liza Lin, Annie Malcolm, Adedoyin Olateru-Olagbegi, Alice Tams, and Chuzhen Wang, as well as the insight of many books and scholarly articles including *Racial Melancholia, Racial Dissociation* by David Eng and Shinhee Han; *Racing Romance* by Kumiko Nemoto; and *Under Red Skies* by Karoline Kan. Thank you to SCIDpda for the opportunity to volunteer with seniors in the Chinatown-International District from June-December 2020.

Thank you to writers in high places who offered support with so many aspects of the existential vagaries of the writing life as well as the business of publishing. I feel so fortunate to call you not only mentors but friends: Steve Almond, Kayla Min Andrews, Cinelle Barnes, Quincy Carroll, Jessamine Chan, K-Ming Chang, Lan Samantha Chang, Alexander Chee, Karissa Chen, Kirstin Chen, Ava Chin, Sarah Cypher, Peter Ho Davies, Danielle Evans, Carolyn Ferrell, Jamie Ford, Garth Greenwell, Jennifer Haigh, Jennifer Haupt, Peter Hessler, Hua Hsu, Vanessa Hua, Gish Jen, Fabienne Josaphat, Rachel Khong, Angie Kim, Sally Kim, Lisa Ko, E. J. Koh, Ananda Lima, Amy Lin, Karin Lin-Greenberg, Kate McQuade, Joshua Mohr, Peter Mountford, Viet Thanh Nguyen, Dominic Smith, Kaitlin Solimine, Belinda Tang, Vauhini Vara, and Kim Zhang.

Thank you to the residencies, conferences, and grants that supported me and the persevering staff who so selflessly facilitated these vital parts of my writing journey: Cathy Linh Che and Ryan Lee Wong at Kundiman; Josh Lambert at Yiddish Book Center; Bob Boyers at the New York State Summer Writers Institute; Randall Nadeau and Charlie Cheng at Fulbright

Taiwan; Levi Fuller and Joan Rabinowitz at Jack Straw Cultural Center; Pam Houston and Karen Nelson at Writing By Writers; Amy Stolls and Katy Day at the National Endowment for the Arts and the judges for the 2022 Literature Fellowship; Donica Bettanin and Lili Stern at PEN America and the judges for the 2023 PEN/Bellwether Prize for Socially Engaged Fiction; Adam Latham, Gwen Kirby, and Leah Stewart at the Sewanee Writers' Conference; Sheila Pleasants at the Virginia Center for the Creative Arts; Libby Pratt and Lisbeth White at Centrum; Jane Hodges at Mineral School; and Jared Jackson and Ricardo Hernandez at Poets & Writers.

Thank you to the generous editors and outlets who published my work or commissioned it to be performed on stage: Nelson Ng at *LOST*; Alec Ash and Tom Pellman at *The Anthill*; Will Murtha and Alex Co at *Sage*; Matt Straus and Drue Mirchand at *Kitchen Work*; Ryan Thorpe at *The Shanghai Literary Review*; Corinne Segal at *Literary Hub*; Jeremy Goldkorn, Kaiser Kuo, and Anthony Tao at *The China Project*; Laurie Rosenblatt at *LEON Literary Review*; Elizabeth Gonzalez James at *The Rumpus*; Jill Wasberg at *International Examiner*; Briana Gwin and Lisa Chen at *The Seventh Wave*; Colleen Kinder and Aube Rey Lescure at *Off Assignment*; Tajja Isen at *Catapult*; Koye Oyedeji at CommonLit; Jen Soong at *ANMLY*; Brandon Stosuy, Rose Lazar, and Emily Simonson at *Sad Happens*; Candace Walsh and Dalanie Beach at *Quarter After Eight*; Wes Weddell at Bushwick Book Club Seattle; Emily Hammond and Jeri Howitt at Stories on Stage Davis; David Chiu, Maryam Chishti, and Jenni Rudolph at The Braid; and Anna Vodicka and Rebecca Richardson at All Classical.

Thank you to the many writerly friendships that have grounded me in community, accountability, and sanity in the years since this book's gestation: Ricki Schecter, Courtney Han, Matt Rennels, Adrian Perez, Brendan Ross, Amy Dong, Josh Charlson, Allison Kingsley, Yvette DeChavez, Elena Dudum, Jane Marchant, Rose Howse, the Rogue Grinders, the 2022 Seventh Wave Spring Digital Residents; the 2023 PEN/Bellwether Prize finalists; the Seattle City of Literature Board of Directors; the 2024 Incubator cohort; the 2025 Debut Babes; and the 2025 Get the Word Out fiction cohort.

Thank you to the dedicated network of literarians who have given me the opportunity to talk about books with a host of talented authors: Kait Heacock and Rick Simonson at Elliott Bay Book Company; Stesha Brandon at Seattle Public Library; Spencer Ruchti at Third Place Books; Alison Stagner, Emmy Newman, and Grace Rajendran at Seattle Arts & Lectures; Alex Chester-Iwata at Mixed Asian Media; and Shin Yu Pai at Town Hall Seattle.

Thank you to my amazing colleagues at The Serica Initiative—Josephine Lau, Anla Cheng, Michelle Maiuri, and Andrea Louie—and all of the inspiring people and organizations I've had the good fortune of meeting through my work. Thank you to Judy Greenspan and Kristy Geslain for the opportunity to explore the multitudes of Asian American storytelling as a producer with WNET.

Thank you to Elisha Zepeda for the gorgeous cover and George Orozco for the beautiful headshot.

To every bookseller and librarian who stocked this book and every reader holding it in your hands. Thank you.

My loving family: Mom, Hannah, and Real—my first writing teacher. My daughter, Juniper, for sleeping just long enough to allow me to finish edits.

Most of all, I want to thank my partner, Meghan. The sacrifices you've made for me to do this thing I love are beyond measure. Every high and low in this journey has landed first, and hardest, with you, but your support has never wavered. Thank you for believing in me far more than I ever could myself.